Books by Melody Carlson

Courting Mr. Emerson

FOLLOW YOUR HEART SERIES

Once Upon a Summertime
All Summer Long
Under a Summer Sky

HOLIDAY NOVELLAS

Christmas at Harrington's
The Christmas Shoppe
The Joy of Christmas
The Treasure of Christmas
The Christmas Pony
A Simple Christmas Wish
The Christmas Cat
The Christmas Joy Ride
The Christmas Angel Project
The Christmas Blessing

courting
mr. emerson

MELODY
CARLSON

Revell
a division of Baker Publishing Group
Grand Rapids, Michigan

© 2019 by Carlson Management, Inc.

Published by Revell
a division of Baker Publishing Group
PO Box 6287, Grand Rapids, MI 49516-6287
www.revellbooks.com

Printed in the United States of America

Library of Congress Cataloging-in-Publication Data
Names: Carlson, Melody, author.
Title: Courting Mr. Emerson / Melody Carlson.
Description: Grand Rapids, MI : Revell, a division of Baker Publishing Group, [2019]
Identifiers: LCCN 2018026774 | ISBN 9780800735272 (paper : alk. paper)
Subjects: | GSAFD: Christian fiction. | Love stories.
Classification: LCC PS3553.A73257 C68 2019 | DDC 813/.54—dc23
LC record available at https://lccn.loc.gov/2018026774

ISBN 978-0-8007-3567-8 (casebound)

19 20 21 22 23 24 25   7 6 5 4 3 2 1

one

George Emerson didn't need anybody. Or so he told himself as he carefully shaved with his straight-edged razor, just like he always did seven days a week at exactly 7:07 each morning. George knew that most men used more modern razors, but this silver implement had been left to him by the grandfather who'd helped raise him. Wiping his razor across a soft terry towel, he stretched his neck to examine his smoothly shaved chin in the foggy mirror. He could see better with his reading glasses, but after so many years of the same routine, George felt certain the job was done right.

As he closed the bathroom window, shutting out the humming "music" of his overly friendly neighbor, George wondered if there was some polite way to avoid Lorna Atwood this morning. She'd been puttering around her yard for the last ten minutes, and George felt certain it was in the hopes of catching him on his way to work.

As he replaced the cap on his Barbasol shave cream and returned his razor to its chipped ceramic mug, a pinging in the kitchen told him that the coffee was done. The automatic-timed coffee maker was one of the few modern perks that George had been talked into a few years ago. But, as with most electronic devices, he still didn't fully trust the fancy machine. What if it got its wires crossed and decided to make coffee in the middle of the night?

George peeked out the kitchen window as he filled his stainless steel travel cup with steaming coffee, only to see that Lorna was now sitting on her front porch. He slipped two thin slices of whole wheat bread into the toaster, removed a hard-boiled egg from the fridge, and poured himself a small glass of grapefruit juice. This was his standard weekday breakfast. On weekends he'd sometimes fry or poach himself an egg or, if feeling particularly festive, he might stroll over to the Blue Goose Diner and splurge on pancakes and bacon, which he'd leisurely consume while reading the newspaper. Although it had probably been more than a year since he'd indulged in that.

But today was Friday, and by 7:27, George's breakfast was finished, his dishes washed. With his travel mug refilled and briefcase in hand, he locked his front door, checked to be sure it was secure, then checked again just in case. Lingering for a moment, he pretended to check his watch, glancing left and right to be sure Lorna wasn't lurking nearby.

The sun seemed high in the sky for late May, but that was only because he'd never fully adjusted to the late-start days that Warner High had implemented last fall. Although it had disrupted his internal time clock, George had to admit that students seemed moderately more awake with an extra hour of sleep.

"Hello, Mr. Emerson," Lorna Atwood chirped merrily.

She popped out from the shadows of her front porch like a jack-in-the-box in Lycra. "Lovely day today, isn't it?"

He peered up at the cloudless sky then nodded an affirmative. "Looks like a good one, for sure."

"Especially for this time of year in western Oregon. Last year it rained all the way through May and June." She hurried over to him with a hot pink coffee cup in hand. Had she coordinated it to match her lipstick? "Now, you didn't forget about my invitation, did you?" Lorna looked hopeful.

George feigned confusion then tapped the side of his forehead. "I'm so sorry, Mrs. Atwood, but I realized that I do have other plans for tonight. I hope you'll please excuse me."

"Oh, well." Her smile remained fixed. "Perhaps another time. With summer round the corner, we should have plenty of chances to get together. I'll just have to take a rain check from you." She peered upward. "Speaking of rain checks, I heard it's supposed to cloud up this weekend. Maybe I can collect on mine then." She winked.

George forced a polite smile as he tipped his head and continued past her small yard. Her lawn was in need of mowing again. Hopefully he wouldn't have to remind her of her rental agreement and that she was responsible for her own landscaping chores. The little yellow bungalow, owned by him, was nearly identical to the one he lived in—except his was cornflower blue. His grandparents had helped him to invest in these little neglected houses in the late eighties, back when real estate had been ridiculously low. He'd purchased the first bungalow for his own use shortly after acquiring his teaching position at the nearby high school. Since he had no interest in driving, it had made sense to live within walking distance of his work. And he'd been employed at Warner High ever since.

With the help of his grandfather's handyman expertise, George had spent weekends and evenings fixing up his little blue house. It provided a good distraction from the dreams that had not gone as planned. Perhaps that was why his grandparents had encouraged him to take on three more little houses—to divert him from his pain and to keep him occupied. Of course, they wisely called it a "good investment." Plus it proved a clever way to increase real estate values in his neighborhood. Buying derelict properties had seemed a bit reckless at the time, especially since residents were fleeing urban neighborhoods, flocking to the "safety" of the suburbs. But in the past decade, the trend had reversed. People returned to town, and rentals in his neighborhood were at an all-time high. His three rental bungalows, just one block away from downtown, never went unoccupied nowadays.

Mrs. Atwood, his most recent tenant, had been overjoyed to get in. Although she'd only been here a few months, George soon learned to exercise caution when engaging with her. The gregarious divorcée could "chat" nonstop if given the opportunity. He suspected her husband had fled in order to attain some peace and quiet, although Mrs. Atwood claimed to be the victim of her ex-husband's "midlife crisis." To be fair, she wasn't bad looking—just talked too much. And tried too hard.

George had performed some minor repairs on the bungalow shortly after she moved in. Grateful for his "improvements," she eagerly invited him for dinner. When he declined, she insisted on baking him her "famous cherry pie." He pretended to appreciate her gesture, but the overly sweet and syrupy pie wound up in the trash since George wasn't big on desserts. Just the same, he penned a polite thank-you note and taped it to the clean pie plate that he discreetly placed on her porch very early the next morning. But since then, her efforts to befriend him had only intensified—and, short of rudeness or dishonesty, he was running out of excuses to decline.

George was no stranger to feminine attempts to *befriend* him, and over the years, he'd learned to take women's flattering attentions in stride. It wasn't that he was devastatingly handsome—he might be getting older, but he wasn't delusional. Even in his prime, back in the previous millennium when his students had nicknamed him "Mr. Bean," George had been aware that he was no Cary Grant. The comparison to the quirky BBC character may have been meant as an insult, but George hadn't minded.

He actually kind of admired Mr. Bean. And George knew the kids' teasing was the result of his buttoned-up attire. His response to kids dressing like gangbangers had been to step it up by wearing nappy ties and sports coats to school—an attempt to lead by example. Not that it had worked. But it was a habit he'd continued and, despite his fellow teachers' preference for casual dress, George liked his more traditional style. Ironically, it seemed the ladies liked it too. At least they used to, and ones like Mrs. Atwood apparently still did.

Now that he was in his midfifties, George suspected that women like Mrs. Atwood weren't attracted so much by his appearance as by his availability. It had never been particularly easy being a bachelor. Sometimes he'd suspected someone had pinned a target to his back. But as the years passed, many began to refer to him as a "confirmed bachelor." Truth be told, George didn't mind the confirmed part—it sounded better than being committed.

"Good morning, Mr. Emerson." Jemma Spencer waved to him as she bounded up the front steps to the school. "Isn't it a gorgeous day!"

"It certainly is." George politely opened the door for her, waiting as the younger woman went in ahead of him. Jemma was new at Warner High. Fairly fresh out of college, she was energetic and strikingly pretty—and, like most of his fellow teachers, young enough to be his daughter. "And how are things going in the Art Department, Miss Spencer?" He paused to show his ID badge at the security check.

"The natives are restless." Her dark brown eyes sparkled as if she were restless too.

"Yes, with only six days left of school, you have to expect that. Especially on a warm, sunny day like this."

"I think I'll take my students outside today," she confided as they continued toward the main office together, "to draw trees or flowers or clouds or butterflies or whatever. Maybe they'll just stare off into space, but hopefully it'll get the ants out of their pants."

He chuckled. "You're a brave woman."

"Not really, it's just that I'm kinda antsy too." She winked as they turned down the hall by the office. "I'm counting the days until summer break."

"Any big plans?" he asked with mild interest.

"My boyfriend and I are going to Iceland," she declared.

"Interesting—"

"Iceland?" a male voice called out from the faculty room. "Did someone say Iceland? I went there for spring break and it was fabulous. Want to see my photos?"

Suddenly many of the younger teachers were talking at once, sharing phone photos, eagerly recounting travel experiences, talking about the lure of Iceland or other exotic locales, and bragging about various offbeat plans for their upcoming summer. In the past, George might've engaged in this sort of enthusiastic banter—even sharing some of his own travel stories—but since he'd made no plans for the upcoming summer . . . or the past several summers for that matter, he kept his mouth closed and simply collected papers from his mailbox and checked the staff bulletin board. Then, without looking back, he quietly exited the noisy faculty room.

As he walked toward the Language Arts Department, George felt old. Not in a stiff, sore, achy sort of way—although he knew the spring had been missing from his step for some time now. He felt old as in outdated—like the dinosaur of Warner High. It was no secret that he was the oldest teacher on staff, or that the administration had been encouraging him to retire the last couple of years. But now he was nearly fifty-five, which sounded dangerously close to sixty, and budgets had been cut once again. His principal knew she could save money by hiring a less senior language arts teacher. George had resisted her in the past. But this year, he'd caved.

After a bad bout of flu last winter, George had given in, announcing that this would be his last year to teach. And now, in less than a week, he would be officially retired after more than thirty years. Not that anyone appeared to put much value on experience nowadays . . . or even care that he would soon be gone.

More and more, George had begun to feel invisible at this school, as if each year diminished his presence. Even the students looked right through him at times. Not that it was so unusual for a teacher to be ignored. As an English instructor he was accustomed to his students' general lack of interest in academia. He tried to impress upon them the need for good writing skills—and sometimes they got it. But thanks to this electronic age, which he detested, there was a complete disregard for spelling and grammar and structure. As hard as he'd tried to make his favorite class—English literature— relevant and appealing, most of his students didn't know the difference between Chaucer and Shakespeare. Even more, they didn't care.

He sighed as he clicked the pass-code pad numbers beside his classroom door. He remembered a time when no doors were locked inside of campus. Now everyone had pass-codes for everything. Security cams and uniformed police abounded—so much so that he sometimes felt like he was teaching in a prison. And to be fair, some of his students might be better off in a prison. He flicked on the fluorescent lights then walked through the stale-smelling classroom. Not for the first time, he wished the high windows could open and get fresh air in here. He'd raised this issue before, pointing out how it might actually help to wake the students up. But thanks to budget challenges, no changes had been made.

As George punched the number code into his office door, he remembered what this school had been like back in the *dark ages*—back when he'd been a student in this very building, back when dinosaurs roamed freely. What a different world that had been. Although the building, which was new and modern back then, hadn't changed much.

But then some things never changed. Over the years he'd observed that teens from every decade bore striking similarities. Peel back the veneer of current trends and fashions and you'd usually discover a frustrated mix of rebelliousness and insecurity. To be fair, his generation had been no different. He remembered the late seventies well. His class had its share of druggies and dropouts and slackers, yet his peers, even all these years later, felt more real to him than today's youth. Of course, it was possible that his memory was impaired by his age, but when he looked back he saw an authenticity that he felt was missing from kids nowadays.

Maybe it was because his generation hadn't been plugged into all these electronic gadgets and devices . . . pads and pods and phones that were attached at the hip of all his students. Even though the school had a policy of no personal electronics during class time, most of the students managed to bend the rules. It really made him feel crazy at times. What happened to connecting with your friends by looking into their faces while conversing? Or using a phone and hearing a real voice on the other end? He didn't understand these shorthand messages they exchanged, with bad grammar and silly little pictures. And the complaints he got when he explained a letter-writing assignment to his class! You'd think he'd asked them to gouge out their eyeballs—or to destroy their mobile phones.

He'd recently looked out over a classroom only to feel that he was gazing upon a roomful of zombies. It was as if they were all dead inside—just empty shells. He knew he was old-fashioned, but he honestly believed that computer technology had stolen the very souls of this generation. Of course, this had simply confirmed what he knew—it was time to quit.

MORGAN COUNTY
PUBLIC
LIBRARY

Phone: 765-342-3451
http://morgancountylibrary.info

You checked out the following
items:

1. Courting Mr. Emerson
   Barcode: 78551000540733
   Due: 2019-10-07 23:59
2. A hero for Miss Hatherleigh
   Barcode: 78551000540606
   Due: 2019-10-07 23:59

YOU SAVED
$37.00
Value of Materials Checked out!

two

Willow West felt unexpectedly nervous as she pinned the visitor's pass onto her lace-trimmed, tie-dyed tunic top. Her grandson, Collin, called this a "hippie shirt," and now she wondered if she should've changed into something more conservative for this visit. Or not. Anyway, it was too late now and she'd already procrastinated coming here for long enough. Really, she should've taken care of this a month ago. But hearing that Mr. Emerson was about to retire put fire to her feet. If she wanted to secure this recommendation letter, less than one week's notice was cutting it close.

Feeling like a fish out of water—or at least swimming upstream—Willow pushed a trail through the hoard of noisy students eagerly pressing toward the school's exits. The smell in the crowded hallway was a combination of sweat, stinky tennis shoes, cheap cologne . . . and what she could only describe as adolescent angst. Or maybe it was just teenage hormones running amuck.

She hurried on, feeling intrusive for being on their and desperately hoping Collin wouldn't spy her a embarrassed or worried that something was wrong. She hadn't even told him of her plan. Well aware of Collin's type A personality and tendency to obsess over small things, she didn't want to disturb him with what he considered her "eccentricities." Her grandson's cautious approach to life was both sweetly endearing and slightly troubling.

As she went past the trophy case, Willow was surprised at how little appeared to have changed inside Warner High. Even the posters looked the same. Other than dropping Collin off here occasionally, she hadn't been inside this building in ages. Not since her own stint here decades ago. She hoped it wasn't a mistake to show up without an appointment. Schools had never been this formal back in her day. Having to produce photo ID and getting her oversized macramé bag checked by a security guard was a real wake-up call. It made her sad to think this was what Collin was subjected to every day, although he probably took it in stride.

Willow paused by the administration area, considering whether or not to ask someone for help, but everyone looked busy and preoccupied. She probably still knew her way around this place anyway. Unless the layout had drastically changed, which she doubted, she knew the Language Arts ...partment was up the main stairs and directly to the right. ... top of the stairs, she noticed a young security guard ...ing her. Willow smiled at him, then felt a sur- ...nxiety—almost as if she expected to be ...ing a rule. It was probably just a guilty ...—perhaps from the time she and ...king weed in the restroom ...grief, what had they been ...urge to giggle as she walked past the uniformed guard and entered the Language Arts Department. She knew she was being ridiculous. That silly weed incident happened in 1980! And fortunately, her pot-smoking era was quite short-lived. She hadn't touched the stuff in more than thirty years. She felt shocked to think it had been that long since she'd been young. Maybe she was delusional, but most of the time she felt like she was still young—more like her late thirties than her early fifties. She smiled to think how many times she'd been mistaken for Collin's mother and had to explain she was his grandma.

She hoped she hadn't come on a fool's errand as she searched for Mr. Emerson's classroom. She probably should've called ahead to be sure he was here. And if he was here, she hoped she wouldn't appear to be a fanatical grandmother by bursting in on him like this. Yet, she knew if there was anything Mr. Emerson could do to help her grandson, it was well worth any amount of humiliation. She finally found the classroom, and peering through the narrow glass window beside the door, she could see that the lights were on. She felt hopeful. Maybe he was still here.

She tried the door but was dismayed to find it locked. What was it with schools these days? Was everything and everyone under lock and key? Feeling intrusive but desperate, she knocked then pounded on the metal door. She could see the door to the office area opening and then, to her relief, a dark-haired man emerged. He was medium height and slender, looking toward her with his head cocked to one side. But now she wondered if she'd gotten the wrong room. For some reason, she'd expected a bald and portly elderly man. But this guy, dressed in a tweed jacket, light-colored shirt, and narrow tie, looked younger. In fact, he resembled a character from a 1960s TV show—or maybe he'd been an extra in *Mad Men*.

"Hello?" He opened the door with a curious but kind smile.

Willow noticed slight touches of gray hair at his temples and fine lines around his eyes, suggesting he was older than she'd just assumed. But there was a youthfulness about him too. "Mr. Emerson, I presume?" She smiled nervously, hoping he'd get the joke.

"I am." His nod was somber as he opened the door a bit wider. "May I help you?"

"I hope so." She stood up straighter. "I'm here to talk to you about Collin West. I understand he's one of your students."

"Yes. Collin is in two of my classes. A fine young man. Are you his mother?"

She beamed at him. "No, no, but thank you. I'm actually his grandmother. I've been raising him for most of his life. We just moved to Warner last winter."

"Yes, I know that Collin is new to the school." He waved her into the classroom. "He's impressed me as an outstanding student. You should be very proud."

She felt a wave of relief. "Oh yes, I am. I think he's absolutely brilliant. But I've been concerned after transferring here from the Bay Area in California. We moved so abruptly, and it's recently occurred to me that Collin won't have all the letters of recommendation that he might need, you know, to start applying for college. I'm afraid I've been negligent."

"He hasn't applied already?" Mr. Emerson frowned. "I thought Collin was a senior."

"Yes, he is a senior. And you're right, he should've been

embarrassed or worried that something was wrong. She hadn't even told him of her plan. Well aware of Collin's type A personality and tendency to obsess over small things, she didn't want to disturb him with what he considered her "eccentricities." Her grandson's cautious approach to life was both sweetly endearing and slightly troubling.

As she went past the trophy case, Willow was surprised at how little appeared to have changed inside Warner High. Even the posters looked the same. Other than dropping Collin off here occasionally, she hadn't been inside this building in ages. Not since her own stint here decades ago. She hoped it wasn't a mistake to show up without an appointment. Schools had never been this formal back in her day. Having to produce photo ID and getting her oversized macramé bag checked by a security guard was a real wake-up call. It made her sad to think this was what Collin was subjected to every day, although he probably took it in stride.

Willow paused by the administration area, considering whether or not to ask someone for help, but everyone looked busy and preoccupied. She probably still knew her way around this place anyway. Unless the layout had drastically changed, which she doubted, she knew the Language Arts Department was up the main stairs and directly to the right.

At the top of the stairs, she noticed a young security guard curiously eying her. Willow smiled at him, then felt a surprising wave of anxiety—almost as if she expected to be apprehended for breaking a rule. It was probably just a guilty flashback from her youth—perhaps from the time she and Shelly Hanson got caught smoking weed in the restroom right around the corner. Good grief, what had they been thinking? She suppressed the urge to giggle as she walked

two

Willow West felt unexpectedly nervous as she pinned the visitor's pass onto her lace-trimmed, tie-dyed tunic top. Her grandson, Collin, called this a "hippie shirt," and now she wondered if she should've changed into something more conservative for this visit. Or not. Anyway, it was too late now and she'd already procrastinated coming here for long enough. Really, she should've taken care of this a month ago. But hearing that Mr. Emerson was about to retire put fire to her feet. If she wanted to secure this recommendation letter, less than one week's notice was cutting it close.

Feeling like a fish out of water—or at least swimming upstream—Willow pushed a trail through the hoard of noisy students eagerly pressing toward the school's exits. The smell in the crowded hallway was a combination of sweat, stinky tennis shoes, cheap cologne . . . and what she could only describe as adolescent angst. Or maybe it was just teenage hormones running amuck.

She hurried on, feeling intrusive for being on their turf and desperately hoping Collin wouldn't spy her and get

Susan Sontag

————•————

Marat/Sade/Artaud

Earlier we followed one critic, Eric Bentley, on an excursion into the world of therapy. Here Susan Sontag considers some of the same ideas, but stays within the framework of theatrical drama—specifically, Peter Weiss's Marat/Sade, *a play within a play within a psychiatric institution.*

> The Primary and most beautiful of Nature's qualities is motion, which agitates her at all times. But this motion is simply the perpetual consequence of crimes; and it is conserved by means of crimes alone.
>
> —SADE

> Everything that acts is a cruelty. It is upon this idea of extreme action, pushed beyond all limits, that theatre must be rebuilt.
>
> —ARTAUD

Theatricality and insanity—the two most potent subjects of the contemporary theater—are brilliantly fused in Peter Weiss' play, *The Persecution and Assassination of Marat as Performed by the Inmates of the Asylum at Charenton under the Direction of the Marquis de Sade.* The subject is a dramatic performance staged before the audience's eyes; the scene is a madhouse. The historical facts behind the play are that in the insane asylum just outside Paris where Sade was confined by order of Napoleon for the last

SOURCE: Reprinted with the permission of Farrar, Straus & Giroux, Inc. from *Against Interpretation* by Susan Sontag, Copyright © 1961, 1962, 1963, 1964, 1965, 1966 by Susan Sontag.

particular neurosis, and so may such matters as the untimely diminution or cessation of its exercise. But its essence is irreducible. It is, as we say, a gift.

We are all ill: but even a universal sickness implies an idea of health. Of the artist we must say that whatever elements of neurosis he has in common with his fellow mortals, the one part of him that is healthy, by any conceivable definition of health, is that which gives him the power to conceive, to plan, to work, and to bring his work to a conclusion. And if we are all ill, we are ill by a universal accident, not by a universal necessity, by a fault in the economy of our powers, not by the nature of the powers themselves. The Philoctetes myth, when it is used to imply a causal connection between the fantasy of castration and artistic power, tells us no more about the source of artistic power than we learn about the source of sexuality when the fantasy of castration is adduced, for the fear of castration may explain why a man is moved to extravagant exploits of sexuality, but we do not say that his sexual power itself derives from his fear of castration; and further the same fantasy may also explain impotence or homosexuality. The Philoctetes story, which has so established itself among us as explaining the source of the artist's power, is not really an explanatory myth at all; it is a moral myth having reference to our proper behavior in the circumstances of the universal accident. In its juxtaposition of the wound and the bow, it tells us that we must be aware that weakness does not preclude strength, nor strength weakness. It is therefore not irrelevant to the artist, but when we use it we will do well to keep in mind the other myths of the arts, recalling what Pan and Dionysius suggest of the relation of art to physiology and superabundance, remembering that to Apollo were attributed the bow and the lyre, two strengths together, and that he was given the lyre by its inventor, the baby Hermes—that miraculous infant who, the day he was born, left his cradle to do mischief: and the first thing he met with was a tortoise, which he greeted politely before scooping it from its shell, and, thought and deed being one with him, he contrived the instrument to which he sang "the glorious tale of his own begetting." These were gods, and very early ones, but their myths tell us something about the nature and source of art even in our grim, late human present.

applying long before this, but Collin doesn't see the need to attend a big college. He insists on going to community college for his first year."

"I see. Well, that's a sensible plan."

"Maybe so. At least for his first year. But I don't want him to set his sights too low. I'm hoping he'll start applying to some bigger schools soon. Maybe after fall term."

"Getting into a bigger college shouldn't be a problem. He's an intelligent young man. I assume he's got a strong GPA."

"Yes. But we still need to get our ducks in a row. Recommendation letters and such. And I just heard you're going to be leaving Warner High." She frowned. "Did I hear it right? You're retiring?"

"That's correct." He nodded with a grim expression.

She frowned. "You look young."

"Well, maybe . . . but it's time."

"Congratulations . . . I guess—I mean, if that's what you want." She studied him, wondering why he appeared melancholy, but controlled herself from asking. She knew her tendency to get overly involved sometimes, and this was not the time.

"Thank you." He rubbed his chin. "I guess I'm still adjusting to the concept."

"Well, life is about more than just work."

"Yes, I suppose so." He frowned.

Willow studied him for a long moment. Something about Mr. Emerson seemed sad and vulnerable . . . almost like a little boy in need of a warm, reassuring hug. And at the same time, she could tell that he was uncomfortable, as if he wanted her to keep a safe distance. "Anyway," she said quickly, "the reason I came here today was to personally ask you for a recommendation letter for Collin."

He slowly nodded, but there was a faraway look in his eyes, almost as if he wasn't really listening. Perhaps he had health problems. Maybe that was his reason for early retirement—not that she planned to probe. At least she hoped not.

"You see, you're his favorite teacher," she continued. "And if you could write a nice letter, I can make copies. You know, to include in Collin's application packets in the event that he applies to some larger colleges. I suppose I'm hoping he'll soon become disenchanted with community college." She leaned forward slightly, trying to discern if Mr. Emerson was really on board or simply lost in his own thoughts.

"Yes, yes." His dark eyes lit up. "That sounds like a good plan. Sensible."

She felt relieved. "Collin truly is fond of you, Mr. Emerson. He's mentioned you a lot. And he loves his English classes. Whether it's reading or writing or whatever. He actually hopes to be an English major. I'm not sure that's a very useful degree, but I've always encouraged him to follow his dreams. And you may already know that he loves to write. He writes short stories and poems—just for his own entertainment." She paused to catch her breath, worried that she was gushing.

"Yes, I've noticed he's a strong writer. That caught my attention early on."

"Oh, good." She set her overloaded macramé handbag on a desk with a heavy thud and sighed deeply. "So you'll help us then? I mean, him—you'll help *him*?"

"I'd be honored to write a letter for Collin."

"Oh, thank you—*thank you*!" Once again, she resisted the

20

urge to embrace him. With his proper manners and buttoned-up appearance, she felt certain Mr. Emerson was not a hugger. Although she could be wrong. For his sake, she hoped she was wrong. "I was so worried about showing up like this, straight out of the blue," she confessed. "Without an appointment, I mean. I'm obviously from a different era. They never had armed guards all over the schools back in my day. To be honest, this place felt more like a reformatory than a high school to me today."

"I've actually had similar thoughts." He looked almost amused.

She waved her hand around. "Can you believe I actually went to high school *here*? Ages ago, of course. But I'm a Warner High graduate. Well, barely." She felt her cheeks growing warm to remember how she'd marched up to receive her diploma while pregnant. Not that she planned to disclose that.

"Really?" His brow creased. "You went to school *here*?"

"Yep. I was a Warner Wolverine." She chuckled. "I graduated in—"

"So was I. A graduate, I mean. Class of 1980."

"No kidding? I was '81." She blinked, trying to recall anyone by the name Emerson. Then, realizing she hadn't properly introduced herself, she stuck out her hand. "I'm sorry, I should've told you my name. I'm Willow West and—"

"Willow *Wild* West?" His hand covered his mouth as if embarrassed. "Sorry, I shouldn't have said that. Please, excuse me."

"That's okay." She gave him an uneasy smile. "It's true, I was a bit of a wild child in high school. I'm sure the word got around. But I eventually grew up." She rolled her eyes.

"Well, mostly. I suppose I don't ever want to grow up completely. And the truth is that my own grandson still calls me
a hippie." She rolled up her sleeve to show him the faded
rose tattoo on her forearm. "He calls this my *gramp-stamp*."
She laughed loudly. "From back in my glory days. I was even
younger than Collin when I got this and he thinks I was crazy.
I suppose the good news is that Collin has absolutely no
interest in doing anything illegal. He'd never get tattooed.
Not that I'd mind so much if he did. Sometimes I wish he'd
lighten up. Not necessarily with tats." She sighed as she
pulled her sleeve back down.

"I know they're painful to remove." He folded his arms
across his front. "Not from experience, mind you."

"No, of course not. You don't really look like the tattoo
type, Mr. Emerson." She tipped her head to one side. "But I
still can't place you. You *really* went to school here?"

"I'd be surprised if you did remember me." His tone was
solemn. "I was pretty quiet. Certainly not part of your crowd.
Although my best friend Greg Walters mixed with—"

"I do remember Greg Walters! And now I remember you
too. You're *George* Emerson." She peered curiously at him.
"I thought you looked familiar and, come to think of it,
you haven't even changed that much. As I recall, you were
rather standoffish then. Studious and serious. But Greg was
fun. He really came out of his shell in high school. Whatever
happened to him? Does he still live in Warner?"

Mr. Emerson frowned. "No . . . Greg passed away about
ten years ago."

"Oh . . . I'm sorry to hear that."

He nodded. "As am I."

"Didn't you have a war hero brother?" She wanted to

22

MELODY CARLSON

change the subject. "Alex Emerson? For some reason, I remember that name."

His brow creased. "Yes, but I'd be surprised if you knew
him. Alex was ten years older than me."

She suddenly recalled why she remembered the brother's
name, but she didn't want to admit it. Unfortunately, she
couldn't think of a graceful way to deflect the conversation.

"How did you know about him?" Mr. Emerson pushed.

"The truth?" She grimaced.

"That's always the best policy, don't you think?"

"Well . . ." She winced inwardly. "My parents were . . .
well, they were hippies. We lived on a commune. And we
participated in war protests sometimes, and this one time,
when I was just a girl, we were visiting my grandparents right
here in Warner. We demonstrated by the Vietnam Memorial
at the city park . . . and I remember reading that name. It
was the most recent one on the stone. And I can't explain
it, but I felt so sad for him. I remember wishing that he'd
never enlisted."

"Alex didn't enlist," Mr. Emerson said soberly. "Do you
recall the Vietnam draft lottery? How they drew birth dates
and numbered them for the draft?"

"Sure." She nodded.

"Well, Alex's birth date was the second date drawn. He
was drafted into the army right after graduation." Mr. Emerson sighed with a faraway look. "He went overseas with a
buzz haircut, shiny combat boots, and a brave smile . . . and
came back in a wooden box."

"Oh . . . I'm so sorry."

"Yes, so was I." He shook his head.

"I really am sorry. You lost your brother and your best

23

friend." Despite herself, she reached out to put a hand on his shoulder. "That must've been very hard."

He simply nodded.

Now she didn't know what to say. She awkwardly pulled her hand down then reached for her macramé bag. "I sort of lost track of this town after high school," she said nervously. "I spent a year in Berkeley but felt like I was floundering. Then my parents talked me into transferring to an art college." She waved her hand in a dismissive way. "But I'm sure you're busy, Mr. Emerson. I don't want to bore you with the silly details of my life. I'm just so glad you're willing to write a letter for Collin." She reached inside of her bag, extracting a slightly wrinkled business card.

"There's no rush for the letter, but I thought perhaps you'd do it before school lets out. You know, so you don't forget. I'm sure you have big summer plans—celebrating your retirement and all." She handed him the dog-eared card. "That's the info for my art studio and gallery. You may have noticed it on Main Street." She pointed to the card. "Named after me. Willow West. Anyway, it's probably the best way to contact me. Or just send the letter to the email address on the bottom. I can print it out."

"Then I'd have to do that before school ends since I don't have public email."

She blinked. "Seriously? No email?"

He nodded. "I'm rather old-fashioned. I view computers as a necessary evil. I use them when I must, like here at school, but you won't find those electronic devices in my home."

"Seriously?"

"I don't even own a cellular phone."

"Wow." She wasn't sure if this was impressive or just plain nuts. "How do you communicate?"

"I have a landline phone that works just fine. And if I need to write a letter, I use a pen, or if I'm writing something longer, I use the same Olivetti typewriter that took me through college."

She grinned. "That's actually sort of cool . . . and very unusual."

"People give me a hard time for it, but I just happen to like it." He shrugged. "And I think my life is less stressful as a result."

"I can understand how it might reduce some anxiety." She put her purse strap over a shoulder. "And if I could get away with something like that, I think I would too. But for my business, well, I feel it's necessary to have an online presence."

He studied the card. "You're an artist?"

"I mostly create textile arts. As well as a little painting, and sometimes I'll dabble in sculpture and pottery—if I'm in the mood for getting muddy." She grinned.

"Interesting."

"Do you *like* art?" She peered curiously at him. He didn't particularly strike her as the artistic type.

"I believe art is like beauty—it's discerned by the eyes of the beholder. I'm certainly no expert, but I know what I like."

She reached into her bag again, pulling out one of the flyers for that night's event. Like her business card, it was slightly rumpled. "Then you might want to come to this."

His brow creased as he read the page. "An art show?"

"Yes. It starts tonight at seven. And there'll be food and music and all sorts of fun things. All the galleries listed there

25

will be open until nine. It's called Final Friday. Kind of ex-perimental, but lots of places do it. I'm hoping it'll work out and we'll do it every month. Warner needs to wake up when it comes to the arts." She smiled. "That's one of the reasons I moved back here."

"To wake up Warner?" His brows arched.

She chuckled. "Something like that." She closed her bag and squared her shoulders. "Well, I don't want to take any more of your time, Mr. Emerson." She stepped away from him, pausing long enough for him to invite her to call him by his first name. But when he didn't, she simply thanked him for his help with Collin's college letter and said a cheery goodbye.

As she walked through the now-deserted hallway, she wondered about Mr. Emerson. He was so completely un-like anyone she'd ever known. And she'd known a lot of characters in her lifetime. But what made this odd man tick? And why did he act so uptight . . . and sad? And—the most pressing question—why did she feel this strange and un-expected attraction to him and what in the world did she plan to do about it?

three

By that evening, George had convinced himself that the only reason he was going to the art walk on Main Street was because it provided him an honest excuse for turning down Lorna Atwood's persistent dinner invitation. He'd told a little white lie by claiming he had other plans. Of course, he'd intended to make his words true by doing something. But now he actually had an activity. The trick would be getting out the front door without crossing paths with her again.

George had donned his favorite charcoal tweed blazer over a light blue shirt and burgundy tie for this evening's festivities. Someone had once told him that wearing blue brought out his eyes. Not that anyone was likely to notice that tonight. But as he peered out his kitchen window to determine if Lorna Atwood was lurking nearby, he felt rather dapper. And seeing that her well-lit porch appeared to be deserted, George put on his favorite fedora then slipped out onto his own porch.

Lorna Atwood had been right about one thing—the

weatherman had predicted showers for this evening, and it was already clouding up. So armed with his sleek black umbrella, George made his way down his walk.

"Mr. Emerson," Lorna called out with a note of victory in her voice. "How nice to see you tonight."

"Good evening," he said crisply, wondering where she'd popped out from and how hard it would be to extricate himself from her company. "Are you going out?"

"As a matter of fact, I am," she chirped. "Since you couldn't come to dinner, I decided to walk into town tonight. I heard there are some activities and live music. Kind of a summer kickoff."

"Oh?" George paused.

"Are we walking the same direction?" she asked. "Perhaps we can keep each other company along the way."

"I, uh, if you'll excuse me, I just remembered something that I forgot inside. Something I needed to take with me tonight."

"I can wait."

"No, no, you go on without me. It will take me a few minutes to get it ready." He tipped his head politely. "Good evening." Then, turning abruptly, he hurried back into his house. Feeling like he'd just dodged a bullet, he was relieved that he hadn't actually lied. He glanced at the clock to see that it was nearly half past seven now. No time to waste.

George went over to his Olivetti typewriter, the same one that had gotten him through college. The letter he'd started typing this very afternoon was still in the carriage and very nearly finished. Without removing his hat, he sat down, typed the last two lines then carefully rolled it out, gave it a solid proofread, and signed his name. As he fanned the page to help the ink to dry, he felt a tinge of guilt. He hadn't really intended to give the recommendation letter to Willow West this evening, but it had provided a handy excuse for avoiding Mrs. Atwood.

Satisfied that the ink was dry, he carefully folded the letter, inserted it into a legal-sized envelope, and penned *Ms. Willow West* on the front. He was curious as to why she'd kept her maiden name but assumed it had to do with being an artist. And it certainly had a rather pleasant ring to it. He slipped the envelope into his jacket's inner pocket and, relatively certain that Lorna Atwood would be well on her way by now, set out to stroll to town.

Because the Willow West Gallery was on the other end of town, George decided to go there first. Hopefully it would lessen his chances of bumping into Lorna Atwood as she wandered through town. Main Street was surprisingly busy with pedestrians meandering along the sidewalks on both sides of the street. Strains of music floated out of some of the shops' opened doors. And the oak trees along the sidewalk were lit up with tiny white lights, giving the town a rather festive appearance.

George felt uneasy as he entered the Willow West Gallery. Almost as if he was an unwanted intruder, crashing a gathering that he'd not been invited to attend. Of course, that was ridiculous because Ms. West had personally invited him. Besides, he had something to give her. The gallery was quite large, well-lit, and attractive, but surprisingly full of people. They were clustered in small groups, and most of them had drinks and appetizers in hand, acting very much like this was a party. Maybe he really was crashing.

With various walls and dividers, the space felt somewhat maze-like, but George attempted to blend in with the art-lookers, pausing to study various paintings, sculptures, and fabric creations. Although a number of them had Willow West's name on the little white description cards, most of the items appeared to have been created by other artists. And the prices on everything sounded a bit outrageous. George could be wrong, but he doubted that anyone in Warner would fork out that kind of money on art.

"George Emerson!"

He turned to see Lorna Atwood directly behind him. Had she followed him here? Was she turning into a stalker? "Oh, hello again," he said a bit stiffly.

"Well, isn't this interesting." She gave him a sly grin. "Here we are at the same event. It seems almost fortuitous. I didn't know you were a patron of the arts."

"I'm here to meet someone." He felt a tinge of guilt again. That was certainly stretching the truth a bit.

"Oh?" Her pale brows arched. "Someone in this gallery?"

"Yes." He continued to move through the maze of divider walls, tilting his head from side to side as if doing a search.

"Who is it you're looking for?" she persisted, still at his elbow.

To his relief, George spotted Willow West now. She was dressed in a flowing and colorful kimono, and her strawberry-blonde hair was piled on her head and secured with what looked like a chopstick. In the back of the gallery, she was surrounded by a small group of people. "Excuse me," he told Lorna. "I see her now." And before she could further

30

question him, he went directly toward Willow and what appeared to be a fan club of admirers.

"Mr. Emerson." Willow's face lit up as he approached and, to his relief, she excused herself from the others and came over to clasp his hand. "I'm so glad you came tonight. Welcome!" Something behind him caught her eye. "Are you here with someone?"

He glanced over his shoulder to see that Lorna was still trailing him. "Not exactly," he muttered, but remembering his manners, he quickly introduced the two women. "Mrs. Atwood is my neighbor," he explained to Willow.

"We were supposed to have dinner at my house tonight," Lorna chirped at Willow. "But Mr. Emerson suddenly remembered a previous engagement." She chuckled. "And yet here we are at the same—"

"Well, we did arrange to meet here tonight," Willow told Lorna in a surprisingly firm voice. "If you'll please excuse us, I'd like to show Mr. Emerson something." And before Lorna could protest, Willow linked her arm into George's and led him around a corner, past a display of pottery, and over to the refreshment table in the corner.

"Thank you," he murmured gratefully. "My neighbor is a most persistent woman."

Willow laughed. "Well, I am very glad you made it tonight." She nodded to the table. "Would you like something?"

"No thank you," he said. "I'm fine."

"Oh?" She studied him closely. "Dieting?"

"What?"

"Watching your waistline?"

"No, nothing like that. I'm just not hungry."

"Not even for this?" She held up an appetizer, smiling coyly as if to tempt him.

He resisted the urge to turn to see if Lorna was nearby, perhaps listening to his awkward conversation. He forced a smile and reached for the cracker and cheese. "Thank you very much."

"This is a nice chèvre." Willow's eyes twinkled.

"Chèvre?" He took a tentative sniff.

"Very light and fresh and made in Oregon."

"Oh?" He took a bite and chewed.

"Chèvre is cheese made from goat's milk."

He blinked as he swallowed. "Goat's milk?"

"Do you like it?" Willow asked innocently.

He tried not to gag over the thought that he'd just ingested *goat's milk* cheese. "I, uh, I guess so." He reached for a cocktail napkin, nesting the remains of his appetizer into it as his cheeks grew warm.

Her turquoise-blue eyes twinkled with merriment. "Such an endorsement."

"Well, anyway, thank you for rescuing me just now." He lowered his voice. "Is my neighbor still lurking nearby?"

"She appears to be intently studying the large bronze in the center of the gallery."

George grimaced. "I, uh, I don't mean to keep you from your guests."

"Oh, don't worry about—"

"But I did bring you something." George pulled out the envelope from his pocket. "For Collin."

"Oh, you dear man!" Willow smiled. "Thank you so much."

Her sincere appreciation warmed him, and he returned

32

her smile. "This is a nice gallery. I didn't look around too much, but it looks like you've accumulated some very interesting art." He studied her closely, noticing how her loose curls framed her creamy face. She really was exceptionally pretty.

"Thank you. It's a work in progress. I started the gallery last fall and I feel like the pieces are finally falling into place." Her brow creased. "I, uh, don't want to alarm you, but it appears your neighbor is heading our way."

"Oh dear." He glanced nervously toward the door. "Perhaps I should just go home."

Willow held up the letter. "I know. Why don't you take this up to Collin? He's in a rather dour state of mind tonight. I couldn't coax him to come down here."

"Oh . . . what's wrong?"

"It's about a girl. I encouraged him to invite her here tonight. Unfortunately, she turned him down." She shook her head. "But if you took this up to him, it might brighten his mood." She offered a stiff-looking smile as Lorna joined them.

"If you ladies will excuse me, I need to deliver this." George waved the letter for Lorna to see.

Lorna looked dubious.

"There's a hallway to the stairs near the gallery entrance," Willow told George. "Apartment three."

Feeling mysterious—as if embarking on a secret mission—George exited the gallery, went up the dimly lit stairway, and knocked on the door with a three on it.

"Mr. Emerson?" Collin blinked in surprise. "What are you doing here?"

George held up the letter and quickly explained. "Your grandmother asked me to give it to you."

"Thank you!" Collin opened the door wider. "Do you want to come in?"

"Sure." George nodded, glancing around the starkly furnished apartment. All was neat and tidy, but it didn't look like the sort of place someone like Willow would inhabit.

"Can I get you something to drink?" Collin asked. "Although I'll warn you, all I have is almond milk and carrot juice and kombucha."

"Kombucha?"

"Yeah. Do you like it?"

"I don't know."

"I was about to have some." Collin opened a fridge that looked strangely bare. "It's passion fruit. Want me to pour you some?"

"I, uh, sure. Why not?" George sat on the bar stool next to the counter, taking in the sparse-looking kitchen as Collin poured a pinkish concoction into two glasses. "So you and your grandmother live here?"

"No, Nana doesn't live here. This is *my* apartment." Collin set a glass in front of George. "She has her own apartment next door."

"You have your own apartment?" George studied the murky-looking beverage with uncertainty.

"Yeah. My own bachelor pad." Collin laughed sardonically. "Not that it does me any good. I'm not much of a party guy. I guess Nana isn't too worried I'll get out of hand on my own."

George took a tentative sniff of his drink. "What is this anyway?" he asked.

34

"Kombucha? Well, it's a fermented probiotic drink."

"Fermented?" George felt alarmed. "Is it alcoholic?"

"No, of course not." Collin chuckled. "It's like Greek yogurt or apple cider vinegar. Good for the gut."

"Oh?" George took a cautious sip. "Interesting."

"My grandmother is kind of a health food nut. I'm used to it, but some people think it's weird."

"How long have you been with your grandmother?"

Collin shrugged. "For as long as I can remember."

"Are your parents living?"

"Yeah, sure. Well, my mom is. I don't really know about my dad."

"I'm sorry." George set down his glass. "I didn't mean to be intrusive."

"Not at all." Collin finished off his drink. "My mom had me when she was just nineteen. Kind of like my grandmother did—I mean, with no dad around. Nana says they were two of a kind. But I don't get that. My mom ran off, but Nana has taken care of me like I'm her own kid."

"Do you know where your mom is? Do you hear from her?"

"Sometimes. She's kind of a groupie."

"A groupie?"

"You know, with a band. The way the story goes, I was a baby and my mom left me with my grandparents to attend a weekend rock concert, then never came back."

"I see."

"I guess she's hooked up with the bass player now. It's a grunge rock band that was popular in the nineties and is making a comeback now."

"Interesting." George forced down the last of his drink,

35

trying not to gag over how slimy it felt as it went down his throat.

"So what do you think of kombucha?" Collin grinned.

"Not my cup of tea." George slid the glass across the bar. "But thanks."

"Well, I guess it's an acquired taste."

George felt a sudden pang of compassion for Collin. "I was raised by my grandparents too," he said quietly.

"Really?" Collin looked at him with interest. "And you turned out okay."

George grimaced, then chuckled. "Depends on who you ask."

"I'll bet your mom didn't run off with a rock band."

"No. She died. Both of my parents did. Car wreck."

"Oh, that must've been rough."

George sighed. "Yeah. But my grandparents were pretty great."

"Mine were too. Poppy wasn't really my grandfather—I mean, by blood relation. But he treated me like he was. He died a couple years ago."

George nodded. So Willow was a widow. The room got quiet and George wondered if he should leave, but then remembered something. "Your grandmother mentioned something about a girl that you wanted to ask out tonight."

Collin's cheeks flushed slightly.

"Sorry." George started to stand. "I don't mean to intrude."

"No, that's okay. Actually I wouldn't mind getting advice from a guy. Nana is great, but she can be over the top sometimes. You know?"

Although he nodded, George wasn't sure he really did

know. Or that he was the kind of guy to give anyone advice on their love life. That was a joke.

"So there's this girl. Maybe you know her. Marissa Thompson."

"Sure, I know Marissa. She seems like a very nice girl."

Collin's face lit up. "Yeah, I think so too. Anyway, Nana suggested I invite her to the gallery show tonight. So I did." His smile faded. "But she said she was busy."

"Maybe she *was* busy."

"I don't know."

"Did you ask her last minute?"

"Yeah. After school today."

"Then you need to give her another chance," George told him.

"But what if she turns me down again?"

"I guess that's life." George glanced at the kitchen clock, surprised to see that it was nearly nine. "But what if she doesn't turn you down? What if she truly was busy tonight and was disappointed that she couldn't spend time with you? And Marissa strikes me as a shy and rather serious sort of girl. Not the kind who would reach out to you. I think it's up to you to give her a second chance, Collin. It's the manly thing to do."

Collin nodded. "I think you're right. Thank you, Mr. Emerson."

George pointed to the clock. "I should probably go. The art walk is supposed to end at nine and I left my umbrella downstairs."

Collin thanked him again for the letter of recommendation while George thanked him for his unusual beverage and made his exit. But as he went back down the shadowy stairs, he wondered about this odd little family. Collin's mother was a grunge band groupie. His grandmother was a hippie. These sorts of people were definitely not George's norm . . . and indulging in goat cheese and kombucha was well outside of his comfort zone.

four

The gallery traffic had thinned considerably, but George decided to use this opportunity to take a better look at the art, slowly making his way back to the refreshment table, where he'd left his umbrella.

"There you are," Willow said cheerfully as she set a cracker and cheese on a napkin. "I hoped you hadn't gone home. Did you see Collin?"

"Yes." He nodded. "We had a nice visit."

She held up a nearly empty cheese plate. "Here, help me finish this off."

George started to protest, but stopped. He didn't mind getting the taste of the kombucha out of his mouth. Even if it was with another strange sort of cheese. At least it didn't look like the goat cheese. "Did you have a good showing tonight?" He took a cautious bite.

She shrugged. "I think it went well."

"Do you actually sell anything during art walks? There were so many people, but they looked more interested in talking than buying."

She chuckled. "We rarely make a sale at these gatherings.

It's more about connecting with the public. But sometimes a customer will return a few days later and make a purchase." She turned to the young woman who was clearing up the refreshment table. "Mr. Emerson, this is my assistant, Leslie. I don't know what I'd do without her."

Leslie grinned. "Good, I hope you never find out."

"How about if you lock up for me?" Willow set the cheese plate down. "I want to go grab a cup of coffee and put my feet up."

"No problem."

George reached for his umbrella. "Then if you'll excuse me, I'll—"

"Don't be so quick," Willow told him. "I thought perhaps you'd accompany me down to Common Grounds."

"The coffee shop?"

"Yes. They're having live music there until eleven. And I'd love a cup of coffee."

"But isn't that place for young folks?"

Willow laughed. "*We* are young folks."

George wanted to challenge this, but decided not to. Instead, he allowed her to lead the way. Perhaps he was simply under her spell, but he soon found himself entering a crowded coffeehouse where what sounded like folk music was playing and most of the crowd looked about half his age.

After a quick discussion at the counter, where George confessed to not being a coffee connoisseur, Willow insisted on ordering and paying for their coffees. "This is my little thank-you for writing that letter for Collin," she said as they settled with their coffees at a little bistro table in a semi-quiet corner.

George never drank coffee past the noon hour, but so many things about this evening were outside of his norm, he decided it didn't matter. And after his first sip, he was surprised. "This is really good," he told Willow. "What is it?"

"Just Brazilian medium roast," she said. "You said you weren't a fancy coffee drinker so I just chose a basic."

"But it's so tasty."

She looked amused. "So, tell me, what coffee do you usually drink?"

"It's just a generic grocery store brand."

"Oh." Her eyes twinkled. "Let me guess—it comes in a can."

He nodded, then took another sip. "Well, thank you for this. It's surprisingly good." He smiled. "But I'm the one who owes you a thank-you tonight."

"Whatever for?"

"For helping me to escape Lorna Atwood."

She laughed. "That woman is really into you."

"So did it take very long for her to get discouraged and leave?"

"I didn't actually see her go, but I'm sure she remained for a good fifteen minutes. She was hanging near the door . . . probably in the hopes of snagging you up again. Did you actually break a dinner date with her?"

"No." He firmly shook his head. "It was never a date. She asked me several days ago and I couldn't think of a good excuse so I put her off by saying I'd think about it. The other day, I told her I had another commitment. It wasn't exactly a lie. I planned to think of something else to do, to make it true. And then you told me about the art walk tonight. It sounded like the perfect excuse to go out."

"But not with her."

"That hadn't been my plan." He frowned. "It's not that she's particularly unpleasant, she's quite cheerful really . . . although she talks a lot."

"She is rather attractive."

"In a cupcake sort of way."

"What?" Her brows arched.

He chuckled. "Oh, that's a bad habit of mine. Not the sort of thing I usually say out loud."

"Tell me more." She leaned forward with an attractive tilt to her head. "What is a cupcake sort of way?"

"The truth is . . . I have an embarrassing tendency to compare women to baked goods." Had he really just admitted that?

"Seriously? And Lorna Atwood is a cupcake? Why?"

"Well, because she's sort of fluffy and a bit too sweet and colorful for my taste."

"Interesting." Willow nodded to a pair of attractive younger women seated nearby. "What about those two? What sort of pastries would you use to describe them?"

He studied them briefly. "Well, I don't really know them so this is pure speculation, but the blonde might be a French cruller and the brunette could be a frosted brownie."

"Hmmm . . . I wonder what I would be."

"A bran muffin," he answered without hesitation, then instantly regretted it. What was wrong with him? He wasn't usually this open and transparent with anyone. Had she cast a spell over him?

She looked dismayed. "Really? That's it? A bran muffin?"

"With raisins." He grinned sheepishly. Naturally, he had

no intention of admitting that bran muffins with raisins were, hands down, his favorite.

"Interesting." She leaned back with a creased brow. "And do you consider yourself to be an expert on baked goods?"

"Not in the least." He grimaced. "The truth is I avoid sweets altogether."

"Both in women and pastries?"

"You have me all figured out."

"Hardly, Mr. Emerson."

"Please, call me George."

"Only if you call me Willow."

"Agreed." He set down his cup and just looked at her. "This has been a most extraordinary evening."

"Really? In what way?"

"Well, I lead a very quiet life. To be honest, I rarely go out at night. And here I am at a coffeehouse at nearly ten o'clock . . . and that's after I've indulged in goat cheese and kombucha."

"Kombucha?" She blinked.

"Collin had me try some." He made a face. "Not exactly my cup of tea."

"No, I wouldn't think so."

"But it was nice getting better acquainted with Collin. I think he and I share some commonalities."

"How so?"

George explained about being raised by his grandparents. "But that's because my parents were killed in a car wreck. I was surprised to hear that Collin's mother is a grunge band groupie. At least that's what I think he said."

Willow's smile faded. "Yes, Josie has led a troubled life. I keep hoping she'll return to her senses and come home.

I even offered her one of the apartments above the gallery. But she declined. Last week, I texted her an invite to Collin's graduation, even offering to cover her expenses, but she texted back that there's a big concert in Fort Lauderdale the same weekend." She glumly shook her head. "It's as if she's forgotten that Collin is her own son."

"That must be frustrating for you."

"Do you have children?"

He shook his head. "Never married."

"Then I doubt you can imagine just how frustrating it is." She sighed. "But then that's life. You can't let it beat you up. And as I remind myself every single day, God knows what he's doing. Even if I don't."

George considered her words. For some reason he hadn't supposed that Willow West was a particularly religious person. It just didn't appear to fit her carefree hippie persona. But, of course, he was no expert on religion. "Collin mentioned that you're widowed . . ."

She slowly nodded. "Asher passed away . . . It'll be three years in October."

"I'm sorry."

"Thank you. He was a dear, lovely man. And we had a very good life together. He was the sort of man who happily embraced each day—right up to his death."

"Was it unexpected? His death, I mean."

"Of course, it was a shock when he was diagnosed with pancreatic cancer. Everything happened so quickly. But at least it gave us time to take care of things . . . to say goodbye. Asher seemed ready to go. But he was only in his midseventies when he passed away."

"That old?" George felt surprised. Willow had such a

youthfulness about her, it was hard to imagine her with someone that much older.

"Yes. I suppose Asher was old enough to be my father. I first met him as a student eons ago." She looked at George with a curious expression. "You know, he was a teacher too."

"What did he teach?"

"English lit. At Berkeley. I was young and idealistic and impressionable. His age didn't bother me in the least . . . not then, anyway."

"Did it bother you later?"

"Only that he grew older faster. And then when he died, I was alone. Well, of course, I had Collin. That made a difference." She brightened. "So you see why I said we are still young, George. Compared to Asher, we are young. With our whole lives ahead of us. So why think of yourself as old? I don't know about you, but I plan to be around for about forty more years. Maybe more."

George wasn't so sure. It wasn't that he had any health problems, but somehow he'd never imagined himself growing particularly old. In fact, he'd never expected to be as old as he was right now. And his age, combined with being put out to pasture with this early retirement, well, it just didn't instill much confidence into what might be lurking ahead.

"I'm afraid our conversation has grown rather somber," Willow said apologetically. "That's probably my fault."

George thought it was more likely his fault, but decided to try a new conversational topic. "It was interesting to see that Collin has his own apartment. I'm sure many fellows his age would be over the moon for that sort of freedom."

She smiled. "Thankfully, Collin is a very sensible young

man. He doesn't abuse his independence in the least. Not so far, anyway."

"And he did point out that your apartment is right next door, so I expect he can't get away with too much."

"Yes. I was fortunate to be able to purchase the entire building, complete with several good rent-paying tenants in the shops below. And besides the apartments above, I also have a nice studio space."

"It looks like you've done some improvements to the property."

"After I did repairs to the exterior and created my gallery space downstairs, I remodeled two of the apartments into a larger single unit. Then Collin helped me to fix up the one he's using. And I'm currently restoring two more for rentals."

"All that renovation must be expensive."

"Thanks to Asher's insurance and selling my properties in San Francisco and Sausalito, well, it was all very doable. And it's been therapeutic to release my creative energies."

George told her a bit about how he'd restored his rental properties. "Although that was years ago. I haven't done much more than repairs and general maintenance for the last twenty years."

They continued to visit, exchanging information, getting acquainted . . . until they noticed that the music had stopped and the coffeehouse was slowly vacating. "I think it's time to go," George told her. "Before they throw us out."

"My goodness." She stood and stretched. "I had no idea it was so late."

When they got outside, it was raining hard. "Good thing I brought this." George opened his umbrella, holding it over her and feeling somewhat self-conscious, but hoping it didn't show. "It appears I am able to escort you home in a fairly dry fashion, madam."

"Thank you very much, kind sir."

As they walked down the now-deserted sidewalk, George began to whistle an old song. Whistling wasn't something he normally did, but nothing about tonight had fallen into the "normal" category.

"Are you whistling 'Singin' in the Rain'?" Willow suddenly asked.

"As a matter of fact, yes," he admitted.

"I adore that old movie!" Now she began to hum along with him, and before long, they were both singing the lyrics as well.

"Here you go, my lady." George made a mock bow in front of the stairs that led up to the apartments. "Thank you for a most memorable evening."

"Thank you." Lit by the streetlamp, she looked at him for a long moment and George suddenly wondered if she expected to be kissed. Good grief, he hoped not! Because, even if he wanted to kiss her—and he wasn't sure—he had no idea how to go about it. It had been so long . . . too long, perhaps.

"Good night," he said quickly. Backing away, he lifted his umbrella and, without another word, rushed away. Had he missed an opportunity just now? Or had he wisely escaped what would've turned into an embarrassingly awkward moment? He argued back and forth with himself as he jumped over puddles and hurried toward home. Perhaps he would never know the answer to such frustrating questions. Perhaps it didn't matter.

Because Willow West had probably figured out that George

was a very odd duck by now. Most likely, she was relieved to be rid of him. For all he knew, she was laughing about the whole thing right now. But wouldn't that be for the best? George had spent most of his life avoiding intimate relationships. For good reason. So why change at this late stage of the game? Why tempt fate?

five

Willow woke bright and early the next day. Although the sun shone brightly, songs from *Singin' in the Rain* still pleasantly wormed through her head as she carried her coffee mug out to her garden terrace. She breathed in deeply the fresh morning air. It felt good to be alive! So good that she began to sing another song from that old Gene Kelly film.

"Good morning, good morning!" she sang as she strolled past the potted plants and flowers, finally settling onto the comfy outdoor sectional that she'd recently added to her outdoor paradise. She sang as many of the lyrics as she could recall then decided it was probably time to see that old movie again.

As Willow sipped her coffee, she replayed the previous evening. The gallery showing had been a pure delight. Much better than the first show she'd had last winter when only three "patrons" showed up. Hopefully last night's visitors would translate into some sales. Not so much for herself, but for the artists who'd consigned their work to her gallery. Some of them, she knew, were really struggling. She wanted to see them succeed . . . wanted the small town of Warner to begin embracing the arts. She felt hopeful.

"Nana?"

"Over here," she called out, watching as Collin made his way through the maze of blooming plants. Wearing his plaid pajama pants, a white T-shirt, and a big smile, he sat down next to her.

"Nice day, huh?" He sipped what appeared to be carrot juice.

"Gorgeous." She peered curiously at him. "And you seem in good spirits."

"I am." He nodded.

"Any special reason?"

"I sent Marissa a text a little while ago." He set his glass down. "I was worried it was too early, but she texted right back."

"And?"

"We are going on a bike ride today." He beamed at her.

"Well, good for you." She patted his back. "Good job on not giving up."

"Mr. Emerson encouraged me to try again."

Willow blinked. "Seriously? Mr. Emerson gives dating advice?"

Collin nodded. "He said to give her a second chance. That maybe she really did have other plans last night. Turns out he was right."

Willow resisted the urge to remind Collin she'd said pretty much the same thing last night. "Well, I'm glad you listened to Mr. Emerson. And how about that letter he wrote—did you read it?"

"I did." His smile grew bigger. "It's really nice. Thanks

for asking him for it, Nana. It almost makes me want to start applying to a bigger college."

"Really?" She felt hopeful.

"Yeah . . . but not until a semester or two at the community college." He grinned. "That's where Marissa is going."

"Aha." She nodded. "Now I get it."

He polished off the last of his carrot juice. "You got anything good for breakfast at your place?"

She grimaced. "I meant to get groceries yesterday, but I got distracted with the art walk preparations. I do have Irish oats, but that takes a while to—"

"That's all right. I already had a bagel and cream cheese."

"Sounds like I should be raiding your larder."

He stood and stretched. "I better get going. I need to grab a shower before I meet Marissa at the park."

She controlled herself from asking why he was showering *before* a bike ride. After all, this was almost a date. Or maybe it was a date. Whatever it was, it was a first for Collin and she was happy for him. "Well, you have fun," she told him. "It's a perfect day for a bike ride."

After Collin left, she felt her own stomach rumbling with hunger. As much as she hated to leave her peaceful retreat up here, she knew she needed to get dressed and go down to unlock the gallery. Leslie had promised to come in early to clean the place before opening.

With no plans to work at the gallery today, Willow dressed casually in jeans, a paisley smock top, and her favorite Birkenstock sandals, then went down to unlock the door just as Leslie arrived. "I'm on my way to get a bite to eat," she told her. "Want me to bring you back something?"

Leslie held up a small brown bag. "I brought my breakfast with me."

"Joel will be here at noon," Willow reminded her. Although Joel was only part-time, he was a great help with bookkeeping and a well-informed salesperson. Willow wished he was willing to be full-time, but she understood. Joel, like her, was an artist and needed time to create.

Satisfied that the gallery was in good hands, Willow headed down Main Street in search of a light breakfast. Smelling a tantalizing aroma from the Muffin Man Bakery, she decided to go inside. As she gazed over the well-stocked glass case, she thought of George's confession about comparing women to pastries. Willow suspected that she would've been offended if another sort of man had made a statement like this . . . but somehow, coming from George, it sounded rather innocent.

"Are those bran muffins?" she asked the girl behind the counter.

"Yes. Fresh out of the oven."

"With raisins?"

The girl grinned. "Yep."

"I'll take half a dozen," she said impulsively.

After paying for the muffins, she headed over to Common Grounds Coffee Company with a specific mission in mind. Munching on a broken-off piece of a bran muffin, which was surprisingly good, she selected a small bag of medium roast Brazilian coffee beans and a coffee grinder, then ordered herself a latte. While she waited for her coffee, she used her phone to look up "George Emerson of Warner, Oregon" and was pleased to discover his address was only a few blocks away.

As she carried her purchases, she continued to nibble on the bran muffin, finishing it off as she came up to his house. It was a charming cornflower-blue bungalow with a tidy, albeit sparse, yard. She felt a little nervous as she stepped up to the front porch. Poor George had been practically stalked by his neighbor last night and here was Willow showing up uninvited this morning. Perhaps she should simply set her gift in front of his door and leave.

"Hello there," a female voice called out.

Willow turned to see Lorna Atwood waving from her front porch. "Oh, hello," Willow called back. "I was just dropping something off for George."

"I think he's home," Lorna said. "At least I haven't seen him venture out."

"Oh, well . . . thanks." Willow turned back, quietly tapping on the door, but preparing to just drop off her parcels and leave.

"Hello?" George opened the door with a bleary-eyed expression.

"Did I wake you?" she asked with concern.

"No, no, of course not." His frown looked confused.

"Here." She held the bags out. "I brought you something and—"

"What's this for?" he asked with a furrowed brow.

She glanced over her shoulder to see Lorna watching with open curiosity. "May I come in?" she whispered.

He appeared to understand. "Yes, of course." He opened the door wider. "Please, come in."

Once inside, she let out a sigh then giggled. "I'm sorry to burst in on you like this, George. But I wanted to thank you for—"

"You thanked me last night." He looked self-conscious as he tucked a slightly rumpled blue shirt into his trousers. Not his previous buttoned-up self. She wondered if something was wrong.

"This is to thank you for something else." She quickly explained about Collin's plans to meet up with Marissa. "He was so happy. And he said it was thanks to you."

George's lips curved up. "Well, that's nice to hear. I'm glad for him."

Willow held out the bakery bag. "For you."

His eyes lit up as he peered inside. "Bran muffins?"

"With raisins."

"Thank you." He nodded.

"That's not all." She held up the other bag. "Coffee."

"But I already have coffee." He nodded toward his kitchen. "I haven't made it yet, but I—"

"If you don't mind, I'd like to make your coffee this morning." She went past him, going into the small but tidy kitchen and examining the coffee maker—even sniffing inside of it.

"Well, that's rather unusual. I can easily make it—"

"Do you have any white vinegar?"

"What?" He pushed his uncombed hair back with a perplexed expression.

"I'd like to clean your coffee maker," she told him as she removed the carafe, setting it into the sink.

"But, as you can see, it's perfectly clean." He ran a finger over the top of it.

"Yes, it's spotless on the outside, but when did you last clean the inside?"

"What?" He frowned.

"Do you or do you not have white vinegar?" she demanded.

He went to a pantry and after a bit returned with a bottle of white vinegar. "Here." He handed it over with a dubious look.

"This will take about ten minutes or so." She poured vinegar into the carafe. "In case you have anything you need to attend to."

"Well, I, uh, actually haven't had my morning shower yet. I slept in today. Not something I normally do."

She smiled. "Sometimes it's good to do things outside of the norm, George. Go ahead and get your shower. I'll take care of everything."

"Well, I, uh—"

"Go on." She gave him a gentle nudge. "Don't worry, I'm not a house burglar. You can trust me. And take your time." To her relief, he didn't continue to protest. Poor fellow, he probably thought she was certifiably nuts. But as she waited for the vinegar water to heat and run through the coffee maker, she knew that purging out his old generic coffee would be well worth the effort.

Willow didn't like to think of herself as a snoop but couldn't help a look around the kitchen as she waited on the coffee maker. The wooden cupboards were painted white but spotlessly clean. The black-and-white checkerboard floors looked old but well cared for. Although there was no dishwasher, the aqua-blue stove and fridge looked like vintage 1950s and were actually quite charming. Other than the coffee maker and toaster, there were no "modern" conveniences on the original countertops. For some reason this wasn't surprising. George was an old-fashioned guy . . . almost like someone from a different era.

Curious as to whether there might be milk or cream for

coffee, she peeked inside the fridge to see that it was adequately, albeit rather spartanly, stocked. Not that she could judge since it was actually in much better shape than her own much more modern refrigerator at the moment.

She removed a carton of eggs, a block of white cheddar cheese, a red onion, and some spinach. While the second batch of just plain water gurgled through the coffee maker, she set to work grating, chopping, and stirring. She paused to grind the Brazilian beans and, while a fresh pot of aromatic coffee brewed, sautéed the onions. Then she added the spinach, eggs, and cheese . . . and scrambled. Leaving her concoction covered on the stove, she got out dishes and mugs and then, peering into the backyard, she noticed a derelict picnic table and decided to transport their breakfast outside.

She'd just gotten it all set up, complete with a canning jar bouquet of blooms that she'd picked from a slightly neglected flowerbed in the backyard, when George appeared with a hard-to-read expression.

"You look clean and fresh." She waved him over. "Breakfast is served."

"But how did you—"

"I hope you don't mind." She filled his plate with the scramble then added a muffin as he approached. "But I was starving. So I just made myself at home." She smiled nervously as he picked up the fresh pot of coffee, pouring it into his mug. "Please, join me."

After he sat down, she said a quiet and nontraditional blessing then picked up her fork. "Dig in before it gets cold." And without further ado, she took a bite. Egg scrambles had always been her specialty and this one was near perfection—although some cremini mushrooms might've improved it a bit.

"This is delicious." George dabbed his mouth with a paper napkin. "Thank you."

"Try your coffee," she said.

He took a tentative sip, then smiled. "This is very good. Is that just from cleaning with vinegar?"

She explained about the freshly ground beans. "But I couldn't bear to put them in an unclean coffee maker. That would spoil everything." She pursed her lips. "It's rather spiritual, if you think about it."

"How is that?" He broke his muffin in two.

"Well, sometimes people look all spotless and clean on the outside, but they're a mess underneath." She chuckled. "In fact, that's almost exactly what Jesus said to the religious leaders of his day."

"What?" George looked clearly confused.

"Sorry." She took another bite. "I didn't mean to preach at you." She tipped her head toward the side fence where a blonde head was peeking over. "And, don't look now, but we have an audience."

"Mrs. Atwood?" he murmured without turning to see.

Willow nodded. "Should I invite her to join us?"

"No." He bit into a muffin and thoughtfully chewed. Then his eyes lit up.

"Better than a cupcake?"

"Most definitely better."

"Do you think I've given the wrong impression by showing up like this?" She lowered her voice. "I mean, for your neighbor."

He grinned. "Well, if you have, I owe you my sincerest gratitude. Thank you very much."

"Hey, I do what I can."

Willow's concerns for crashing in on him like this slowly evaporated as they pleasantly visited and dined in the sunshine. Although she suspected that George was still somewhat dumbfounded by her actions, she felt that he was enjoying himself . . . and the food too. "This has all been so unexpected," he said as they finished up. "But much appreciated."

"I'm glad you liked it."

"I had a rather sleepless night," he confessed. "I normally don't drink coffee beyond the noon hour. I'm afraid it kept me awake."

"You're sure that was the coffee?" Willow hid her smile as they carried the breakfast things back into the kitchen. George insisted on cleaning up, and she felt a fresh wave of pity for this man. He lived such a barren and colorless existence. Almost as if he'd gotten stuck somehow, or perhaps had a primal fear of fully participating in life. Whatever it was, she felt more determined than ever to get to the bottom of it. But she suspected it wouldn't be easy. It would probably require a lot of gentle pushing on her part. And perhaps some less-than-gentle prodding too.

six

George felt bewildered as he hurried to wash up the breakfast dishes. Willow hadn't appeared eager to depart and, although he hated to leave dirty dishes in the sink, it didn't feel very hospitable to let her sit alone in his living room. Even so, he couldn't just leave the kitchen like this. Willow might be a good cook, but she certainly left a huge mess behind.

George wasn't quite sure why it made him so uneasy to think of Willow roaming around his little house. He didn't have anything to hide. But it was disturbing to think she'd gone through his fridge and cupboards and such. Equally disturbing to imagine her out there "making herself at home." Truth be told, George was not the ideal host. In fact, he'd never been a host at all. As much as he liked Willow, she certainly did push him from his comfort zone.

"Well, that will do for now." He joined her while still holding a damp dish towel. "I'll finish up later." He dried his hands on the towel then folded it.

"You're sure I can't help?" she offered from her position on his small sofa.

"No, thank you." He looked nervously around the room.

In the sunshine, he could see several surfaces with a slight layer of dust. He resisted the urge to use the damp dish towel to wipe it now. Probably not a hospitable move.

"I've just been admiring those gorgeous cabinets." Willow stood, going over to the wall of cabinets that George and his grandfather had built more than twenty years ago.

"Thank you."

"I've tried to imagine what you keep in there." She grinned. "I suspect it's books, but I've resisted the urge to peek."

"You can look." He opened the cabinet nearest to him.

"Oh my goodness!" She rushed over to see it more closely. "Vinyl records—there must be hundreds of them." She turned to him. "You're a collector?"

"Only by default. The oldest ones belonged to my grandparents. My grandfather was a jazz aficionado. My grandmother loved the crooners—Sinatra, Crosby, and such."

"But these are from the sixties and seventies." She removed an album. "Beatles?"

"Those belonged to my brother."

She continued to look through them. "The White Album? You have the Beatles White Album?" She carefully removed it from the cover. "In mint condition too."

"My brother had most of the Beatles' albums."

"Amazing." She slid the album back into place. "Do you ever listen to them?"

He opened the next cabinet to expose an old turntable and speaker system. "I used to occasionally, but it's been a while." He honestly couldn't remember the last time he'd turned the stereo on.

"Oh, you should enjoy them, George. Music is good for the soul."

He considered this. "Well, maybe with my retirement, I'll have more time for that." That, of course, was absolutely silly. George always had plenty of time.

"And what's behind these doors?" She pointed to the other end.

"Another collection." He felt a little embarrassed, but he opened the door anyway.

"VHS tapes?" She chuckled. "Are you kidding?"

"Most of these belonged to my grandparents."

"What wonderful old classics." She perused the spines. "You've got all the Katherine Hepburn–Spencer Tracy films. And here are all the Cary Grant ones. And Fred Astaire and Ginger Rogers. These are delightful films."

"My grandmother loved old romantic movies."

"And here are the westerns." She continued to the next shelf, reading off titles.

"My grandfather's."

"And Alfred Hitchcock." She pulled out *North by Northwest*. "One of my all-time favorites."

"Those were my collection."

"You're a Hitchcock fan?"

He nodded.

"When did you last see this?" She held up a copy of *The Birds*.

"I don't know. Years ago."

"So you don't watch these much?"

"Maybe now that I'm retired . . ."

"Do you have a VHS player?"

He opened the next cabinet door to reveal an old-fashioned TV and a VHS player. "I assume it still works," he murmured.

She slid the tapes back into place. "Well, I hope someday

you'll invite me over to watch some of these with you." She smiled warmly as, one by one, she closed the cabinet doors. "I'll bring the popcorn."

"I'll keep that in mind." He shifted his weight uncomfortably. On one hand, he did enjoy her company. On the other hand, it was highly disturbing. He wasn't sure how much he could take of this. He resisted the urge to run a finger around his collar . . . to loosen it in order to breathe better.

"How about these last two doors?" Willow asked.

"As you suspected." He opened both doors. "Books."

Willow ran her hand across the smooth surface of a wooden door. "These cabinets really are beautiful, George. Do you know what kind of wood this is?"

"Cherry." He explained how he and his grandfather had built them.

"You're kidding." She examined the cabinets more closely. "You're a craftsman, George."

"My grandfather was."

"But if you helped him, you must've learned a thing or two."

He shrugged. "Yes, I suppose I know the basics of cabinet building. But I haven't really dabbled in it much since then. That was decades ago."

"I suppose you need a well-equipped workshop," she said, "to produce pieces like this. As an artist, I understand the need for space and tools."

"I have a workshop."

She looked around the small room. "Where?"

"Oh, it's not here," he explained. "It's at my grandparents' house."

"But I thought they'd passed away years ago."

"They did, but they left me their house. And my grandfather's workshop is still there, complete with all his tools."

"Do you think you'll put them to use?" she asked. "I mean, after you retire."

"That's a thought."

"I'd love to commission some cabinets like these," she said. "They wouldn't even need to be this beautiful, although I wouldn't protest if they were. But I desperately need storage cabinets for my studio." She peered curiously at him. "Any chance I can entice you to make some for me? I'll pay you well, George. And perhaps I'd even make you breakfast again. Or maybe dinner. I'm great with Italian food."

"Oh, well, I don't know. I'm not sure I could really make what you want. I'm out of practice and—"

"I'm sure you could produce something that would work. As I said, I only need storage cabinets for my studio. They could be made out of simple plywood and I wouldn't complain. Right now I've got supplies strewn all over the place."

"I'll think about it, Willow. Maybe after next week."

"Yes, of course." She pursed her lips. "I'm sorry to be so pushy, George. It's just that I'm just so impressed by the craftsmanship here." She studied him closely. "Do you *enjoy* woodworking?"

He considered this. "I did."

"Then perhaps you would again." She stepped back with a sigh. "Now I'm afraid I've worn out my welcome. I should probably be on my merry way."

George felt torn. On one hand, he'd be relieved if she left . . . on the other hand, well, he wasn't sure. "Would you like to see my grandfather's workshop?" he asked suddenly. "I had planned to walk up there today. I usually check on my grandparents' house on the weekend."

"I'd love to see the workshop," she exclaimed. "Is it nearby?"

"About half a mile. On Talbot Hill."

"Talbot Hill," she said in a teasing tone. "Isn't that where all the rich snobs live?"

He shrugged. "I don't know. My grandparents weren't snobs."

"Sorry. My grandparents probably said something like that. They lived on the wrong side of the tracks. Literally." She laughed. "So, what are we waiting for?"

"Do you mind walking?"

"Not at all."

He smiled. "I don't have a car."

"Seriously?"

He opened the front door. "Never saw the need for one."

"Interesting." She followed him outside, waiting as he locked the door. And since she was watching he refrained from checking it twice. "Let's go."

As they walked toward Talbot Hill, he told her a bit about his grandparents. "I never thought of them as that well off, but I guess they probably were. My mother's side of the family owned the lumber mill in town."

"You mean Rockwell Lumber?"

"That's right. When I was a kid, the mill nearly shut down, thanks to all the government's logging restrictions for spotted owls and such. My grandfather was always complaining about how the government was running him out of business. So to my way of thinking, my grandparents weren't really that rich."

"So are you saying your grandparents were the Rockwells?"

"That's right. My mother's parents."

Willow peered curiously at him. "I thought the Rockwells were quite wealthy. Does that mean you're rich?"

"No, no . . . that was long ago. The timber industry tanked when I was in high school. My grandfather sold the mill. I think that's what paid my college tuition. The buyers kept the Rockwell name and retooled the mill to manufacture doors and windows. From what I hear they're doing quite well nowadays."

"What about the Rockwell house?" she asked. "Is it on the historic register?"

"No."

"I noticed the house looks a little run-down and neglected. Did your family lose that too?"

"No. That's where we're going right now. That's where my grandfather's workshop is located. They left the property to me."

"You're kidding. That's *your* house?"

He barely nodded, still stuck on her previous comment. "So do you really think the house looks run-down and neglected?"

"Sorry, I didn't realize you're the owner, George." She grimaced. "But I always loved that house. Whenever I see it, I wish that someone would show it some love and fix it up. Most of the other historic homes on the hill have been restored." She poked him in the arm with a teasing look. "Maybe you'll have time for that, once you're retired."

"I'll have plenty to keep me busy before long." As they turned up his grandparents' street, he felt suddenly overwhelmed. Almost like he was drowning—or about to. Like he couldn't catch his breath. What was he doing with this woman? And taking her to see his grandparents' house? Had he lost his mind?

Willow was interesting, but rather intense. Perhaps too intense for him. What would she say when she saw his family home up close? What if she criticized or made too many suggestions—or laughed? He knew he wouldn't handle that very well. Especially after a sleepless night. What if he turned grouchy and defensive and spoke his mind? He wished he hadn't invited her along and desperately tried to think of a way to derail this now. He was about to make an excuse to go back home when he heard a jangling sound.

"That's my phone." Willow paused to reach into her jeans pocket. "Sorry." She peered down at it. "Oh, it's the gallery—I have to take it. Excuse me."

Wanting to be polite, George stepped away from her, trying not to eavesdrop as she talked to her assistant about something that sounded urgent.

"I'm sorry." Willow repocketed her phone. "That was Leslie. She needs me at the gallery. I need to head back to town."

George nodded, feigning disappointment. He actually felt enormous relief. "No problem."

"Some other time then?" Willow smiled hopefully.

"Of course." George thanked her again for the breakfast and they said goodbye. Feeling that a weight had been lifted, he continued on toward his grandparents' house. Somehow he needed to put the brakes on this friendship with Willow. She was nice enough and part of him was seriously intrigued. But a larger part of him was horrified and terrified and stressed beyond words. Willow West was just what he did not need in his life. She was the type who would poke and prod and stir things up. Although he didn't like to compare her to Lorna Atwood, she was not completely unlike his pushy neighbor. Women like that were troublesome. George had spent the last three decades avoiding that sort of trouble, and he didn't intend to start inviting it now.

Besides, he reminded himself as he went up the hill to his grandparents' house, he had the end of school and his retirement to think about. He had one week to empty his office, calculate his students' grades, and say a final farewell to his career. He didn't need a demanding relationship to complicate things.

seven

It didn't take long for Willow to take the hint. George Emerson was giving her the cold shoulder. She'd called his house after church the next day, inviting him to join her and some friends for tea on her terrace, only to be told he had "other plans." Then, on an after-dinner walk with Collin on Monday, they'd "casually" strolled down George's street. Collin spotted George sitting on his porch, but by the time they got closer, George had disappeared inside. He probably thought she was stalking him. And maybe she was.

Despite her dismay, Willow knew she had to let it go. Really, did she need someone like George Emerson in her life? She had so much going on, so many projects to complete, the gallery to run, new friends to spend time with . . . Why would she bother with someone who appeared to want to hold her at arm's length anyway?

And yet, each day in the following week as she went about her business, she thought about Mr. Emerson. In the morning, she made excuses to walk with Collin partway to school in the hopes of spotting him. And in the afternoon, after school had let out, she would often take a stroll through town, hoping to spy him on his way home. Maybe she really was a stalker. It was embarrassing.

• • •

George was surprised at how much he'd managed to accumulate in his office at school. Mostly books and paperwork, because he'd long since given up on displaying personal items there. He'd kept a few framed photos at first, but students' comments eventually motivated him to remove them. Either the kids would poke fun at something or become overly interested. He soon learned it was best to leave his personal life—as if he had one—at home. Still, by Wednesday, as he was lugging yet another heavy box of books through the school's foyer, he felt weary to the bone.

"Mr. Emerson." Mrs. Malcolm paused to hold the door for him. "That looks like a heavy load."

He nodded and, thanking her, passed by. "Books."

"Hopefully you parked nearby."

"No car," he huffed as he went down the front steps

"No car?" She sounded shocked as she followed him down. "Don't tell me you're going to lug those books all the way home like that."

"That's my plan."

"Not if I have anything to say about it." She pointed to the parking lot. "Let me give you a ride."

George was too tired to object. "Thank you, Mrs. Malcolm. That would be most welcome."

She led him to a blue sedan and, after he was comfortably

seated, he let out a long sigh. "I feel like I'm getting very old," he confessed.

"I heard you're retiring."

"Yes. I didn't feel old enough for retirement before. But now I think it's probably for the best." He paused to give her directions to his house.

"But you're not that old."

"I'll be fifty-five this summer."

"That's not very old."

"So I keep hearing."

"I just turned forty-five."

He turned to look at her. He would've guessed her to be older. Not that he planned to say as much. "It won't be too long before they'll start pressuring you to retire," he warned her. "What with the recent budget cuts and all."

"Well, I've been considering it anyway. When my husband passed away, I had planned to quit. But my son encouraged me to keep working. He thought it was good for me. I don't know."

"I suppose if there's something else you want to do . . . retirement could be good."

"Aren't you looking forward to it?"

"I'm not sure. I suppose I am right now. I don't know how I'll feel by September."

"Yes, there's something to be said for our line of work— especially when you're single and living alone."

"What do you mean?" he asked.

"Well, you spend the whole day surrounded by people. Some that can be very obnoxious and irritating and stressful. You know what I mean?"

He nodded.

"Then you go home to your nice, calm house with no one interrupting or challenging you. No laughing or teasing or stomping about. Just peace and quiet." She let out a long sigh. "Well, it makes you grateful."

"I suspect you're right about that."

"Even if all you have to look forward to is a microwave meal. It's still a relief to dine in a peaceful place." She chuckled. "Although I'll be having homemade beef Stroganoff tonight."

"Homemade beef Stroganoff? Isn't that a lot of work?"

"I made it yesterday for my sister's birthday. She loves my Stroganoff. Anyway, I've got loads of leftovers." She turned to him. "Hey, do you like beef Stroganoff?"

"I used to. My grandmother made it, but I haven't had it in ages."

"Then you must have some tonight."

"Well, I, uh, I don't know, Mrs. Malcolm—"

"Please, call me Patty."

"Well, it's just that—"

"I won't take no for an answer. Let this be my retirement gift to you. I even have leftover birthday cake. Trust me, you won't be sorry. We will dine in style tonight."

George didn't know how to dissuade her, and she'd already turned her car in a direction that he could only assume was toward her house. Besides that, he'd only had an apple for lunch. He was hungry. Hopefully she made a good Stroganoff.

Before long, she was driving through a neighborhood where every tan and beige house looked exactly like the next one. He was about to ask her if she ever got lost in the maze of identical dwellings, but then she turned in to a driveway.

"Here we are," she said cheerfully. "This is going to be such fun." She led him into a living room with tan walls and an enormous beige sofa shaped like an L. "You make yourself comfortable while I get things ready," she said. "And don't mind the cats."

"Cats?"

"Yes, there are three of them. Sammy and JoJo are very friendly. But Gordie, well, not so much."

George swallowed nervously as he sat on the sofa. He was not terribly fond of felines. And that was putting it mildly. Oh, he'd liked an amazing cat once . . . but his cat, Buddy, had been one in a million. He'd never known a cat like that since. He hoped Patty's cats would sense his chilly attitude and keep a safe distance. But before long, a large, furry cat was rubbing against his legs, coating his dark blue pants with white hair—and another scrawny gray cat hopped onto his lap and was suddenly kneading his thighs with sharp claws that felt like they could draw blood. Did these animals carry diseases? When was his last tetanus shot?

"Oh my," Patty declared. "It looks like you've met my babies. That's Sammy on your lap and JoJo down there." She set a plate of cheese and crackers on the table. "Help yourself to appetizers while I go heat up the Stroganoff."

As desperately as George wanted to bolt for the door and dash home, he knew it was pointless. Not only was his box of books still in the back of her car, this subdivision was at least five miles from town. Best to just get this over with . . . as painlessly and quickly as possible. He was about to reach for a cracker when the fuzzy white cat leaped onto the coffee table and began to sniff at the plate.

George's appetite vanished. Just as JoJo helped himself to a piece of yellow cheese, George pushed Sammy from his lap, rescued the plate of appetizers, and carried them into the kitchen.

"I thought I should come keep you company," he told Patty. "Do you mind?"

"Not at all." She smiled as she slid a pan into the oven. "My late husband always liked to sit in the living room while I fixed dinner. I assumed you'd like that too."

"Not particularly." George sat down at the breakfast bar. Eying the appetizers, he tried to remember which side of the plate the cat had been working on, hoping it was safe to eat from the other side. He was about to take a cracker when, once again, the big white cat leaped—clear up to the breakfast bar. "What!" George jumped in surprise.

"Oh, JoJo," Patty scolded gently. "You know you're not supposed to jump on the counters." She chuckled. "At least when we have guests." She shooed the cat down then apologized to George. "Cats are impossible to train. And to be honest, I don't mind them. Do you like cats, Mr. Emerson?"

"Well, I, uh—"

"And do you mind if I call you George? Mr. Emerson is such a mouthful."

"No, no, I don't mind." George wanted to say what he did mind—and that was ill-mannered cats. To distract himself, he looked around Patty's kitchen. It was one of those modern ones with silver appliances and black stone countertops that felt strangely cold and showed off JoJo's white hairs. As George leaned down to blow over the countertop, sending some of the lightweight cat hairs flying, he noticed the pigs. They were everywhere. Pig potholders, pig salt-and-pepper shakers, a pig cutting board, and a pig cookie jar, just to name a few. "You appear to like pigs," he said absently.

"Oh yes. I adore pigs. I grew up on a farm and raised them for 4-H projects."

"Interesting." He couldn't think of anything less appetizing in a kitchen. Well, except for cats maybe.

"Some people think pigs are dirty, but they are actually rather clean."

Probably cleaner than cats, George thought as JoJo jumped onto another part of the kitchen counter. At least pigs would be limited to the floor. He suddenly imagined a herd of miniature swine crawling about the floor. Patty continued to chatter away, clearly delighted to have company and, although George tried to act congenial, his head was beginning to throb with a headache . . . and the never-ending evening continued.

By the time they were seated at the dining table, with cats still roaming around his ankles, George felt slightly ill. He tried to maintain small talk about school and whatnot as he poked at his not-quite-hot beef Stroganoff. He wasn't sure if it was him or the food, but it all tasted bland and heavy and greasy. Nothing like his grandmother used to make. And when Patty mentioned her sister's leftover birthday cake, George patted his midsection and claimed he couldn't eat another bite.

"I'm afraid this last week of school has worn me out," he told her.

"I know what you mean," she said. "I'm still not done with grades."

"So, perhaps we should call it a night."

To his relief, Patty was already going for her purse and car keys, and soon they were on their way, with Patty cheerfully carrying the conversation as she drove.

"I'm so glad we got to spend this time together," Patty declared as she pulled up to his house. "Even if it was a relatively brief dinner. I hope you'll come over again, George. And it won't be leftovers next time. I make a mean meatloaf, if I do say so myself. Maybe after you're settled into your retirement and aren't feeling so worn out." She turned to smile at him. "Because I suspect we have a lot in common."

"Well, thank you again." He got out of the car. "I'm sure you need to get back to finish your grading." He retrieved his box of books from the backseat. "I'll see you at school tomorrow." Then, without waiting for her response, he closed the door and hurried toward his house. He couldn't remember the last time he'd been this glad to get home. Patty was right about one thing. A peaceful, calm, and quiet house—preferably without cats—was most welcome at the end of a long day.

As he set the box of books down on his coffee table, George felt like he was not only a confirmed bachelor, but he was a lost cause when it came to women. "Let this be a lesson to you, Mr. Emerson," he said aloud as he set his books into the bookshelf section of his cabinet. "Keep yourself to yourself . . . unless you want trouble."

But as he closed the cabinet, he suddenly remembered how Willow had run her hand over this very door. He remembered some of the feelings he'd experienced while being with her . . . at the coffeehouse . . . in his own backyard over breakfast. It was nothing like the way he'd felt with Patty tonight. He shuddered to think of Patty's insufferable cats and homely pigs. He wondered what Willow's habitat might be like. She probably kept tropical birds . . . or a peacock perhaps.

eight

Toward the end of the week, Willow felt like she'd managed to put thoughts of George Emerson behind her. For the most part anyway. She'd almost convinced herself that they were just too different to ever be truly compatible. Some claimed that opposites attract, but what about staying power? How could you sustain a relationship with someone so completely different? It was ridiculous.

"Do you want to come to Mr. Emerson's retirement party this afternoon?" Collin asked Willow on Thursday morning. He was about to head off for his last official day of high school. "It was in yesterday's announcements. Everyone's invited. Teachers, parents, kids, custodians, lunchroom ladies." He chuckled as he picked up his book bag.

"Oh, I don't know."

"Come on, Nana," he urged. "I have a feeling that Mr. Emerson doesn't have many friends. It might mean a lot to him if we went."

"So, you're going?"

"Sure. My way of thanking him for that letter."

"What about baccalaureate tonight?"

"That's not until seven. Mr. Emerson's party is at 3:30. In the school library."

"Well, I suppose if I'm not busy . . . I could come." Even as she said this, Willow wasn't so sure. Besides the fact that she had nothing in common with Mr. Emerson, he appeared to have sent her a clear and distinct message. He was not interested in her. Not in the least.

Still, Collin's invitation stuck with her all morning. By midday, she knew she should go. After all, George had been an excellent teacher for Collin and he'd written the letter she'd begged from him. Shouldn't she at least show her gratitude? Plus, she suspected that Collin was right. A man like George probably had few friends.

As she poked around her messy studio, attempting to organize the clutter and chaos and still wishing for those big cherry cabinets, she got an idea. She'd take George a little retirement gift. Okay, it wasn't exactly little, but she felt it would be perfect. Something to perk up George's stark little bungalow. Oh, he might very well hate it. But that would be his problem. Now if only she could find where she'd tucked away that stack of oversized paintings.

Willow dug around the piles and boxes, creating even more messes, until she finally unearthed some old paintings that she'd wrapped in a drop-cloth. She thumbed through the canvases until she found it. She'd painted this in college. The subject had been a rusty old turquoise-blue pickup truck. She'd set it in an overgrown field of bright orange poppies. Something about those two bright colors had spoken to her back then. And she actually still liked it. But this painting was large and cumbersome—not something she cared to display in her gallery and too big for her apartment.

She couldn't explain it, but something about the piece reminded her of George Emerson. Perhaps it was metaphorical. The broken-down yet charming pickup was going nowhere—and although George wasn't exactly broken-down, he did act somewhat stuck. But the cheerful optimism of the prolific poppies encompassing the truck promised better things, happier days. Anyway, she hoped so.

She wasn't sure how George would react, but something about the truck and poppies had George Emerson written all over it—and she was determined to present it to him today. As she wrapped it in kraft paper, prettily tying it with strands of dyed raffia, she was glad that her signature was obscured by the frame. That way if George sincerely hated it, he needn't be concerned that she'd take it personally.

As she loaded the canvas in the back of her SUV, she chuckled to herself. Whether this was a white elephant gift or an insult, she wasn't sure. But as she parked near the high school and extracted her bulky package, she realized she didn't particularly care. Let George sort it out.

Willow had dressed a bit more conservatively today. For her, anyway. This morning she'd donned an off-white dress and espadrille sandals. She'd perked the ensemble up with turquoise and coral beads, silver bangle bracelets, and big hoop earrings. Some might think her ensemble too youthful for a woman her age, but Willow had never concerned herself with conventions. If she felt good—what else mattered?

Although she did feel slightly conspicuous as she went through the security station, she told herself it was only because she was going in while everyone else was rushing out. She quickly explained to the security guard that her parcel contained a gift for Mr. Emerson's retirement party. "Nothing toxic or dangerous or explosive," she teased. "Well, unless someone hates art."

The guard gave the package a few pokes and squeezes then finally nodded. "I guess we won't need to open it. Have a nice time."

She thanked him and proceeded toward the library. Her plan was to be congenial but not overly personal. She would simply present her gift and chat a bit, then make an excuse to leave shortly thereafter. That would satisfy Collin, and George would probably be relieved to see her go. But when she got to the library, which she'd expected to be filled with well-wishers, there was no sign of a party.

"Can I help you?" a woman with a bored expression asked.

"I thought there was a retirement party for—"

"Oh, that's in the conference room." The woman nodded toward the back.

Willow thanked her then headed back. As she got nearer to the open conference room door, she expected to hear voices, but like the rest of the library, it was eerily quiet. She entered the conference room, expecting to be greeted by crepe paper banners and colorful balloons, but all she saw was a sheet cake on the table with a handful of stiff-looking people congregated around it.

Relieved to see Collin and Marissa were there, Willow smiled brightly at George. "Happy retirement, Mr. Emerson!" She held out her parcel. "A little something from Collin and me." She winked at her grandson. "Well, not exactly little."

"Thank you." George's smile looked more forced than usual. "It was very nice of you to join us."

"Open it," someone said.

"Yes, of course." George stiffly took the package from her. "Please, have some cake, Willow. It has lemon filling."

As Willow helped herself to a piece of cake, George opened the package. To Willow's relief, there were several oohs and aahs from the party guests as the paper fell away. But George looked stunned as he stared at the painting—and not in a good way. "Thank you," he solemnly told her. "This is very thoughtful."

Willow attempted some lighthearted small talk, but no one in this group was particularly congenial. Or perhaps, like her, they were simply uncomfortable—and suddenly the "party" began to break up. Excuses about cleaning out classrooms and preparing for tonight's baccalaureate ceremony were made and, before Willow could excuse herself, it was simply her and George and Collin standing in front of the half-eaten cake.

"I'm not sure how I'll get this home," George said as he carefully folded up the wrapping paper. "I walked and—"

"I'll drive it home for you," Willow offered him. "I'll just leave it on your front porch."

"Thank you." He looked at her with a hard-to-read expression. It looked like a mixture of apology and discomfort and perhaps, unless it was her imagination, longing. "I already have a large box to carry home." He explained how he'd been taking portions of books and papers home with him each day. "I hope to get the last of it by tomorrow."

"We can give you a ride," Collin declared. "Nana's got lots of room in her SUV."

"That's a good idea," Willow agreed.

"I'll help you carry stuff down from your office," Collin suggested. "Maybe we can get everything out today. Then you won't have to pack anything tomorrow."

"That'd be nice." George sounded genuinely grateful. And just like that, it was arranged. Collin and George would go get his things and Willow would park her car out in front and wait for them.

But after Collin helped load some boxes in back, he explained that Marissa was waiting to meet up with him. "Later," he called as he closed the rear door. "I'll see you at baccalaureate, Nana."

So it was only George and Willow, driving toward his house in awkward silence. Fortunately it would be a short ride.

"I can hardly believe that Collin is graduating tomorrow," Willow said in an attempt to fill the void. "It seems like only last week, I was walking him into his first grade classroom."

"I feel a bit like that regarding my retirement," he said quietly. "I think I'm sort of in shock."

She glanced at him with a sudden surge of empathy. "How many years did you say you taught?"

"Next year would've been my thirtieth."

"Wow. I've never done anything for that long."

"What about marriage?" he asked. "Didn't you meet your husband in college?"

"Yes, but we didn't get married right away. We dated awhile, then broke up, then got back together. We'd just celebrated our twenty-first anniversary before Asher passed." She parked in front of George's house, turned off the engine, and smiled at him. "I think it's very admirable that you taught school for that long, George. Congratulations. Well done!"

He looked at her with misty eyes. "I guess it's really hitting me now. I can hardly believe tomorrow is my last day. I didn't expect to feel this emotional about it. Or maybe it's just the letdown of that pathetic retirement party." He made a sad attempt at a smile. "Pretty sorry affair, wasn't it?"

"I was a bit surprised at how small it was," she confessed.

"Probably fitting." He opened the door.

"Well, it's a busy time." She got out. "What with baccalaureate and graduation and all." As he carried his boxes into his house, she brought in the painting. But now she was feeling guilty. "You know, George, if you don't like this piece, I will understand. I realize that art is very subjective and—"

"I do like it," he insisted.

"But I won't be offended if you don't want it hanging here in your house," she said. "To be honest, I was feeling rather smug about giving it to you earlier. But now I feel a bit embarrassed and I'm—"

"Embarrassed?" He held up the canvas with a confused expression. "This is a beautiful gift, Willow. I will treasure it."

"Really?"

He carried it over to his gray sofa. "Do you think it would look good here?"

She studied the colorful painting on the barren white wall. Normally she wasn't a fan of paintings above sofas, but for some reason this looked right. "Yes, it looks just fine there, George. Perhaps a bit lower though." She explained the general rule for hanging art at eye level. "Do you really like it?" She grabbed up a pencil, preparing to mark a spot for a nail.

"I love it."

Willow felt dumbfounded as she marked the wall with a tiny X. He loved it? Although she didn't know George well, she knew that he was a very sincere person. He wouldn't say he loved it if he didn't.

He leaned the painting against the couch then turned to her. "Thank you very much, Willow. It was most thoughtful."

"You're very welcome. Again, I congratulate you on your career, and on your retirement. Hopefully the best is yet to come."

His brow creased, but he simply nodded. Feeling she'd worn out her welcome—again—Willow excused herself and made a hasty exit. She had no intention of pushing George too much. She felt certain she'd overdone it last weekend. Probably overwhelmed the poor man. It was just her way.

Less is more, she reminded herself as she drove home. As usual, she parked in the back lot, then went around to the front of the building to enter. She was about to go up to her apartment when a lone figure standing next to the gallery caught her attention. The woman's hair was the color of eggplant and she had on shabby jeans, tall black boots, and a worn leather jacket. Was it possible?

"Josie?" Willow called out.

"*Mom!*" Her daughter turned then rushed to her. "I thought you'd never get home."

"What are you doing here, honey?" Willow hugged Josie then held her at arm's length, looking intently at her face. Still pretty and somewhat youthful, but there was a hardness there too. Life had etched itself into Josie's features.

"Collin's graduation." Josie dropped a half-smoked ciga-rette to the sidewalk, grinding it under her heel. "You invited me to come. *Remember?*"

"But you said you couldn't—"

"Yeah, well, I changed my mind." She jerked her thumb down the street. "And Garth is here with me. He just went to get us some coffee." She nodded toward the gallery. "And that snob in there apparently didn't appreciate my presence, so I've been hanging out here and feeling like a bag lady."

"Didn't you tell her who you were?"

"No. Why should I?"

"Well, it's just that—"

"So, do you have a place for us to stay? Our junk's in the rental car parked out back. And I'll warn you, it wasn't cheap to get here, but I promised Garth you'd pay him back. Right?"

"Yes, of course." Willow nodded, trying to conceal her concerns. It sounded like a good idea a few weeks ago to have Collin's mother at his graduation. But she hadn't considered the boyfriend. Suddenly she felt unsure. "You and Garth get your bags from the car, and I'll go unlock the apartment for you. And I must apologize. I didn't realize you were coming, so the apartment's not really ready for guests."

"Don't worry. We're used to roughing it." Josie laughed.

As Willow hurried upstairs, she suspected that was true. Still, she'd hoped to have the apartment in better shape for Josie. She unlocked the door then hurried around to open the windows and let some fresh air inside. She'd stored some furnishings in here, but wanting to do some remodeling and repairs and painting, nothing was in place.

She bustled about, attempting to move some things, make some pathways, create a semi-habitable space. She was just sliding a chair into the living room area, when she heard the sound of voices. "Hello?" Josie called out.

"In here." Willow waved them into the apartment and Josie introduced her to a tall, skinny man with a goatee and what looked like thousands of dollars' worth of tattoos. "This is Garth," Josie said proudly. "The bass player for Black Night."

"I'm happy to finally meet you," Willow told him. "I'm sorry this apartment isn't set up for guests." She pointed to pieces of a bed leaned against a wall. "Maybe you two can help me get that set up in the bedroom."

"Don't worry, Mom." Josie tugged off her jacket, tossing it onto the chair. "We'll take care of all this."

"Sure." Garth nodded. "We'll just flop the mattress on the floor. And then we'll flop ourselves onto it and take a nice long nap."

"Yeah. We took the red-eye from Florida," Josie explained as she nudged Willow toward the door. "Then we drove here from Portland. Believe me, we're exhausted."

"Well, Collin's baccalaureate is at seven, but we should probably leave here around six-thirty to get good—"

"I thought graduation wasn't until tomorrow." Josie frowned.

"It is tomorrow. Baccalaureate is a different ceremony," she said from the doorway. Of course, this was all foreign to Josie. She'd missed out on these things by insisting on getting her GED in lieu of a traditional diploma. "Baccalaureate is like a spiritual send-off for the graduates. A blessing of sorts."

86

"Well, maybe we can skip that," Josie told her. "We're pretty wiped out."

"Okay." As Willow closed the door, an unexpected wave of sadness washed over her. Had Josie really come to see her son . . . or did she just want a free vacation and a place to crash for a while? Willow didn't mind so much for her own sake. It was simply good to see her daughter's face. But she did not want Collin to be hurt by Josie's callous attitude. Besides that, she knew that her grandson disliked surprises. Somehow she had to break this to him gently—and quickly. He barely knew his mother and it would not go well if he felt blindsided by her unexpected appearance.

Grateful that Leslie and Joel were handling the gallery for the next few days, Willow went into her own apartment and sent a text message to Collin. Not wanting to say too much, she simply stated that a surprise was waiting for him at home. Then she tried to put together some sort of plan—a way to allow Collin some time with his mother and her boyfriend . . . a way to break the ice without too much drama. She decided to start with an informal dinner before baccalaureate tonight. Hopefully Josie and Garth would be awake and feeling sociable by then.

As Willow started getting things ready for a simple dinner, Collin called. "So what's up?" he asked. She quickly explained about Josie and Garth.

"You're kidding." Collin didn't sound the least bit enthused.

"I know it's kind of a shock," she said carefully. "I was pretty surprised too."

"I don't really want to see her," he declared.

Willow sighed. If only they'd had more time . . . more warning. "I understand how you feel, but I thought we could have a quiet little dinner with them before we go to bacca-laureate. We'll have to keep it short and sweet."

"I told Marissa I'd take her out for tacos and then we'd go to baccalaureate together," he explained. "I planned to meet up with you afterward."

"Oh." Willow felt dismayed. "Well, I guess that's okay. Maybe we can spend some time with your mother and Garth tomorrow. You don't have school."

"I don't have school because it's senior skip day," he reminded her. "I told Marissa that we'd bike out to the lake and rent some kayaks."

"That sounds nice." Willow tried to think of an alternative plan. "Well, how about if I plan a little celebration for *after* graduation?"

"But Marissa and I plan to go to the all-night party."

Willow was actually glad to hear he was engaging in all these social activities—and knew that it was probably thanks to Marissa. Still, it made Josie's visit here rather awkward. "But I thought the all-night party didn't start until ten," Willow said. "Couldn't you spend a little time with us before that? You could bring Marissa too. And maybe invite some of your other friends."

"Yeah, I have so many friends," he said sarcastically.

"Well, you could invite Spencer and Will. And I'll invite some friends," she told him. "I know Leslie and Joel would like to come. And the weather forecast is good—we could hold the party out on the terrace. You know how pretty it is up there with all the patio lights in the evening. I'll bet Marissa would like it too."

"Okay," he reluctantly agreed. "I'll ask Marissa and Spencer and Will."

"Thanks, Collin. I'll get right on it. And I'll see you at baccalaureate." As she hung up, she felt relieved. It would actually be easier not to deal with this tonight. And tomorrow, well, it was a new day. Hopefully it would all work out by then.

nine

George hadn't really planned to attend the baccalaureate service or graduation, but at the last minute he decided it might be a nice way to end his career. A way to say farewell to his students. Not that anyone would notice. But he hadn't been to one of these ceremonies in years and this would be his last chance to participate as a faculty member. Why not go for it?

George suspected that most attendees would be dressed in today's ultra-casual style—aka T-shirts, flip-flops, and holey jeans—since most of his students' parents didn't dress much differently than their kids these days. Even so, George decided on his lightweight gray suit. It would be warm in the gymnasium, but he wouldn't feel comfortable in anything else.

As he adjusted his navy tie in the living room, he stared absently at the painting now hanging above his sofa. It had been kind of Willow . . . but his feelings toward the artwork were decidedly split. On one hand, this large, colorful painting felt like an unwelcome intruder in his calm and understated space, the sort of thing he would normally refuse and reject. But on the other hand, that old pickup was almost exactly like the one his brother had driven in high school. It was uncanny. Certainly Alex's truck had been in better shape than this one. At least it had been back then. But, unless George was mistaken, the pickup in the painting was the same model and year. Even the color was the same. Alex had loved that pickup. He and Grandpa had worked hard to restore it. And George had been only seven, but he'd loved the pickup too. He still remembered riding around town in it with his big brother that last summer. Before heading off to boot camp Alex and Grandpa had placed the pickup on blocks to remove the shiny chrome wheels and tires, so that they'd be in good shape when Alex came home. Except that Alex never came home . . . and the pickup was eventually sold.

George felt a lump in his throat. He couldn't remember such an emotional day. Not in years. He attributed it to his retirement. After all, it was the end of an era. Best to take everything in stride, take a deep breath and just keep moving. Attending baccalaureate would provide a good distraction for him. Well, unless he broke down in tears there. That would be humiliating.

He checked his watch to see it was still a bit early to head out, but he wanted a good seat. For him that meant on the aisle in a lower row. George disliked sitting in the bleachers almost as much as he disliked being stuck in the midst of a crowd. He suspected he suffered from claustrophobia, because he hated tight spaces. An overly crowded room always felt unbearably hot to him—even in winter. And it always felt like there was insufficient air. During school assemblies, he would simply stand on the sidelines, as if to guard the exit, until the program ended.

George stepped outside, locked his front door and, as usual, checked it twice. He glanced furtively over his shoulder to see if Lorna was lurking nearby. To his relief, she was nowhere to be seen. So he slipped down the front steps and headed off to the high school. It was a balmy evening, warm enough that he should've worn a summer-weight suit. But if he wanted to get a good seat, it was too late to go back and change.

Not many people were in the gymnasium by the time he arrived, and to his relief it was still fairly cool. He knew how hot and steamy it would become before the service was over. Especially up in the nosebleed seats. But a number of smart people, like him, had arrived early to secure the best seats. Many of them were elderly or unable to scale the bleacher steps, and already the bottom row was filling up.

George exchanged greetings with a couple of fellow teachers then took an aisle seat in the second row, close to the rear exit. To fill the time, he proceeded to read the program. If he'd had a pen on him, he might've edited it. Only a few tiny typos, but it didn't reflect well on the academia of the school. Well, he doubted many people would notice. Certainly not the students. And probably not their parents, either.

George watched as people began pouring into the gymnasium. A few hurried to get seats, and his bleacher row was quickly filling up, but most of the people looked uncertain, meandering about with questioning looks until an usher pointed them in a specific direction. But it was the woman in the white lacy dress that caught George's eye. Her beads, bracelets, and earrings made for a gypsy-like appearance, but the porcelain complexion and strawberry-blonde hair piled carelessly on her head suggested something altogether different.

George was caught off guard when Willow lifted her hand. Was that wave meant for him? Had he been staring at her? Had she noticed? George gave a cautious wave and Willow's face broke into a wide smile as she came directly over. "Room for one more?" she asked pleasantly.

"Certainly." He stood and moved aside so she could sit down. He knew that was the gentlemanly thing to do, but in all honesty he simply wanted to preserve his spot on the aisle. And now that his row was full, he needn't worry. "How are you doing?" he asked politely.

"I'm fine, thank you. Although it's been a busy day."

"Lots going with graduation preparations?"

"Yes. And then my daughter showed up out of the blue. That sort of threw me for a loop."

"Your daughter? Is that Collin's mother?"

"Yes. She and her boyfriend arrived this afternoon. I wasn't expecting them and didn't have anything ready." She fanned herself with the program. "I've been scrambling to get it together. Getting them bedding and linens and what-not. Then making a fast grocery store run. My, it feels good to sit down."

"Are they here?"

She explained they'd been up all night and were too tired, but he suspected by her expression that she had her doubts. "They'll come to graduation tomorrow."

"Was Collin happy to see his mother?"

"He hasn't actually seen her yet." She frowned. "To be

honest, I'm a bit worried. He wasn't too happy to hear she'd come."

"That must be difficult."

She nodded. "I wish I'd had more warning. I could've prepared him better. And I don't know what he'll think of the boyfriend."

"Is he the one who's in the grunge band?"

"Yes, and you know how conservative Collin is. I don't know how that will go." Her eyes lit up. "George, would you do me a gigantic favor?"

George blinked. "What do you have in mind?"

"I told Collin we'd have a little celebration tomorrow night. You know, after graduation. It's really just my way to get him to spend some time with his mother. I thought if I invited a few people, well, it might sort of soften things. Unfortunately, Collin doesn't have many friends." She placed a hand on his arm. "George, if you would come, I would be so grateful. And I know Collin would be pleased."

"Well, I, uh . . . I suppose I could come by."

Her face brightened. "Thank you so much."

The school orchestra began to play and the seniors started to file in, filling the chairs down on the gym floor. Before long the principal welcomed everyone, and a clergyman opened with a prayer.

As the service continued, George was aware of two things. He wasn't suffering too badly from his usual claustrophobia, and it felt unexpectedly reassuring to have Willow next to him. He wondered if the two things were somehow connected. As a result, the service didn't drag on as long as he recalled from the past.

"That was very nice," Willow said at the conclusion.

"Yes." He nodded, watching as the crowd began to fill the floor of the gymnasium. "And now, if you'll excuse me, I, uh, I feel the need to get outside in the fresh air."

"So do I." Willow stayed with him, navigating the crowd until they were finally exiting the stuffy room. "Oh, it feels much better out here."

"You don't like crowds?" George asked.

"Not so much." She inhaled deeply. "It's funny because I used to love being packed in like sardines for a concert or event. But the older I got, the less I liked it. This wasn't so bad tonight, but it felt awfully warm in there." She fanned herself with the program. "Although it's lovely out here." She smiled at George. "We're supposed to have the same good weather all weekend. I'm so glad you agreed to come to our little soirée after graduation tomorrow night. I plan to have it out on the terrace."

"Terrace?"

"Outside my apartment." She grinned. "It's actually the rooftop, but I've turned it into an outdoor space." She tapped his lapel. "And it will be casual dress, so please wear something comfortable."

He wanted to say that suits were comfortable . . . to him.

"I plan to be barefoot."

"Barefoot?" George grimaced. Did she expect him to do the same?

She laughed. "Don't fret, George, I won't make you shed your shoes. But warm nights like this just make me long to be barefoot." She stretched her arms toward the sky. "Kind of like skinny-dipping—it's so freeing."

George felt alarmed. What sort of woman was this?

"Dear me, I'm afraid I've shocked you." She smiled coyly.

"But don't you worry, we'll all be properly clothed tomorrow night. I promise." Willow waved to someone behind him. "There's Collin now. And Marissa too."

George stayed long enough to greet Collin and Marissa and then, excusing himself as if he had someplace he needed to be, he went on his way. But as he slowly walked home, he wished he'd lingered a bit longer. What was wrong with visiting with friends on a warm summer evening? Willow probably thought her talk of bare feet, skinny-dipping, and such had unhinged him. And maybe it had . . . momentarily. But he'd recovered.

Well, he'd just have to make up for tonight's lack of sociability at tomorrow night's celebration. Perhaps he would even "dress casually," whatever that meant. After all, he usually wore a short-sleeved shirt and khaki pants when he mowed the lawn or did chores. Perhaps something like that would work.

As he went into his house, he reminded himself that the party was to honor Collin's graduation, which probably meant that George should bring him a gift. Although he had no idea what that would be. Anyway, that would have to wait until tomorrow afternoon since Friday was still a school day. Why they bothered to hold classes was a mystery to George. What with senior skip day and the school feeling more like a zoo than a place of learning, it wasn't as if the students gained anything from the "last day of school." But at least George could console himself—it truly would be the last day of school . . . for him.

•••

Willow didn't know what to expect as she and Collin went upstairs to their apartments, but for some reason she hadn't expected to smell smoke.

"Is there a fire?" Collin asked with concern.

"Goodness, I hope not. I don't hear any smoke alarms." She quickly unlocked her door and sniffed. "Not in here. Let's check your apartment."

"Seems okay to me." Collin turned to her. "Where is my mom staying?"

Willow pointed to apartment number four, then knocked on the door. "I don't know if there's a smoke alarm in there," she told Collin. When no one answered, she pulled out her key, unlocked the door, and opened it to see smoke. "Hello?" she yelled with concern. "Anybody here?" As she and Collin burst into the apartment, she recognized the smell. "Are you smoking pot?" she demanded as she spotted her "guests" in the living room. Josie was in the chair and Garth was lounging on the mattress that was still on the floor.

"Doesn't anyone knock around here?" Josie asked.

"I did knock," Willow told her. "But we smelled smoke and got worried." She glanced around. "And I realized there's no smoke alarm up here."

"Good thing." Garth laughed. "We might've set it off."

"I don't want you guys smoking," Willow told them.

"Really?" Josie narrowed her eyes. "For your information, we're adults."

"I know. But I don't want you to smoke in here. For one thing there's no smoke alarm and this is an old building. Our apartments share walls and a fire would be devastating to everyone. Not to mention the gallery below." Willow went into the kitchen to turn on the fan above the stove. Then to the bathroom where she turned on another fan. She felt seriously aggravated. Not only had they been smoking pot, the apartment was a mess with their stuff thrown all about and wet towels tossed on the bathroom floor as if they expected "housekeeping" to show up. Still, she knew it would do no good to lose her temper.

"What are you doing?" Josie asked with irritation.

"Just letting some air inside," Willow told her.

"Why are you so mad?" Josie frowned. "In case you haven't heard, pot is legal in Oregon. What's the big deal?"

"Like I said, I don't want any kind of smoking in here. Not cigarettes or joints or anything that burns. If you need to smoke, you'll have to go outside. I want you and Garth to make yourselves at home—and it appears you're doing so—but please respect the rules. No smoking." She lowered her voice. "And keep in mind that your son is here."

"No, he's not."

"What do you mean?"

"He left without even saying hello. Bad manners, if you ask me."

Willow had to bite her tongue. "Well, he's probably worn out. There's been a lot going on this week. Tomorrow's senior skip day and he probably wants to get to bed now."

"Right." Josie scowled at her. "Maybe we shouldn't have come."

"Maybe you should've given us more notice," Willow told her. "Anyway, let's not worry about that anymore." She placed a hand on Josie's shoulder. "I'm actually very glad you're here, honey. It's wonderful to see you. But, please, do *not* smoke in here. Take it outside. Can you make sure Garth understands that too?"

Josie just shrugged.

"I have some spare smoke alarms." Willow went into the living room. "I'll get one and put it up. It's actually required by law, but because no one was using this apartment, I hadn't installed it yet. I'll be right back." Although Willow had extra smoke alarms still in their boxes, she decided to get one from her apartment to save time. While she was there, she put together a bag of groceries that she'd gotten for them before going to baccalaureate. Just some basics and snack foods, but hopefully it would show them that she really did want them here.

To her relief it smelled less smoky when she returned to the apartment. Garth had disappeared and Josie was digging through a backpack. "I have some food for you guys." Willow set the bag down. "Some things should be refrigerated." When Josie didn't respond or come over, Willow used this opportunity to set the smoke alarm on top of a kitchen cabinet—out of sight just in case someone tried to disable it. "I'll go ahead and put the orange juice and milk and cheese away," Willow called out as she removed items from the bag. "I figured you guys would want to do some meals on your own."

"So you just want us to stay in our room like naughty children?" Josie's tone was sarcastic. "Out of sight, out of mind?"

"Not at all." Willow smiled. "In fact, you're welcome to come to my apartment for meals if you'd like. I thought I'd make us a simple dinner before graduation tomorrow night. And then we'll be having a little party after graduation. Just snacks and dessert. Out on the terrace."

"There's a terrace?"

"Yes, but it's only accessible from my apartment." Willow made her way to the door. "But you're welcome to use it, honey. In fact, I'll put an ashtray out there."

"If it's not too much trouble." Again with the sarcasm.

Willow reached for Josie's hand. "I know that you and I have had our problems, Josie. But as I've said before, I'm sorry that I wasn't a better mother."

"You mean by abandoning me to my grandparents for the first thirteen years of my life?"

"I was barely nineteen when you were born, Josie. And not very mature. It took me a while to grow up. Trust me, I would've made a terrible mother during your early childhood." Willow wanted to point out that she'd been raising Josie's son for most of his life, but she knew that would get them nowhere. "I hope someday you'll be able to forgive me."

Josie shrugged. "It doesn't matter."

"It matters to me." Willow was still holding her hand and attempted to hug her, but Josie ducked away. "Well, I'll leave you to it then. Unless you want to visit some more tonight. If so, feel free to come to my apartment. I don't usually go to bed until elevenish."

Willow felt a cloak of sadness as she returned to her apartment. Josie was thirty-five but still acted like an adolescent, and Willow was afraid that she was to blame for most of it. She made a cup of jasmine tea and took it out to the terrace, mulling over the years and how they'd gotten stuck in this frustrating place. Would they ever get beyond it?

Willow knew Josie still held it against her that she'd spent her first thirteen years with her grandparents then been removed from their home against her will. When Josie was a baby, it felt like the best solution to leave her with Willow's parents. It allowed Willow time to go to college . . . and grow up. And even though Willow's parents weren't exactly conventional, they had a comfortable home, a source of in-

100

come, and food in the fridge. Willow's mother had been delighted to take in her granddaughter. So much so that a few years later, when Willow had gotten her bachelor's degree and a job and finally felt ready to raise her child, her parents refused.

Her mother had insisted that Josie, who was about to start school, was better off with them. She had friends and a puppy . . . and "no child should be raised in a smelly city." After much discussion, they persuaded Willow to let them continue to raise Josie. And to be fair, Josie looked perfectly happy with them.

It wasn't until shortly after Willow married Asher—and Josie had become a smart-mouthed adolescent—that Willow's parents suddenly changed their minds. They'd already been through Willow's wild teenage years and weren't eager to do it again. Naturally, Josie had been angry to leave her friends and move to the Bay Area.

Willow had tried to be a good mother. She'd exposed Josie to all the culture San Francisco had to offer. And Asher, although claiming he was too old to parent, had done his best as well. But the middle school years were a never-ending battle. Josie seemed determined to be miserable—and since misery loved company, she was determined to drag Willow and Asher along for the ride. Admittedly, their parenting skills weren't top-notch, but not for lack of trying. Willow was constantly encouraging Josie to try new activities— whether it was art or theater or dance or martial arts. Josie would go to a few sessions then either get kicked out or refuse to go. By the time she was fifteen, Josie was so defiant and disrespectful that Willow worried she'd wind up incarcerated. Despite thousands of dollars spent on counseling and therapy, and various labels applied, Josie pulled farther and farther away.

During the counseling years, two labels were routinely attached to Josie. Borderline and narcissistic personality disorder, depending on the therapist. Although Willow had been opposed to medical treatment, she eventually gave in to the psychiatrist. Naturally, Josie used this as an excuse for abusing drugs, although she later confessed that she'd already been using. After getting kicked out of school during her junior year, Josie had begged to get her GED and move out with some friends. When she threatened to run away and live on the streets, Willow had given in. For a while, Josie's life seemed to improve some. She actually got her GED and a barista job. Then she met Zeke . . . and got pregnant. Willow had encouraged Josie to let her baby be adopted by a loving family. But Josie had insisted she and Zeke could handle it, and for almost a year they did. But a few months after Collin was born, it had all unraveled. Drugs entered the picture, a social worker was called, and Collin was removed from their home.

At Josie's request Collin was "temporarily" placed with Willow and Asher—and for the next few years he was bounced back and forth. When Josie was doing "well" she would convince the court she was ready to be a responsible parent. And then it would fall apart. Finally, when Collin was almost four, Josie ran off to become a full-time band groupie, and the court awarded full custody to Willow and Asher. Although it hadn't been exactly easy becoming full-time parents, it had been well worth it. Collin, who appeared to have been "born old," had never been a problem. He and Asher became the best of friends. Willow really had nothing to complain about in that regard. Collin had enriched their lives.

She sipped her now lukewarm tea. Fourteen years later . . . here they were—Josie still acting like an adolescent while her teenaged son was on the cusp of responsible adulthood.

ten

George's last day of school went much as expected. Teachers were harried and distracted. Meanwhile the students were literally climbing the walls. Leo Brandt fell while scaling a column in the courtyard and after being transported by paramedics, the staff later learned he'd suffered a broken collarbone. By the end of the day George was so fatigued that he actually welcomed the onset of his "retirement."

As he walked home, his steps felt sluggish. All he really wanted was a nice, long nap. Perhaps he would skip tonight's graduation ceremony after all. The idea of another evening in a hot, stuffy, noisy gymnasium had no appeal. Because he'd promised Willow, he would still attend Collin's party afterwards, but perhaps he would make an excuse to depart early. He could blame it on last-day-of-school weariness.

As George walked through town, he pondered what he might give Collin for graduation. What did teenagers like these days—well, besides those addictive electronic gadgets? Of course, Collin was not a typical teenager. The young man had good sensibilities. George paused outside the Book Nook. He hadn't been in there in years but had always liked the cozy little shop. And as he pushed open the door, he immediately felt welcomed by the jingling of the bell and the dusty aroma of books. They carried both used and new books here and, unlike other bookstores, the Book Nook had not succumbed to the pressure of hawking cheap trinkets for impulse buying. Nor had they added an espresso bar.

"Can I help you?" a middle-aged woman asked.

"I'm not sure." He rubbed his chin. "I think I'm looking for an Emerson book."

"Ralph Waldo Emerson?"

"Yes. But I don't want a paperback or even a new hardback edition if I can avoid it. I'd prefer an older copy. Not one that's terribly old or dear, but something that feels substantial. It's for a graduation gift."

"We just got in some lovely used books this week. And I believe there were a couple of Emerson titles in the bunch." She led him to a section in back, pointing to a shelf. "Here you go."

George eagerly reached for Emerson's *Essays: First Series*. "This looks perfect." He carefully opened it, checking its spine and page condition. He paused to scan the list of essays, which he almost knew by heart. "'Self-Reliance' is in here," he told the woman. "One of my favorites."

"I haven't read it," she admitted. "But self-reliance sounds like a good topic for a graduate."

He nodded as he turned it over to see the price. Although it wasn't cheap, he felt it was worth it. Collin was the kind of young man to appreciate something like this. "I'll take this."

"Would you like me to wrap it for you?" she asked at the register.

"Yes, that'd be nice."

"Do you want to inscribe it first?"

He considered this. "No, no, I don't think so. I suppose I'm old school. I've never liked writing in books. Especially a collectible one like this."

"Would you like a gift card—they're free with purchase." She pointed to a nearby rack of small cards. And while she wrapped the package, he neatly penned an Emerson quote inside the card. It was from "Self-Reliance"—a line that he'd memorized in college, and which sounded well suited for Collin.

A foolish consistency is the hobgoblin of little minds, adored by little statesmen and philosophers and divines. Ralph Waldo Emerson

He still liked the ring of those words . . . and yet, as he slid the little card into the little envelope, he felt the jab of hypocrisy. Had his years of careful living turned him into a "little mind"? And if so, what could he do about it?

* * *

Although Willow was determined to remain patient in dealing with her prodigal daughter, it was a growing challenge. Not only had Josie and Garth attempted to turn Willow's terrace into their personal smoking lounge, they'd left trash and personal items strewn about. Willow had reminded

Josie that she would be busy getting things ready for Collin's graduation party, hoping that even if Josie didn't want to help, she might at least not turn the party area into a garbage dump.

"What are you making?" Josie paused in Willow's kitchen.

"Caprese skewers," Willow said. "Just grape tomatoes, fresh basil, and a chunk of fresh mozzarella. You layer them like this on a skewer and—"

"Great." Josie reached for a handful of the skewers that Willow had just made. "Garth loves caprese salad."

"Would you like to help make some?" Willow asked.

"No, you look like you have it under control." Josie opened the fridge. "Mind if I grab a couple of sodas to go with this?"

"No. Maybe you'd like to load some into the cooler by the door and take it out to the terrace with you."

"That's okay. This will be fine for now."

"I meant for the party," Willow said a bit tersely.

"But that's not until after graduation. Why bother with it now?"

"Because we'll be leaving for the ceremony in about twenty minutes," Willow explained. "I'd hoped to have things mostly set up and ready for when we get home."

"It's not like you're having a lot of people here." Josie was still foraging in the fridge. Apparently the pizza that Willow had ordered for them an hour ago hadn't cut it. Willow bit her tongue as she watched Josie helping herself from the appetizer trays that Willow had carefully put together earlier. "You told me it's gonna be like a dozen people. Looks like you're going to way too much trouble."

"I'm doing this for Collin," Willow said. "He's worked

so hard in school. He never even complained about moving up here last year. And he's taken lots of AP classes and maintained an outstanding GPA. I just want to celebrate that—"

"Oh, I get it." Josie slammed the fridge door closed. "Like, *hint-hint*, Josie. You were such an academic flop. Such a disappointment."

"I've *never* said that." Willow set her knife down with a bang. "Not once."

"You don't have to, Mom. It's written all over your face. You think I'm a loser. Admit it."

"I'm sorry if that's your perception, Josie. I, of all people, am aware of the challenges you've faced. Your life hasn't been easy. And I take the blame for some of that and want you to know that—"

"You should take the blame!" Josie grabbed a bag of unopened chips then stormed back out to the terrace where Garth was waiting.

Willow blew out a long sigh. All she wanted to know right now was, how long did they plan to stay? So far Josie had barely said anything to her son. Although to be fair, Collin had kept a very low profile on the home front. After senior skip day ended, he'd texted Willow that he was taking a long nap. Then, just a few minutes ago, he'd sent another text, informing her he was walking to school for the pre-graduation meeting. But his message was clear—he wanted to avoid his mother.

It was equally clear that Josie was not here to support her son. Worse than that, it almost felt like she wanted to sabotage this evening's festivities. Or maybe Willow was just imagining things. It was no secret that Josie came with bag-

108

gage . . . and Willow was well aware that *hurt people hurt people*. But she hoped and prayed that Josie wouldn't hurt Collin tonight of all nights.

Willow thought back to the conversation she'd had with Garth earlier. Unlike Josie, who'd slept in until noon, Garth had actually joined Willow on the terrace for coffee rather early this morning. They hadn't talked of anything terribly specific or important, but Willow got the feeling that Garth had a good sense of empathy. She also got the impression that he was losing patience with Josie too. Perhaps he could help to keep Josie in line this evening. As if that were possible. Willow checked the clock to see that it would soon be time to head over to the school. She was already dressed in a long paisley broomstick skirt and a lacy peasant top. Of course, this had invited Josie's criticism. "Still dressing like a boho gypsy?" she'd teased. "I thought you were too old for that."

Willow set the last of the appetizers in the fridge, removed her apron, and, with trash bag in hand, went out to do some last-minute damage control on the terrace. "Are you guys about ready to go?" Willow paused as she emptied the ashtray.

"Isn't it too soon?" Josie asked.

"I'd like a good seat." Willow picked up the crushed pizza box and several empty beer cans from the six-pack that Josie had brought in earlier. "I'd like to leave in about ten minutes, honey. In case you need time to freshen up or anything." This *was* a real hint, since Josie was still wearing the same grubby jeans and stained rocker T-shirt that she'd had on yesterday. Her long, dark hair looked greasy and matted and she had smudges of eyeliner beneath her eyes. Not that Willow planned to mention any of this. She was determined to avoid confrontation—at all cost.

Garth finished the last of his soda, handing the can over to Willow. "I think I'm gonna take a pass on the graduation thing. I don't really know Collin and—"

"If I'm going, you're going," Josie shouted at him.

"Why?" He frowned at her. "He's your son."

"That's why we came here, Garth, to go to my son's graduation."

"That's not why I came here," he declared.

"I'll let you two sort this out," Willow said nervously. "I want to freshen up a little, and then I plan to head out. If you don't go with me, maybe we can meet up there." She could hear them arguing as she hurried back inside. Normally, Willow didn't like to bother God with every little thing, but as she brushed her teeth, applied a bit of coral lipstick, and rubbed some lavender lotion into her hands and elbows, she silently prayed for God's grace over tonight's celebrations. They would certainly need it.

George felt uncomfortable and conspicuous as he walked through town in his "Saturday chores" uniform of a short-sleeved light-blue shirt and khaki pants. Oh, everything was perfectly clean and pressed, but it wasn't what he'd normally wear to a social gathering. Not that he'd attended many, for certain. Not outside of school functions anyway. But he wanted to respect Willow's request for "casual attire." Also, he didn't want to be the victim of "foolish consistency" of his own "little mind." He was still struggling over that Ralph Emerson quote.

When he left the house, he'd been worried that gradua-tion might still be going and that he'd arrive too early for the party, but judging by the lively traffic through town, he felt certain that it was over. And when he got to the doorway that led up to the apartments above the gallery, there were balloons in the high school's red and gold colors and a sign that said COLLIN'S PARTY UP HERE—WELCOME!

He followed red and gold streamers up the stairway to where a door was wide open and another sign said COME IN AND CONTINUE TO THE TERRACE. He could hear music playing as he walked through what was a surprisingly at-tractive apartment, albeit a bit cluttered with multiple pieces of artwork and lively colors. But it was a nice, wide-open space with clean white walls and what looked like a recently remodeled kitchen. All in all, the space was rather inviting. But it was what he saw when he went through the opened French doors that almost took his breath away.

It was the scent that first hit him—green and herbal and fresh. Then he took in the delicate white lights and hanging lanterns that illuminated the outdoor garden. The effect was surprisingly elegant, like something out of an old classic film. As George slowly walked past small potted trees and flow-ers and plants, he got the impression of a fairyland in the nighttime. A water feature with an angelic sculpture was lit with a soft pinkish light. George then saw a pathway lined with lanterns, leading him toward the sound of voices and opening out to a seating area where there appeared to be about a dozen or so people gathered.

"George, you made it." Willow came over to greet him, proceeding to introduce him to the others. He recognized Willow's gallery assistant, who was there with her husband.

And, of course, he already knew Collin and Marissa. Marissa's mother was there as well as a couple of Willow's artist friends. But it was the dark-haired girl with the angry countenance that made George uneasy. "This is my daughter Josie and her boyfriend, Garth." Willow sounded like she had a slight strain to her voice.

"Pleased to meet you all," George told everyone. Then he turned to Collin. "Congratulations on your graduation." He handed Collin his present. "A little something to commemorate this occasion."

Collin thanked him, then proceeded to read the card and carefully unwrap the package. "An Emerson book from Mr. Emerson," he said happily. "Thank you so much. I've read some Ralph Waldo Emerson, but I'm not sure I fully understand his philosophy."

"I would be surprised if you did. Although I've been acquainted with him for decades, I don't fully understand it myself," George admitted.

"But I like his thoughts on living and thinking independently," Collin said. "He's not one to follow the crowd."

"I thought you might appreciate that." George smiled. "I know I do."

"Well, a lot of us don't want to follow the crowd," Josie said a bit sharply. "But then not everyone can appreciate other people's forms of individuality." She glared at Willow, as if her words were aimed toward her. "Some people insist on shoving us into their narrow-minded expectations."

Willow didn't respond to her daughter's jab and, taking George by the arm, led him over to a table loaded with appetizers and drinks. "Please, fix yourself a plate." She pleasantly explained what there was to choose from, obviously in an attempt to distance herself from her caustic daughter.

"Thank you." As George began to select some bits and pieces, he could hear Josie still taunting her mother. And then Collin spoke up.

"I don't think you're a true individualist, Josie."

"What do you mean by that?" she snapped back.

"Well, think about it," Collin said calmly but firmly. "You're just a follower."

"I am not."

George turned, cringing to see Collin facing off with Josie. Clearly he had no respect for his "mother," but George hated to see them getting into a sparring match. Everyone else watched with wide eyes.

"You've devoted your life to being a groupie to your boyfriend's grunge band," Collin said plainly. "That makes you a follower."

Josie's boyfriend let out a loud snort of laughter. "He's got you there, Josie."

"Shut up!" she growled at him. "The only reason I follow your stupid band is because my own mother threw me out and disowned me—just because I was a single mother."

"Oh my." Willow shook her head. "Please, Josie, let's remember this is a celebration for Collin and—"

"It's okay, Nana." Collin waved a hand at her. "If Josie wants to make a scene, I think she should bring it. Maybe it's about time we had this out. But first of all, I want to refute what my birth mother just said. I might've been just a kid, but I remember what happened." He turned to the other guests. "My grandmother never disowned her or threw her out. The truth is that my birth mother never wanted to be a mother. She was always dumping me with my grandparents. Then when I was four, she abandoned me for good. She left to follow a band. She was supposed to come back the next day, but she just disappeared—for days. CPS eventually turned over custody to my grandpa and—"

"*Your* grandpa?" Josie challenged. "Asher wasn't even related to you, Collin."

"Maybe not by blood, but he treated me far better than you ever did," Collin shot back. "He was a father to you too, Josie, but you didn't even come to his funeral." He shook a fist. "And I wish you hadn't come for my graduation either."

"Big surprise there." Josie narrowed her eyes at Willow. "You've obviously poisoned him against me." She turned back to Collin. "But beware, my son, you come from a long line of messed-up people. Children having children is a big, fat mistake." She pointed to Marissa, who was watching with wide eyes. "Maybe you're the one I should warn since a teen pregnancy would—"

"That's enough!" George said loudly. Everyone turned to him. Feeling almost as if he were in the classroom attempting to restore order, he continued. "I think we've all heard enough, Josie. My understanding is that this party is to honor Collin, and if you can't participate in that, I think you should excuse yourself." To George's surprise, everyone began to clap. Even Josie's boyfriend. And just like that, Josie stormed out.

"I'm sorry," George muttered to Willow. "I didn't mean to overstep my bounds just now. I suppose my inner teacher just took over. Please—"

"Don't apologize." She smiled brightly. "You have no idea how much I appreciate your intervention."

"I do too," Collin told him. "Thank you, Mr. Emerson."

"Okay, everyone, let's not let Josie's bad manners ruin the party," Willow said loudly. "We still have a lovely cake and lots of food and drinks. I think we should all make a toast to our two graduates."

George smiled stiffly as he lifted his fluted glass of sparkling cider in a toast, but he felt like a fish out of water and longed to slip out unnoticed and forget this whole evening. To his relief, Willow invited him to help her get some things from the kitchen.

"I really don't know what came over me," he said quietly as she loaded his arms with chilled soda cans.

"I don't either, but it was wonderful," she told him. "You have no idea how difficult it's been with my daughter these past couple days. I feel terrible to confess this, but I cannot wait for Josie and Garth to leave."

"When are they going?"

"Garth mentioned tomorrow." Willow slid open the freezer drawer.

"It's hard to understand how such a fine young man . . ." George stopped himself, realizing he was about to insult Willow. After all, Josie was her daughter.

"Yes, I know what you were about to say, George. And I take some of the blame for my daughter's bad behavior. Not all of it, mind you." She removed a carton of ice cream with a stiff-looking smile. "It's a long story. Maybe someday, if you're interested, I'll tell you about it."

As George followed her back outside, he wondered . . . Would he ever hear that story? Did he even want to hear it?

Did he want to continue his involvement in this somewhat eccentric and unpredictable family? Again, he felt torn. On one hand, he knew he should run fast and hard in the opposite direction. But on the other hand . . . there was Willow.

eleven

Willow was pleasantly surprised that George stayed so long. She hoped it wasn't out of pity. The other guests, although they tried to hide it, had obviously been disturbed by Josie's abrasive attack and, one by one, began excusing themselves. Marissa's mother was the first one to leave, although she had a good excuse since she'd offered to drive Collin and Marissa to the bowling alley for the start of the senior all-night party. So the fact that George not only lingered but also offered to help her clean things up was rather touching.

"Your apartment is really nice," he told her as he carried in the last of the party things. "Very homey."

She thanked him then grimaced. She could hear the sounds of Garth and Josie next door—in what sounded like a heated argument.

"Is that normal?" George asked with a furrowed brow.

"I honestly don't know." She paused to listen. "I mean, I've heard them argue, but not quite as loud as this." She cringed at a crashing sound. Had someone thrown something . . . or was it something worse?

"Do you think your daughter is in any danger?"

"I'd be more worried about Garth," she confessed. "Josie's temper is pretty volatile. You saw a sample of that earlier." Still, the truth was she didn't know.

"Would you like me to go over there and say something to them?" George asked.

Willow blinked in surprise. "You'd really do that?"

He sighed. "I taught high school for nearly thirty years. I know a thing or two about these things."

She set the last of the leftovers in the fridge. "Yes, I suppose you do. It's just that I don't see you like that, George. You act like such a quiet and mild-mannered gentleman."

He nodded. "Well, now that I'm retired, I hope to enjoy a quiet and mild-mannered sort of life."

Willow tried to read his expression. She knew the noises coming from the next apartment were disturbing him. But as much as she appreciated the offer, she didn't really like the idea of him getting into the middle of some nasty domestic squabble. She jumped to hear the door slam, followed by loud footsteps going down the stairs. "Maybe they'll cool off now." She smiled gratefully.

"Well, then I guess I will say good night. Thank you for a most memorable evening."

She shook her head. "I wanted it to be memorable. But not because of Josie's hissy fit."

George looked concerned. "That's not what I meant." He pointed toward the terrace. "I guess I didn't mention it, but your outdoor space is quite wonderful, Willow."

"Really? You like it?"

"I felt like I'd been transported to someplace else," he said with sincerity. "Someplace truly beautiful."

"Thank you!" She beamed at him. "You have no idea how much that means to me. And I hope you'll come see it again, George. It's quite different in daylight. But still lovely, I think."

He thanked her and said good night, and as she watched him go down the stairs, she wondered about Josie and Garth. Should she check on them? Perhaps, since it was so quiet over there, it was best to let sleeping dogs lie. But, she decided, as she closed and locked her door, if they got into it again, she had no problem calling the police to come check on them.

As Willow continued cleaning up after the party, she was relieved to hear footsteps, more quiet and controlled, coming up the stairs. Then she heard a door open and close, followed by silence. Hopefully Josie and Garth had patched things up. And hopefully they would leave first thing tomorrow morning, just like Garth had assured her they would do.

Willow, not for the first time, felt like a failure as a mother. As she got ready for bed, she replayed parts of Josie's hostile speech in her head. Of course, she knew it was mostly untrue. Except for the fact that Josie may have convinced herself it was true. What if Josie truly thought that Willow had shoved her away? Perhaps Willow had sent signals like that to her daughter. After all, Josie had a knack for making life difficult for everyone around her. Surely, despite how hard they'd tried, there must've been times when Willow and Asher had lost their patience and voiced their disappointments. They were only human. Still, what parent hadn't made similar mistakes? And not all children turned out like Josie. But Josie was thirty-five. Wasn't it high time she took responsibility for her choices and actions—as well as the consequences that followed? Wasn't it time that Josie grew up?

As Willow got into bed, she prayed that God would help her to love Josie better . . . unconditionally . . . and she prayed that Josie would learn how to receive such love. Then, feeling completely exhausted—as if the past few days had taken about ten years off her life—Willow went to sleep.

When she woke up, it was to the sound of pounding on her door. Thinking it was the middle of the night and some calamity had befallen her, she leaped out of bed and ran to answer it. As she raced through her living room, she was surprised to see it was daylight outside. And past eight o'clock. Worried that something might've happened to Collin, she jerked open the door to see Josie standing there with a tearful face.

"Do you know where Garth is?" she asked with desperate eyes.

"No." Willow shook her head. "I just got up."

"Well, he's gone. His stuff is gone. The rental car is gone. He's gone!"

Willow waved Josie inside. "Perhaps he went to get gas. It's a long drive to Portland and—"

"No!" Josie shook her head. "He left me. I *know* he left me."

"But he—"

"He threatened to leave me last night," Josie continued. "But I didn't believe him."

Willow felt her heart sinking as she picked up her shawl, wrapping it over her cotton nightgown. "Did you try to call him?" she asked.

"His phone is off."

"Well, don't jump to conclusions." Willow went into the kitchen to start a pot of coffee. "It's early, honey. Garth knows you like to sleep in. It's possible that he simply—"

"He left me, Mom!" she shouted.

Willow didn't answer as she filled the machine with water. "Don't you get it?" Josie continued. "He. Left. Me!"

Willow still didn't respond. Instead she ground the beans, poured them into the filter, set it in the basket, and then turned on the coffee maker. With a deep sigh, she turned to look at Josie. "Well, I suppose it's possible he left you."

"What am I going to do?" Josie demanded.

Willow simply shrugged. "What do you want to do?"

"I want Garth!" And now Josie began to rant and swear, blaming Willow for everything. "If I hadn't come here—for you—Garth and I would still be together."

Willow wanted to set Josie straight, to point out that Josie was a spoiled brat who had treated Garth badly—treated everyone badly—and that Josie was probably only getting what she deserved . . . but then Willow remembered last night's prayer to love Josie without conditions. "I'm sorry that Garth left you . . . if that's what really happened. And I truly hope that it's not. But I'm still here for you, Josie. I love you, and I'm willing to do whatever I can to help you."

"You can't help me. No one can help me." Josie burst into fresh tears. Willow went around to the other side of the breakfast bar and, knowing this could backfire, wrapped her arms around her daughter. "God can help you, Josie. And it's possible I can too." To Willow's surprise, Josie didn't pull away or curse at her. Instead she went limp as a noodle and just cried. Willow held her until she finally stopped and stepped away.

"I need to go," Josie said gruffly, wiping her nose on her sweatshirt sleeve. "I need to get out of here."

"Where will you go?" Willow asked.

"I don't know. Just away from this horrible little town." Josie spat out some off-color words. "And away from you!" And then she stormed off.

Although she felt dismayed, Willow wasn't surprised. This was typical Josie. Still, she felt curious. Had Garth really abandoned Josie? If so, where would Josie go? What would she do? Other than Willow and Collin, Josie probably had no one to turn to. Willow's parents had washed their hands of their difficult adult granddaughter years ago—between band trips, Josie had worn out her welcome in their Arizona condo. After that they'd moved into a "senior commune" down near Monterey where residents had to be sixty-five or older.

With no college education or vocational training, Josie's only option was some minimum-wage job that probably wouldn't last long. She had no way to support herself. Willow remembered her prayer . . . unconditional love. Did that mean she needed to encourage Josie to remain here in Warner? But wouldn't that make life miserable for everyone?

As Willow quickly dressed, she remembered how one of Josie's counselors would often tell Willow that "it's time for tough love." That was probably what he'd advise today. But Willow had never been good at tough love. That had been Asher's territory. Somehow he'd been able to draw a line without turning it into an emotional battle. Even when Josie would try to push his buttons, Asher would never engage. He'd simply remain firm . . . his no meant no. But sometimes Josie turned her blame game onto her mother. Willow would want to be strong, but if Josie pushed long and hard enough, Willow would either cave or go running to Asher for reinforcement.

Grateful that Leslie and Joel were working the gallery today, Willow decided to go for a walk to help clear her head. Before she left, she tapped on Josie's door. Part of her was worried that Josie had already left . . . and part of her was worried that she was still here. Josie answered the door with puffy red eyes. "What do you want?" she growled. "Haven't I left soon enough for you? Are you going to throw me out?"

"No, that's not it." Willow kept her voice even. "I only wanted to tell you that you're welcome to stay here, Josie. And if I can help you figure things out, I'm willing to—"

"Thanks but no thanks!" Josie slammed the door.

Willow stepped back and, taking in a deep, calming breath, headed down the stairs, where she was met with Collin. She forced a smile. "Back from the all-night party?"

"Yeah. They had a big breakfast at the high school, but Marissa and I were so tired we decided to pass. I just want to sleep."

"Good idea." Willow couldn't resist the urge to hug him. "Have I told you lately how much I love you?" she asked with tearful eyes.

"What's wrong?" he asked with concern.

"Oh, it's nothing much." She quickly explained about Josie still being here. "Garth took off without her. I told her she can stay on, but she sounds determined to go."

"Good." Collin's countenance turned dark. "The sooner the better."

Willow simply nodded. "Get some rest." Then, feeling slightly lost and disoriented, she continued down the street

. . . until she found herself at the Muffin Man Bakery purchasing bran muffins.

George felt surprisingly refreshed and content as he went about his usual Saturday chores. Although he knew he could now perform these chores on any day he chose, there was a comfort in routine. And despite his concern over Emerson's quote about "little minds," George wasn't ready to change his habits yet. Perhaps he never would. Another, less intellectual quote that his grandmother liked to repeat, usually for his grandfather's sake, fit George as well. *You can't teach an old dog new tricks.*

George had just finished putting his white load of laundry into the washing machine when he heard the doorbell. He was concerned that it might be Lorna Atwood, since she'd been waving at him over the backyard fence while he'd checked the oil and gasoline in the lawnmower, forcing him to postpone the lawn mowing for a bit. George peered cautiously around the corner of the kitchen to get a glimpse through the door's high window. But instead of the pale platinum hair he expected to see, it was strawberry-blonde. He dropped his empty laundry basket and hurried to open it.

With a very forlorn expression, Willow held out a small white bag. "I—I brought you muffins." Her eyes glistened with tears. "To thank you for your help last night and—and—" Her words were choked by a sob.

"Come in." He gently tugged her inside, closing the door quickly lest Lorna was looking.

"I'm sorry," she said. "I'm kind of a mess today."

"It's okay." He led her to the couch, helped her to sit. "What's wrong?"

She blurted out about Josie being abandoned by Garth and how they'd exchanged some hurtful words. "I think she's going to leave, but I told her she can stay. And then I told Collin—and this is what hurts so badly. He was so cold about it. It sounded like he truly hates her. Although I don't really blame him, I can't bear to think of him so full of hatred for anyone. Especially his own mother. And I—I was just so confused. I went for a walk in search of some clarity. Then I got muffins . . . and here I am."

George got up to fetch a box of tissues, setting it on her lap . . . wondering what to do or say. This certainly was not his area of expertise.

Willow blew her nose and then stood. "I shouldn't have come like this. I have no right to burden you with my problems. I'm sorry, George. I'll go now."

"Don't go." He attempted a sympathetic smile. "I'm your friend, Willow. You can talk to me."

"Really?" She stared at him with a doubtful expression.

"I realize I'm not very experienced at this." He shoved his hands into his pants pockets. "But I can try."

"But I don't want to take advantage," she said. "Like I said, my life is messy, George. And yours is so tidy and neat. And I know you like it that way."

He nodded. "That's true."

She looked at the painting he'd hung over the sofa and her lips almost curled into a smile. "That looks nice there."

"Yes, I'm getting used to it."

"I'm actually surprised that you hung it at all. I thought it might be out on your back porch or given away by now."

George held up the bakery bag. "How about some coffee to go with these?"

"That sounds nice."

As George went into the kitchen, he realized he'd need to make some fresh coffee. "I, uh, I don't really know how to make that special coffee you brought me," he confessed as he set the bran muffins on a plate.

"What?" She frowned as she joined him. "You don't know how to make coffee?"

"I know how to make *my* kind of coffee," he explained. "But I don't know about those whole beans. Do you measure them before or after you grind them? How much do you use per cup? How long do you grind them? And is there anything else I should know?"

Willow's weak smile grew stronger, although George suspected it was at his expense. "It's very simple," she said. "Let me show you." Then, without even measuring, she filled the grinder with beans and began to operate it. "Probably about thirty seconds," she said as it whirred noisily. "Then you just dump it in like you would your other coffee."

"Without measuring?"

She shrugged. "I just wing it, but you can measure if you like."

"How much?"

Willow's creased brow suggested she questioned his sensibilities. "Whatever you normally use should work."

So he got out his mini coffee scoop and meticulously measured, leveling off the top before pouring it into the filter. "It does smell good," he admitted as he turned on the coffee maker.

"See how easy that was."

"I guess." Still, he wasn't sure. It might not turn out right.

"And coffee beans stay fresher longer than ground coffee." She closed up the bag. "Just keep this in a cool, dark place." She ran a hand over his kitchen table. "Should we sit here?"

"Sure." He set the muffin plate in the center of the table. As he fetched paper napkins, a pair of small dishes, and coffee mugs he tried to remember the last time anyone had sat at this table with him. Probably his grandmother . . . nearly twenty years ago. He was about to admit this to Willow then stopped himself. She probably already thought he was rather strange. Why reinforce the concept?

Before long, they were having muffins and very tasty coffee. Sure, it wasn't how George normally spent his Saturday mornings, but he reminded himself that he was retired now. There were bound to be some changes ahead.

twelve

Over coffee and muffins, Willow asked George about his small kitchen dining set. The table had a plastic laminate top with an aqua-blue-and-silver pattern and was trimmed with chrome. The matching chrome chairs were upholstered in what appeared to be the original aqua-blue vinyl upholstery. Obviously vintage, the set had to be more than fifty years old, and yet it was in mint condition.

"My grandmother gave it to me when I bought this house—along with these appliances. For as long as I can remember, she'd had those pieces in her kitchen, although this set had four chairs back then. But besides my brother and me having lunch occasionally, we rarely ate in the kitchen. My grandmother was very proper and felt meals should be served in the dining room."

"That must've been nice." Willow sighed.

"How did your family have meals?"

She chuckled. "Well, I think I've told you that my family was quite nontraditional. I suppose my parents were ahead of their time. Early hippies. I was raised on a communal farm."

"Oh yes, I do recall you mentioned that once. I thought perhaps you were jesting."

"Not at all. It was a real commune with shared gardens, shared chores, shared meals—the works."

"Did you have siblings?"

"Yes. An older sister, but she hated commune life. She left the farm when she was fifteen." Willow shook her head. "I haven't seen her since."

"But you went to high school at Warner?"

"My parents moved back here. It was my mom's hometown and I think there were some problems at the commune. Plus my parents were worried about my education and that I'd end up running away like my sister. Unfortunately, I was so independent and wild, I was a handful for everyone. And then when I got pregnant with Josie, well, my parents insisted on raising her while I went to college. I have to give them credit for helping me get my education, but I sometimes wonder if it might've been better for Josie if they hadn't."

"How's that?"

"Well, when I finally finished college and got on my feet, Josie was about six. I wanted to have her with me, but my mom convinced me she would be better off with them. And maybe she was . . . although I suspect they spoiled her some. Probably an attempt to make up for where things went wrong with my sister and me. Of course, it all unraveled for them when Josie became an adolescent and started to rebel. That's when my parents shoved her off on Asher and me. And by then . . . well, we tried, but I think it was too little too late."

"Do you think that's why Josie is, uh, the way she is?"

Willow explained about the counselors and shrinks that

Josie had seen during her teens, about the diagnoses and treatments. "But nothing really helped."

"I've had students like that," George admitted. "More so, it seems, in recent years. It makes me question the state of the world. Are we degenerating? If so, is it due to environmental factors . . . or just a general decaying of humanity?"

"Those are big questions." Willow set down her empty coffee cup. "Speaking of big questions, I'm curious about your interest in Ralph Waldo Emerson. Besides the name connection, do you really embrace his philosophy?"

"I did in my youth. But to be honest, it's been years since I really studied his works. Although I still believe in independent thinking and living freely."

"Living freely?" She frowned at the immaculate kitchen around them. She hadn't failed to notice how carefully George kept everything in its place. So much so that she felt certain he had some form of obsessive-compulsive tendencies—although she was reluctant to ask.

George sighed. "As freely as one can, I suppose."

"From my understanding, Ralph Waldo Emerson was an atheist," she said cautiously. "Do you embrace that as well?" Although she hoped that George would say no, she knew it wouldn't be a deal breaker in their friendship. Not at all.

"I suppose I'm an atheist." He frowned. "To be honest, I don't give religion much thought."

"I used to be an atheist," she confided. "But looking back I believe it was simply a cry out to God for him to prove to me that he was real."

"And did he?"

"Yes." She nodded. "Most definitely."

"So now you have no doubts?" George looked skeptical.

"Well, I'm human. Of course, I have doubts. But my faith outweighs them."

"So do you believe *everything* in the Bible?" he asked.

"I'm not much of an expert on the Bible, but I'm not sure I take it all literally."

"Really?" George looked genuinely surprised.

"Oh, I believe it's inspired by God. Although there are parts of the Old Testament that I don't understand. But I do love the New Testament. Especially the words of Jesus. Those Scriptures ring true and clear to me." She cringed slightly. "I'm sure my theology doesn't line up with a lot of well-meaning Christians. To be honest, I'm not usually this open about my beliefs. Although I do chat with God about these things."

"You chat with God?"

She chuckled. "Well, yes. I try not to wear him out with every little thing, but if I need to talk to him, I do."

"Interesting."

She felt somewhat embarrassed. "I'm not usually this transparent with people about my faith. Well, except for Collin. He makes fun of me sometimes. But I just remind him that we're all on our own spiritual journeys and as long as we're moving forward, we really shouldn't compare ourselves to each other. And we shouldn't judge."

"This is all very interesting." George rubbed his chin. "I've never heard anyone talk like that about religion. My grandparents were very involved in church. As was my mother. But as I grew older, I identified more with philosophies like Ralph Waldo Emerson's. He had little use for religion or God. Felt they were like crutches that crippled people. I began to feel the same way as I grew older. Religion let me down. So why should I trust in it? That's the first step in living independently."

"Independently of God?" she asked.

He slowly nodded.

"I suppose I thought I was rather independent too," she admitted. "But at the same time I was uneasy inside . . . and, I think, rather lonely."

"Lonely?" George's brow creased, but his gaze was intense. "You do not strike me as a lonely sort of person, Willow."

"No, I suppose not. But I believe I was lonely for God. I had this hunger. Nothing filled it up. Not my family, not my art, not the adventures I sought. It was only when I invited God into my life that the empty place was filled." She looked at George to see that, although he was still listening, he appeared confused.

"I've said too much." She stood, gathering up their dishes. "And I've used up too much of your time—on your first official day of retirement too." She smiled. "But I do thank you, George. I feel ever so much better now. I suppose I needed to preach that little sermon to myself. Thank you for graciously listening." She set the dishes in the sink. "Can I help you wash—"

"No, no, this is a one-man job." He studied her closely. Probably still trying to make sense of all that she'd just said. Poor man.

"Then I will let you get back to your day. And I better go home and find out what's going on with Josie. Hopefully she hasn't disturbed Collin with her troubles . . . or burned the place down."

"What?" George looked alarmed.

"Oh, she's a smoker. And she keeps forgetting my rules

to take it outside." She glumly shook her head. "Thank you again, George. You're a good listener."

As Willow walked home, she felt concerned. Oh, not so much that Josie would be smoking in the apartment. Willow felt worried that perhaps she'd said too much to George. Overwhelmed him once again. And so she prayed for God to straighten things out with George. After all, these matters of faith were between them. And then, as she got nearer to her building, relieved to see no smoke or fire engines, she prayed for Josie, imploring God to help her lost child find her way. Because, for certain, only God could do that.

George washed and dried the dishes and wiped down his kitchen. Then, suddenly feeling bone-tired and weary, he sat down in his easy chair in the living room and stared up at the painting of the pickup in the poppies. He felt discombobulated. That was not a word he'd ever used to describe himself before. But he felt so thoroughly confused, bewildered, perplexed, and befuddled . . . only *discombobulated* really fit.

He knew it was because of Willow. This feeling of being turned upside down and inside out only happened when he spent time with her. Even when he'd enjoyed being with her, he always was left with a very unsettling feeling when it was all over and done with. He wondered if that was similar to how an addict felt. Did they get a sense of enjoyment while strung out on their destructive substance of choice, then experience a terrible letdown afterward? And, really, was he comparing his friend Willow to cocaine? If she was like cocaine, shouldn't he be keeping a safe distance from her?

Thinking about such things only made him more confused. So George got out of his chair and, instead of mowing the lawn or putting his wet laundry into the dryer, like
he knew he should do, he walked to town. He went into the
hardware store and, after looking about for a bit, purchased
a hammock. One of those ropey ones that looked as if someone had tied hundreds of knots.

"Are you certain this is sturdy enough to safely hold me?"
he asked the sales clerk as she rang it up. She was a hefty
woman, so he thought she should know.

She just laughed, assuring him it was sturdy enough to
hold a much heavier person. "Or even two people." She gave
what looked like a flirty wink.

George paid her in cash, then, with his hammock under
one arm, marched triumphantly toward home. He'd never
owned a hammock before. Never even been in one that he
could remember. But for some reason, the idea of being retired with time to relax and unwind . . . well, it seemed to
suggest that a hammock might very well be a necessity. Now
if he could just figure out how to safely hang the contraption.
And hopefully in a spot where Lorna Atwood wouldn't be
able to gape over the fence at him.

As George turned down his street, he wondered . . . Was
he lonely? Certainly, he spent plenty of time alone. He'd be
spending even more time alone now that he was no longer
a teacher. But spending time in solitude didn't necessarily mean he was lonely. Had Ralph Waldo Emerson been
lonely? Or had he simply embraced a lack of companionship as a sign of true independence? Perhaps George would
lie in his new hammock and read one of his old Emerson
books. He could just imagine himself like that. A man of

leisure reading up on philosophy. Now wouldn't that be something!

However, as soon as George got inside his house, he felt compelled to finish his laundry. He'd never let it sit in the washing machine this long before. As usual, he removed the laundry items one at a time, giving each piece a firm shake before placing it in the dryer. These appliances were thirty years old, but according to the repair man who serviced them from time to time, the new models—thanks to all their electronic gizmos—were not nearly as dependable or as easily fixed as these old ones.

With the laundry situation under control, George went out to the backyard to scope out a good place to hang his hammock. The options were decidedly limited. And no spot promised the privacy he'd hoped for. He was just measuring the distance between a pear and apple tree when he noticed that his lawnmower was still sitting by the back porch, ready to go.

Naturally, even though the grass wasn't very long, George felt compelled to mow and rake the yard. And then it was time for his final load of laundry—sheets and towels. By the end of the day, his new hammock, still encased in its plastic, remained where he'd set it on his back porch. Perhaps he would hang it tomorrow.

• ◦ •

Despite Josie's claim that she did not want to remain in Warner, by the end of the day, she was still here. And even though the stress level was higher than ever, Willow was actually somewhat relieved. She knew Josie was a powder keg. But she also knew that Josie needed help. Now if she could only get Collin to understand.

"All I know is that I can't stand to be around her," Collin told Willow as the two of them had a quiet dinner out on the terrace. Fortunately, Josie had declined Willow's invitation to join them, claiming she wanted to be alone right now. After spending the last few hours in Willow's apartment pacing angrily about—raging about her selfish boyfriend and this "stinking small town" and her horrible life and even the hot, humid weather—Josie looked like she'd worn herself out. But before she stormed off to her apartment like a wounded victim, she loaded herself up with leftovers from last night's party. There were no worries she would go hungry.

But at least Josie was still here . . . and still talking. For some reason that gave Willow hope. It had been a relief to dine alone with Collin—except that his nose was seriously out of joint. "I don't see why she's still here," he said sullenly as they finished up their meal.

"I understand your feelings," Willow said quietly. "I'll admit that Josie isn't easy to be around. And I don't expect you to spend too much time with her. All I want is for you to remain somewhat neutral. It won't do any good to engage with her. Not right now anyway. She's too hotheaded for a civilized conversation."

"It's hard to remain neutral when someone attacks you."

"I know." Willow cringed to remember how nasty Josie had been to Collin when he'd popped in to talk to Willow this afternoon. She'd treated him more like a brother than a son. As if they had a sibling rivalry going on. Naturally, Collin had been hurt. "I'm sorry she's being so difficult."

"Even Mr. Emerson got fed up with her." Collin brightened. "Wasn't that awesome how he stood up to her last night?"

"It was certainly surprising."

"Maybe she needs people to stand up to her," Collin suggested. "Maybe she's run roughshod over everyone all these years, and now it's time for her to get hers. I'll bet that's why Garth left. He couldn't take it anymore."

"You could be right about that. And it's possible she needs people to stand up to her like you're saying. I'm just warning you to go easy for now. But you're smart, I'm sure you'll figure out the best way to interact with her."

"Meaning she's going to be here awhile?" He frowned.

"I don't know for sure. But she doesn't really have anyplace else to go. No one else who will take her in."

"But she acts like she hates us. And she says she hates this town. What good is it for her to stay in Warner?"

"I honestly don't know. All I know is that she needs to be loved—unconditionally."

"Well, don't expect *me* to love her." Collin set his glass of iced tea down with a bang. "I hate her."

"I know. You've already told me that. I'm just asking you to be patient."

"Right now, all I want is to avoid her. That reminds me of something. You know how you wanted me to work at the gallery this summer?" he asked. "I've been rethinking that."

"Why?"

"For one thing, if Josie's living here, I want to keep a distance from her. But besides that, Mr. Emerson mentioned something last night. I told him I wanted to work this summer, and he said there's a HELP WANTED sign in the bookstore. I thought maybe I'd go apply for a job there. You know how much I love books. I think I'd fit in better there than in the gallery. Besides, I really don't know much about art."

"You know a lot about art, Collin. You grew up with it all around you. Besides my art, I took you to all the galleries in the Bay Area and—"

"I know. That's not what I mean, Nana. The truth is I'm not that interested in art. No offense. I mean I like your art. But art in general, well, it's just not that important to me. Not like books and literature."

"Then, of course, you should apply at the bookstore." Willow forced a smile for his sake. "They'd be lucky to get you."

"And it might diminish the chances of bumping into my mother. For some reason I cannot imagine she'd show her face in a bookstore. She probably doesn't even know how to read."

"Oh, Collin." Willow chuckled. "But you're probably right about her lack of interest in books."

"So you won't be mad at me for not working in the gallery?"

"Not at all, Collin. I really do want you to do what's best for you. But now I better start looking for someone to help out. From what I hear, town gets busier in the summer."

"Maybe Josie would like to work for you." Collin snickered like this was a great joke.

"That might actually work."

"You gotta be kidding, Nana. You'd let Josie terrorize your customers?"

"Valid point." Willow cringed to imagine Josie tearing into some unsuspecting visitor to the gallery.

"Hey, maybe Marissa could work for you. She's looking for a summer job. And she actually *likes* art."

Willow brightened. "That, my boy, is not a bad idea. Why don't you tell Marissa to pop in and talk to me about this? I mean, if she's genuinely interested."

Collin's eyes lit up. "Do you like her, Nana? Not just for my sake. I mean do you *really* like her?"

Willow smiled. "I do like her. Very much. From what I've seen she's a kind, thoughtful girl."

"And she's intelligent."

"Sounds like what I need in the gallery. I just hope she's interested."

"I'll go call her right now." Collin collected their empty dishes. "Thanks for dinner. Want me to help clean up in the kitchen?"

"No, you go call Marissa. That's helpful enough."

After Collin left, Willow remained out on the terrace. It had been an extra warm day, but a slight western breeze brought a refreshing coolness with it, and the sky was just getting rosy with the promise of a beautiful sunset. Willow took a slow, deep breath, leaning back on the padded lounge chair with tired contentment. Everything had been so crazy and hectic these past few days, she relished this quiet moment to herself, up here in her lovely garden with the gurgling sound of the nearby fountain. How perfectly delightful to be alone.

thirteen

By Sunday afternoon, following about an hour of measuring, calculation, and careful contemplation, as well as two trips to the hardware store—first for chain lengths, then for S-hooks—George managed to hang his hammock between the pear and apple trees. But getting into the contraption presented a whole new challenge. The confounded thing would simply not remain in place. Each time he was about to climb in, it would sway precariously away from him, and he would barely escape. Finally, after several unsuccessful attempts, he was nearly settled when the obstinate hammock suddenly flipped over, dumping him to the ground. George stood up, clenching his fists in frustration and controlling the urge to spew some unsavory language.

Clearly it was time for a showdown. It was either him or the hammock. George took a deep breath and, steadying himself, backed up toward the hammock. He then gripped it tightly with both hands, one on each side, and eased his backside onto it. So far so good. Next he cautiously lifted his legs, shifted his weight, and gingerly leaned back. George could feel his heart racing as he lay there as rigid as a stick, waiting for the unruly hammock to exert its will against him, but nothing happened.

Determined to relax, George tried to ignore the strings that felt like they sliced through his back. But before long his head began to throb as well. How in the world was a hammock supposed to be relaxing? And how was he supposed to swing the wretched death trap when even the slightest motion threatened life and limb?

After a few minutes, deciding he'd had enough, George swung his legs downward, but this motion sent the hammock into another dizzying spin, landing George on all fours in the grass and sputtering like a lunatic. As he stood up, brushing grass from his trousers, he could hear loud giggles coming from the direction of Lorna Atwood's side of the fence. Naturally, she'd been witnessing this whole fiasco.

Trying to maintain a slight shred of dignity, George tipped his head toward her. "Good afternoon."

"Looks like you're having some trouble with your hammock," she called out.

He sighed as he went over to speak to her. "Yes, it seems I'm not a hammock sort of fellow." He held up his hands. "For some reason I thought that it would be a relaxing way to pass the time with my newly acquired retirement. But now I'm ready to dump the whole works into the trash can."

"Don't do that," Lorna said. "You just need to get the hang of it."

"It nearly hung me."

"There is an art to using a hammock," she explained. "Believe me, I had one for years at my previous house. I would've brought it here with me, but I couldn't find an appropriate place to hang it in the yard. Although I am considering one of those free-standing ones."

"Well, if you had a place to hang a hammock, I would offer you that one."

"What you need, Mr. Emerson, is a hammock lesson." She beamed at him. "And I am just the one to give it to you."

"Well, I don't know."

"Come on," she urged. "With a few handy tips, you'll soon discover the wonders of good hammocking."

"Hammocking?" He frowned. "I don't think that's a word."

She just laughed. "Meet me at your front porch—and I will give you a free training session." And then she hurried away.

Knowing he had little choice, George went through his house, but as he opened his front door, he was already concocting an excuse to send his "helpful" neighbor on her way. "Thank you for—"

"Don't mention it," she said as she forced her way into his house. It was the first time she'd been inside, and she brazenly looked all around. "Looks like this is the same floor plan as my house, but not quite as cozy looking." She grinned. "More like a bachelor pad, eh?" She was already leading him through the kitchen and out to the backyard. "Lesson number one," she said with authority. "We need to lower your hammock a bit." Already she was adjusting the S-hook and chain on one side. "Take it down a couple of links," she instructed him.

"But this is so low," he countered. "Won't my backside be dragging in the—"

"Trust me. It's just right. Next you need a lightweight

rope." She pointed to a lower branch of the apple tree. "We'll tie it there. It should be long enough to comfortably reach nearly to the ground."

"Whatever for?" Did she want him to hang himself?

"It's a pull rope," she explained. "You dangle it over your hammock and give it a little tug to set your hammock swinging."

"Oh?" He nodded. "That makes sense."

"Besides that, you need a nice, thick blanket or two."

"But it's not cold—"

"To lay on top of the hammock," she said. "It's to pad you from these strings. I had a hammock just like this and, believe me, those strings will leave nasty welts all over the back of you. Not pretty."

"Oh yes, that is a good idea."

"And then you'll want a nice, soft pillow for your head."

He nodded. "You really do seem to know hammocks." He wondered if he should've been taking notes.

"And then you might want to place a little outdoor table out here. Not so close that you'll knock it over, but close enough to set a cool drink or some reading material or sunglasses. You know, the comforts you'll want while relaxing."

George looked at his neighbor with fresh appreciation. "You have clearly given this much thought."

"I told you I was experienced." She chuckled. "So let's go inside and gather the things you need, and then I'll show you the best way for getting in and out of a hammock. I thought you almost had it, but then, well, you saw what happened."

Convinced this woman knew her stuff, George allowed her back in his house, and before long they had gathered up an old quilt made for him by his grandmother when he was a boy, a soft feather pillow, some clothesline, and even a TV tray. With Lorna's assistance, they soon had everything all set up outside.

"I must say this almost looks inviting," George admitted as he stood back to look. "But I'm not sure . . . I really don't relish the notion of being dumped on the ground again."

"That's why you need to learn the proper way of entering and exiting a hammock. Let me demonstrate. Your technique for getting in backwards was good. But you need to do it like this." With her back to the hammock, she grasped it with both hands, easing herself to a seated position. Then she went down sideways and carefully rolled over, smiling as if this were nothing. Next she reached for the clothesline and gave it a little tug. "There. See? Easy peasy."

"Hmm."

"And here is how you get out." She reversed what she'd just done and was now on her feet. "See?"

"I, uh, I guess so."

She straightened out the mussed quilt and fluffed the pillow. "Your turn."

Uncertain he wanted to attempt such a feat with an audience, he was about to decline. But remembering that she'd witnessed his earlier humiliation, George decided to give it a try. He cautiously backed up to the hammock and proceeded to imitate her steps—and, to his surprise, it worked.

"Voila." She clapped her hands then handed him the loop that she'd tied at the end of the clothesline.

He gave it a cautious tug, lying stone still as the hammock gently rocked from side to side.

"How is it?" she asked.

He felt himself beginning to relax. "Not bad."

"Now all you need is a drink and a good romance novel." She giggled. "At least that's what I usually go for."

"Maybe I should practice getting out," George said. "Just in case."

"Good idea."

George played the steps in his head, reversed from how he'd gotten in, and hoping he wasn't about to splat on the ground, he went for it. To his pleased astonishment, he wound up on his feet. "I think your suggestion for lowering the hammock was most helpful," he told her. "Thank you very much for the lesson."

"You are very welcome, Mr. Emerson."

"Why don't you call me George," he said a bit sheepishly. "After all, we're neighbors. No reason we can't be friends."

"Well, thank you, George." Lorna smiled. "And I feel I should apologize. I realize that I can be overly enthusiastic at times. My girlfriend Karen reminded me of this a few days ago. So if I've overwhelmed you with my enthusiasm, I hope you'll accept my apology."

"Thank you." He nodded. "I must admit to liking a quiet life. When someone comes on too strong, I tend to retreat the other direction."

"And I've noticed that you're involved with your artist friend, Willow West. She seems quite nice."

George didn't know how to respond. On one hand, it would be a convenient way to discourage unwanted advances from his "overly enthusiastic" neighbor, but on the other hand, it was disingenuous. "Willow is a good friend," he said honestly. "But sometimes she can be overly enthusiastic too."

Lorna grinned. "Well, then I'm in good company." She waved. "Now I'll leave you to your hammock and your peace

145

and quiet. But if you ever need anything, George, you know where I live."

———— •••• ————

On Sunday, instead of raging at everyone about everything, all Josie did was sob and wail. Willow honestly didn't understand how a person could cry that much. But Josie wasn't faking it. Her tears were real. By that afternoon, Willow felt seriously concerned that her daughter could be dehydrated from shedding so many tears.

"I made you a pitcher of iced green tea," Willow said after Josie opened the apartment door. Her nose was red and swollen and her eyes were so puffy they looked like slits. "Are you okay?"

"Of course, I'm not okay," Josie declared. "I miss Garth. I feel like someone chopped off my leg. I don't know how I can go on without him."

"I'm sorry." Willow handed her the pitcher. "Is there anything I can do to help?"

"Get Garth back." Josie peered at her hopefully, as if she really thought Willow could perform such a magic trick.

"Have you tried to call him?"

"I think he's blocked me."

"Oh."

"Maybe you could call him, Mom."

"I don't know."

"He wouldn't have your phone blocked."

"I wouldn't know what to say, honey. And I honestly don't think I should get in the middle of your—"

"Then let me use your phone," Josie begged.

Against her better judgment, Willow gave in. "You have

146

to use it in my apartment," she insisted. "And keep the call short. If he really wants to talk to you, ask him to call you on your own phone."

"Okay," she agreed.

But, back in Willow's apartment, the call to Garth was very brief—and then Josie was crying all over again.

"I'm sorry." Willow exchanged her phone for a handful of tissues. She controlled herself from saying something trite—like *sometimes life is tough* or *sometimes doors close*. She knew platitudes would do no good. Instead, she simply hugged Josie . . . and felt relieved not to be shoved away. Maybe that was progress.

"I don't know what I'm going to do," Josie flopped down on Willow's sectional, clutching a batik pillow to her chest. "I feel so lost."

"I'm sure you do." Willow sat down across from her, silently praying for help.

"What will I do, Mom?"

Willow concealed her shock. Josie was asking her for advice? That was new.

"Tell me, Mom," Josie pressed harder. "What am I supposed to do for the rest of my life?"

Willow took in a cautious breath. "Well, for starters, you can only live one day at a time."

"What is that supposed to mean?"

"When Asher died, I felt lost," she confessed. "But a friend reminded me that we can only live one day at a time."

"But I don't even know how to do that." Josie blew her nose. "I feel like I'm dying inside."

"I know." Willow tried to gather her thoughts. "You need to take baby steps, Josie. That means moment by moment.

147

Like—step one—you get up in the morning and just breathe deeply. Then—step two—you brush your teeth and—"

"I never brush my teeth in the morning."

"Well, that's just an example." Willow frowned. "But maybe it's time you did." She continued suggesting steps. "You just think about the moment you're in, Josie—and you do your best. You don't worry about what's happening next . . . or tomorrow . . . or next year. And before long, you begin to feel better."

"I'll never feel better."

"I know it feels like that now. But, trust me, I felt like that after losing Asher. In time . . . it got easier."

Josie looked up. "I'm sorry I missed his funeral, Mom."

Willow felt a clutch in her chest. "Thank you, honey. That means a lot to me. You know . . . Asher really loved you."

She nodded. "I know."

"And, even though I made lots of mistakes, I loved you too. I still do."

She nodded again, and for a long moment they both just sat there. Then Willow's phone rang. It was Marissa. They'd met for coffee and an interview this morning and Willow had offered her a job, instructing her to call this afternoon to discuss her hours.

"Can I call you back?" Willow asked. Marissa agreed. But when Willow turned back to Josie, she could tell that what had felt like the start of a tender moment had evaporated.

"I'm sure you have places to go and people to see," Josie said sharply. "Don't let me and my problems keep you from it."

"I actually don't have anywhere to be or anyone to see," Willow assured her. "Leslie and Joel are working the gallery

148

until closing. And that was Collin's girlfriend, Marissa, on the phone. I've hired her to work at the gallery this summer."

"Marissa is going to work for you?" Josie scowled with disapproval. "Isn't she awfully young?"

"Young, but motivated. And she loves art."

Josie frowned. "I thought maybe I could work for you."

"Really?" Willow studied her closely. Was Josie just playing her? Willow was well aware of her daughter's ability to manipulate people when she wanted something.

"I need money—I mean, if I want to get out of here."

"But you don't need to worry about that today," Willow assured her. "You'll have a place to live and food to eat. When you're ready—and hopefully it won't be long—we can talk about the possibility of you working for me. Or perhaps you'd rather look for a job someplace else in town."

"I don't really care where I work."

"Do you have, uh, much work experience?"

Josie rolled her eyes. "I've worked before. Okay, no big, fancy jobs. But I've flipped burgers, cleaned cheap hotel rooms, slung beer . . . and a few other jobs that you probably don't want to hear about."

Willow tried not to look shocked.

"Don't worry, I haven't done *that*."

"I didn't say anything."

"All I meant was that I've done jobs I'm not that proud of. Just temporary stuff. I've been a dancer in clubs . . . sold my blood . . . I've even panhandled when we were broke and the band needed gas money. People are more generous to women. But that's not the sort of crud you'd put on a job application."

"Is there any sort of work that you feel you'd like to do? Perhaps something you could be trained or go to school for."

"I am *not* going back to school," she declared. "Never again."

Willow held up her hands. "That's fine. I wasn't really expecting an answer from you. But maybe it's something you could think about . . . while you've got time on your hands. Maybe it's time to dream a little. Dream about what you'd like to do or be."

"Dream?"

"Why not?"

Josie snuggled down into the corner of the sectional. "Maybe I should take a nap here and try to dream. Your apartment's lots nicer than where you've got me holed up. I think I'll move in here."

Willow suppressed aggravation. Why wouldn't Josie want to take up residence in Willow's apartment? It was comfortable and pretty and clean . . . with a well-stocked fridge. But the amenities would deteriorate quickly if Josie had her way. And before long, they'd be at odds over it. "I have a better idea," Willow said.

"What?"

"Well, you want to earn some money, right?"

Josie cautiously nodded.

"And I need work done on the apartment you're using."

"What kind of work?" Josie's eyes narrowed.

"Like what I've done in here. And like what Collin did to his apartment. We ripped out the carpets and linoleum, refinished the wood floors, painted walls and cabinets . . . just basic renovation stuff." Willow waved a hand. "But the result is a place like this."

150

Josie glanced around with what looked like genuine interest.

"The payoff for you would be to stay in a much-improved space. That apartment has the potential to be quite nice. But when the work was done, I'd expect you to keep it clean and neat. I mean, if you remained here in town."

"I don't know." Josie frowned.

"And don't forget, I'd pay you fair wages for your work."

"But I don't know how to do any of those things."

"I can show you. So can Collin. It's mostly just plain elbow grease and dogged determination." Willow knew it would be a miracle if Josie agreed to this idea—and put in the effort. She also knew it was probably just the sort of work Josie needed right now. But how to get her on board? Willow recalled how reverse psychology had sometimes worked on Josie as a teen. Would she fall for it now?

Willow shrugged. "But it's okay if you want to pass on this, Josie. It's a lot to take on and you're probably not in great condition. You have to be physically fit to do that kind of work. It's very demanding and—"

"I'm in good shape."

"But it's a big undertaking, honey. You might not have it in you to—"

"You could at least let me try," Josie protested. "It's possible that I'm more capable than either you or Collin thinks. Yeah, sure, I haven't been at my best these past few days, but it's been pretty stressful around here. You can at least give me a chance to show you what I can do."

"Yes, of course. I just want you to understand right up front that it's a lot to take on."

"Why don't you let me be the judge of that?"

"Fine. How about we get started tomorrow?"

"Fine." Josie's jaw jutted out. "What do I do first?"

"The carpet and linoleum need to be pulled up. And I'll have to arrange for a Dumpster." Willow reached for a notepad, starting a to-do list. One for her and one for Josie. She knew that this plan could completely fall apart or blow up in her face, but what was the worst that could happen? Even if it wasn't done right, Willow had planned to gut that apartment anyway. If Josie could invest some real energy and time into it . . . well, maybe it could be a win-win for everyone. Or else it could all go up in smoke. Willow added "install more smoke alarms" to her list.

fourteen

At the end of his first week of retirement, George was uneasy. Perhaps even antsy. As he went about his usual morning chores, he tried to pinpoint why he felt like this. Having time off in summer was nothing new to him. But even reading in the hammock had gotten a bit old. While sweeping the kitchen floor, he thought perhaps it had been errant not to plan some sort of travel event—something to commemorate the end of his teaching career. He remembered how teachers before him had boasted of the exciting globetrotting they planned to do in their retirement. As he returned the broom to the closet, George wondered if he should be contemplating going somewhere.

But George had traveled a lot in his forties. Always on organized tours, of course. Where every minute and mile had been spelled out on a detailed agenda that George would begin studying in midwinter. Over the course of a decade, George had stepped onto every continent, and his passport boasted colorful stamps from dozens of countries. Traveling had always been a bit stressful, but when fall came, he recalled how his "adventures" had impressed his fellow teachers. Of course, these trips had been the result of his friendship with Brad and Tracie. Owners of Wilson Travel, they always recruited George for their annual summer trips—mostly to balance the tour groups, since there'd always been a majority of single women. But Wilson Travel had folded with the economy, and George hadn't been on a tour in more than ten years.

George sometimes saw ads for group tours in the local newspaper. He'd read them with amusement but never enough interest to respond. In fact, the very idea of getting on a plane and going to another country sounded rather horrifying to him right now. The honest truth was that George had no desire to go anywhere. But why was he so unsettled?

As George cleaned his coffee maker, his thoughts wandered to Willow West . . . again. These musings, which had become habitual, were most unwelcome. They popped in and out, uninvited, throughout his day until he finally decided that since there was little he could do about it one way or another—why not simply give in?

He made a small grocery list, wondering what Willow was doing right now. Probably working at her gallery. He could imagine her dressed in one of her exotic outfits, casually chatting with a customer as quiet classical music played in the background. Not a bad sort of life. But was her obnoxious daughter still tormenting her, or had Josie moved on by now? And had Collin gotten that job at the bookstore? The owner had called George as a reference and, naturally, George had spoken favorably.

Maybe George should stop by on his way to the grocery store. Maybe he'd even buy a book—something outside of his normal reading habits. That could shake things up. As he gave his counter a final wipe down, he wondered if Willow was planning any more exotic parties to be held out on her wonderful terrace. The weather forecast for the weekend was good. He could imagine her and her artist friends up there in the moonlight. There'd be music and laughter. They'd probably dine on fancy hors d'oeuvres and drink fine wine—having an enjoyable evening. All of this, though out of his comfort zone, was still rather intriguing. But George had been determined to put some time and space between himself and Willow. That relationship, even when it was enjoyable, had grown too close for comfort.

As George changed into a clean white shirt—without a tie—he felt a deep longing . . . a need to escape. Not this house necessarily. Or even the small town of Warner. No, George felt the need to escape himself. But as quickly as that feeling swept over him, he pushed it away. With his shopping bag folded neatly inside of his dark trousers pocket, he headed to town.

His first stop was the Book Nook, where, to his dismay, Collin was not working. George considered inquiring, but the salesclerk was busy. So without even browsing for a book, George continued on his way. Next stop was Mabel's Market. He'd been shopping there for as long as he could remember. Even when old Mabel sold the small grocery store to the Patel family and moved to Florida, George had remained a faithful customer, primarily for two reasons. First, it was near enough to easily walk to and from, and second, they carried a limited selection of merchandise, which helped prevent confusion and distraction. George could easily gather the items on his list and be on his way.

During the school year George habitually shopped on

Wednesday afternoons and Saturday mornings. But since this was summer—and now that he was retired—he planned to adopt a more flexible schedule.

"Good day, Mr. Emerson," Mrs. Patel said politely. "How are you this fine morning?"

"Very well, thank you." George picked up a shopping basket.

"We have some lovely fresh fruit today. Kiwis, papayas, pomegranates, pineapples." She waved a hand over the produce section.

George scanned the colorful display of fruit before picking up his standard fare—two slightly green bananas, two red delicious apples, and two oranges. "This will do, thank you." He nodded to her then continued to the dairy section. As he made his next selections, he wondered why he ever bothered to make a shopping list since he always purchased the same things. But it felt good to have the slip of paper in his pocket—just in case he got rattled or distracted and forgot.

With his shopping bag weighted down with groceries, George headed for home, but instead of turning down his street, he paused, glancing down Main Street to the Willow West Gallery. Perhaps he could simply pop in and say hello. He could ask Willow how things had gone with her daughter. Hadn't he offered her his friendship? And yet he hadn't had a conversation with her all week. What kind of friend was that?

So, convinced that he was overdue for a casual encounter with his friend Willow, he entered the gallery and instantly wished he'd worn a tie. The sound of pleasant music greeted him, as well as the aroma of something he couldn't quite identify. Something spicy but sweet.

"*George?*" Willow practically ran into him as she rushed around a corner, carrying what looked like an old-fashioned wooden toolbox.

"Hello." He stepped aside since she appeared to be in a hurry.

"What are you doing here?" Her tone was flustered, but then she smiled. "I'm sorry, that doesn't sound very hospitable, does it?"

"It looks like you're busy." George noticed her paint-stained overalls and tie-dyed T-shirt. Not exactly the sort of ensemble he'd imagined she'd be wearing in her gallery.

"Yes. I'm helping Josie." She tipped her head toward the door. "I just wanted to slip in and out of here to get this." She held out the toolbox. "I wanted to make a quick getaway before any customers had a chance to see me like this. Want to make a quick exit with me?"

"Sure." He nodded, following her out the door and into the shadows of the nearby stairwell. "I only popped in to say hello," he told her. "I hadn't talked to you for a while."

"I know." She set down the toolbox and pushed a loose strand of hair into the blue bandana that was holding it away from her face. "In fact, I was just thinking of you this morning."

"You were?" For some reason he felt surprised.

"Yes. I was remembering that lovely cherry shelf-unit you made."

"Oh yes. I'm actually considering doing some woodworking again. You'd suggested as much. And perhaps it's a good idea." He smiled. "In fact, I'm thinking that if my skills aren't too far gone, I'll consider making that storage unit you mentioned."

"That's wonderful. But I'd actually hoped to ask your advice about the project I'm working on right now."

"What are you working on?"

"Well, Josie and I are renovating the apartment she's been occupying." She lowered her voice. "I sort of convinced her to stick around here . . . by enticing her to work for me on it."

George felt a small wave of concern. Josie was such an unpleasant person. Wouldn't Willow and Collin be better off without her? "So how is that going?"

"Well, we've had our ups and downs. I won't say it's easy." She glanced up the stairs. "But I think it's worth the effort. And I've even gotten Collin to help out some."

"That's interesting." George shifted his shopping bag to the other hand. "So, he didn't get the bookstore job?"

"No, he got it. But he doesn't start until tomorrow, so I offered to pay him for helping Josie with the apartment this week." She gave a sheepish smile. "I suppose it really has more to do with them learning to get along than anything else. But it seems to be working."

"That's good."

"Anyway, we're trying to figure out what to do with the kitchen cabinets today. Originally I had planned to completely gut the kitchen and order some cabinets online. But Collin thinks they can be fixed." Willow pointed to George. "But we need someone with some woodworking skills."

"I see." George was trying to think of an excuse to make a hasty escape now.

"Would you have time to take a quick look?" she asked. "Give us your expert opinion?"

"I'm not an expert."

"Compared to us you are."

He held up his bag. "I have my groceries. Perishables, you know."

"Yes." Her smile faded. "I understand. I shouldn't have asked. Besides that, it's sort of crazy up there. Paint and messes everywhere. My apologies." She brightened. "But it is good to see you, George. I hope you're doing well." She pointed to his bag. "I'll let you get on your way with that. Hopefully you don't have ice cream in there. It's already pretty warm out."

Now he felt guilty . . . and perhaps something else he couldn't quite identify. "How about this, Willow," he said. "I'll just run my groceries home, put them away, change into some, uh, woodworking clothes, and come back. How does that sound?"

"Really?" Her eyes lit up. "That sounds wonderful!"

As George hurried toward home, he felt—once again—torn. On one hand, he wanted to maintain this connection with Willow. On the other hand, well, it could quickly turn overwhelming. Especially with her daughter involved in the mix. He tried not to consider the ramifications as he put away his groceries then changed into khaki pants, a plaid short-sleeved shirt, and his old shoes. As he headed back to town, he gave himself permission to simply survey the cabinets, give his opinion—if he had one—then excuse himself to go home . . . to peace and calm and quiet.

George had just knocked on the door when he heard yelling. Tempted to turn and make a run for it, he jumped when the door jerked open. Josie stood there in a paint-streaked tank top and shorts—and a sour expression. In her hand was a paintbrush that was dripping right onto the floor. "What do you want?" she rudely asked.

"Your mother asked me to—"

"Mr. Emerson." Collin hurried over. "Come in. Nana said you were coming."

"Why?" Josie demanded. "We don't need another person in here. It's already too crowded." She glared at Collin.

"You're painting in the bathroom," Collin told her. "Nana said Mr. Emerson was coming to look at the kitchen cabinets."

"Like I already said, the kitchen cabinets need to be torn out," Josie told him.

"I don't agree," Collin countered. "I think they're sturdy."

"But this is MY apartment," she yelled. "I should have the—"

"It's Nana's apartment," Collin yelled back. "She's only letting you—"

"*Where is Willow?*" George asked loudly.

"She went to the hardware store for something," Collin said tersely. "Hopefully she'll be back soon—before Josie takes over completely."

George looked from Josie to Collin—both scowled darkly. What kind of hornets' nest had he just stepped into—and what was the best way to handle it? He turned to Josie. "I don't want to interrupt you from painting your bathroom." He pointed to her dripping paintbrush. "By the way, that's a nice shade of blue."

Josie brightened slightly. "Really? You like it? I picked it out myself."

"It reminds me of the Mediterranean Sea," he told her.

"Have you actually been there?"

"I have." He nodded.

"Mom and Collin both think this color is too much." She

160

gazed wistfully at the brush. "But I like it. I guess I better get back to painting."

"Good for you." He looked at Collin. "Well, since I'm here, why don't I take a look at those cabinets?"

Collin appeared to relax a bit as he led George through the maze of paint buckets, boxes, and miscellaneous messes, stopping in the kitchen. "These cabinets are the same as the ones I had in my apartment," Collin explained. "Mine were pretty beat up and Nana didn't think they were worth saving." He opened a cupboard door that wasn't closing properly. "But these look pretty solid to me. I mean, with some fresh paint and minor repairs. And I already washed them. What do you think?"

"Well, I'm not really an expert." George tested a few drawers and doors. "But I do like the idea of restoring old things." He told Collin a bit about his houses and how he'd managed to salvage a lot of original features. "They built things better back in the old days. And I agree with you. These are worth saving."

"Great."

"It'll take some work." George explained how all the hardware needed to be removed. "But as you take off the doors and drawers, be sure to number them so that you can get them back in the right places." He checked a hinge. "I think the main problem is this hardware. Some old hardware is worth cleaning and reusing, but these are shot. Much easier to replace them with new ones." He was about to show Collin how to easily remove a door when Willow came in.

"Mr. Emerson says we can salvage these cabinets," Collin told her. "He's going to help me."

George wanted to correct Collin regarding his "going to

help" comment, but decided to let it go for now. After all, he was here to help. But only to get them started on the right path. Not to do the actual work. At least that was not his intent. After all, he was retired—a man of leisure. And, like Josie had emphatically pointed out, this small apartment was already overpopulated with people and personalities.

However, a strange thing happened as George showed Collin some simple steps, explaining the need for sanding, prepping, painting . . . he no longer wanted to leave. So it was that, while Willow helped Josie work on the blue bathroom, George remained in the kitchen, instructing Collin—step by step—and working alongside him. He even began to list what was needed to complete the project.

"Now it's time for sanding." George picked up a piece of heavy-grade sandpaper that he found in a toolbox, showing how to fold it and use it to smooth the rough edges of a cupboard door. "We'll need some higher-count paper too." He explained how the grade numbers of sandpaper worked. "Higher numbers are finer paper, which you use last." He added this to his list. "After we're done sanding, we'll be ready for paint. Has a color been chosen yet?"

"That's Josie's territory." Collin rolled his eyes. "And her taste is a little, uh, over the top."

"Well, I suppose if this is going to be her space . . . she should like it."

Collin frowned. "But she keeps saying she hates Warner," he whispered. "So I don't see why she gets to choose everything. What if she leaves and then someone wants to rent this place, but hates these colors?"

"Then I'm sure they'll look elsewhere or repaint."

"How's it going?" Willow asked as she and Josie came into the kitchen.

Collin told them they needed to get paint and a few other things. Josie grabbed up a pack of color samples and began to spin through the swatches. "I like this." She held up a bold orange-red tone. *Pimento.*

"Like that nasty stuff in green olives?" Collin wrinkled his nose.

"I like it." Josie turned to George. "What do you think?"

"Well, it's certainly lively." A color like that in his kitchen would drive him to distraction.

"Cool. I think a kitchen should be lively."

"When you get the paint, make sure you tell them it's to go on wood cabinets," George told them. "And a gallon will be more than enough."

"While you're still here, can you take a peek at the bathroom vanity?" Willow asked him. "I'm not sure if it can be saved."

George went into the small bathroom, blinking at the bold bright-blue paint, then stooping down to examine the vanity. "Like the kitchen cabinets, I think the main problem is the hardware. Replace it, give a coat of fresh paint, and you should be good." He glanced at Josie. "I don't know what color you're considering for this, but white would be a nice, fresh contrast with your blue walls."

She tilted her head to one side then nodded. "Yes, that's a good idea. It will make the blue stand out more. And maybe I can get some cool knobs for the vanity."

Willow tossed George a grateful look. "I'll head back to the hardware store for paint. Anything else we'll need?"

He held up the little list he'd been making.

"Want to come along?" she asked. "We could get those items while they're mixing paint."

As they walked down Main Street in their work clothes, George felt conspicuous, but Willow, in paint-splattered overalls, seemed oblivious to the curious glances tossed their way.

"I think you're right that this project is good for Josie," he told Willow. "She seems different to me."

"She comes and goes. Right now, she acts okay. But she and Collin have been going at it, off and on, all week long. To be honest, I was a little worried that she would lash into you, but you must have won her over."

"Maybe for the time being."

"You got that right." Willow sighed. "Being around Josie is like living in a minefield. You never know what will set her off."

"Similar to teaching high school."

Willow chuckled. "So, you really are more cut out for this sort of thing than I had assumed."

"I enjoy helping Collin," he told her. "He's a hard worker."

"I'm selfishly sorry he got that bookstore job. When he starts work tomorrow I lose my best laborer."

"I feel somewhat to blame for that," George confessed.

"Well, maybe I can guilt you into filling the gap for him." She gave him a sly look then laughed. "Just kidding, George."

"Oh." He opened the hardware store door for her and, with list in hand, proceeded to gather hardware and sandpaper while she ordered the paint. Before long, they were headed back with their purchases.

"Do you think getting that apartment done will encourage Josie to remain in Warner?" George asked.

"I honestly have no idea what that girl will do—from one

moment to the next." She shook her head. "But since I like to live in the moment, well, I suppose I should just enjoy the ride."

George wondered how anyone could possibly enjoy the unexpectedness of living around someone like Josie on a full-time basis. But then again, Willow appeared to thrive on craziness, unpredictability, and stress. And with Josie she would get plenty of that. For the life of him, George couldn't fathom how Willow could stand it.

fifteen

Back at the apartment, George was pleased to see that Collin was about half done with the first round of sanding. "I'll go over this with the finer paper now." George picked up one of the sanded doors. When he was done, he wiped it with tack cloth, then showed the results to Collin.

"Wow, that really makes a difference," Collin said. "That's smooth."

"The smoother we get it, the nicer the paint will go on."

"How did you learn all this stuff?" Collin asked. "I mean, I always think of you as an English teacher—very proper in your suit and tie."

George explained how he and his grandfather had spent a few summers working on George's rental properties. "After my grandfather retired from the lumber business he had time to get serious about woodworking. Turned out he was quite the handyman too. He taught me a lot."

"My grandpa wasn't very handy," Collin said. "If something needed to be fixed around the house, he'd just call in someone else to do it."

They were just getting ready to start painting when someone knocked on the door and Willow announced it was time for a lunch break. She'd ordered sandwiches and salads from the local deli. No one said much as they sat around on paint buckets and crates to eat. George wasn't sure whether they were too weary to converse or simply at odds, but it was a relief when everyone got back to work. Willow and Josie got busy painting in the bedroom. Not surprisingly, Josie had chosen another bold color for that. George took a peek, trying not to cringe at the purple-fuchsia tone that would've kept him awake at night. But at least Willow had talked Josie into a nice milky white for all the doors and wood trim. That might help.

George and Collin painted the kitchen cabinets pimento, with Collin making a few vampire jokes, but before long they got into a steady assembly-line rhythm, visiting pleasantly as they worked, which helped the time pass more quickly.

Finally, surrounded by a sea of red doors and drawers, George and Collin paused to survey their accomplishment. "Good work," George declared with satisfaction. "Now these will need time to dry. I wouldn't recommend putting on hardware until tomorrow."

"Then we're all done?" Collin asked.

George checked his watch, surprised to see it wasn't yet four. "What about the bathroom vanity and cabinet? That shouldn't take long."

Collin let out a low groan, but before long, they had the bathroom cabinet dismantled and, while George removed hardware, Collin got to sanding. With both of them working, they had it knocked out by five thirty.

"Nicely done," he told Collin.

"So we're finished now?"

"You appear quite eager to quit." George eyed Collin. "Big date tonight?"

Collin grinned. "Marissa and I are going to a movie."

"Aha." George nodded. "Well, you better get moving, young man. Might take some hard scrubbing to get that pimento paint out of your fingernails."

After Collin took off, George washed the paintbrushes in the bathroom sink. He could hardly believe that he'd stayed here this long. But there was something surprisingly satisfying about it this day. A reminder of when he and his grandfather had worked together so many years ago. Only today, George had played the "grandpa" role.

"This looks great," Willow declared as George laid the cleaned brushes on a rag. "And the kitchen cabinets too. You and Collin do good work. Thank you."

As he washed his hands, he explained that the paint needed to dry before the pieces could be put back together. "And I know Collin is working at the bookstore tomorrow, so how about if I come back and put the cabinets back together?"

"Oh, George, that would be wonderful! That's so generous of you."

They discussed what time to meet up and then George excused himself to leave, but Willow walked down the stairs with him. "I'm sure you must be worn out," she said. "But if you were interested, I would love to fix you dinner—as a thank-you. I have a couple of lovely grass-fed organic New York steaks. Well, unless you're a vegetarian." She grinned. "I used to be vegetarian, back in my thirties. Now I enjoy a good piece of red meat from time to time."

"Steak?" George felt his stomach rumble. "Uh, will Josie be dining with you too?"

Willow frowned. "I haven't invited her. To be honest, I could use a Josie break. But I'm sure she'll want to spend the night in my apartment since hers is still such a mess." She held up a finger. "How would you feel about me bringing my steaks to your house to cook?"

As tempting as a New York steak sounded, George wasn't sure he wanted Willow to cook them in his tidy little kitchen. The smell, the smoke, the grease, the mess, the stress . . . it just wouldn't be worth it. "I'm not really set up for fancy cooking in my kitchen," he confessed. "To be honest, I've never made a steak there myself."

She blinked in surprise. "Oh . . . okay. How about a rain check then? And just so you know, I'm a very good cook. With a good oven and good broiler, I can make a mean steak. Even better on an outdoor grill."

George was still reluctant to give up on that steak. "I have an idea," he said without really thinking it through. "My grandparents' house has a big, well-equipped kitchen. My grandmother was an excellent cook and—"

"That's perfect!" Willow's eyes lit up. "I'd love to see the inside of that house. And it will give me a break from Josie. What time should I come?"

Of course, now George began to second-guess himself. He'd never taken anyone into his grandparents' house since they'd passed. Aside from his visits when he'd dust and sweep and vacuum the main rooms, no one ever went in there. But Willow was already enthusiastically going over her menu, and he knew it was too late to change his mind. They agreed to meet at seven. That would just give George enough time to grab a quick shower then get up there and make sure all was in order. But as he hurried home, he had serious misgivings. This felt like a big mistake.

———•◦•———

Willow could hardly believe it. Not only was she going to see the inside of the Rockwell Mansion, she was going to fix dinner up there. Who would've thought it! Of course, it was entirely possible that before the evening ended, George could regret the whole thing. He could resent that she'd pushed him some. But without pushing that man, he'd probably be stuck in the mud indefinitely. Besides, he was about to get a really great meal out of this.

As she drove up the hill, cleaned up and wearing a comfortable caftan, she felt surprisingly energized. Today had been a good day. And this evening had the potential to be even better. But as she parked in front of the majestic house, she felt dismayed. The place looked so secure and closed up and uninhabited. Had George even arrived yet? Even worse, had he changed his mind? She'd suspected by his expression that he'd been unsure of his suggested plan, but she hadn't given him the chance to back out.

As she got her bag of dinner ingredients from the car, she knew that George wouldn't be comfortable having her up here. But she also knew that George wasn't comfortable with much of anything outside of his norm. By now, Willow felt fairly certain that George had some form of OCD. Naturally, she hadn't mentioned this to him. Not yet anyway. Perhaps one day, when their friendship was more solid, she would.

She went up the front porch steps. Although people referred to this house as the "Rockwell Mansion," it wasn't exactly huge by today's standards. A hundred-plus years ago, it would've been. It was a handsome brick house with Edwardian architecture that gave it a dignified look. It had three stories and a generous wraparound porch. Although it appeared solid and maintained, it had a look of neglect about it. Or perhaps it was sadness. Maybe the house was simply lonely. Willow hesitantly rang the doorbell. To her surprise, George answered.

"Oh, you're here!" she exclaimed.

"I said I'd be here." He opened the door wider.

"Yes, but I wondered if you'd change your mind."

He gave her a curious look, but let her in. "I was just starting to open up some windows," he said. "I'm afraid it's a bit stale in here."

Willow looked around with wide eyes. The foyer was about the size of her whole apartment. An enormous brass chandelier hung from the high ceiling, illuminating the marble floor, a dark Persian rug, and an elegant entry table with a large Chinese vase in the center of it. "This is beautiful," she told George.

"According to my grandfather, nothing has ever changed in this space. Even the wallpaper here is original."

She took in the dark, somber colors. "Interesting."

"Some of the other rooms have been updated somewhat over the years. Not necessarily improved, but made more comfortable, I suppose."

Willow admired the wide staircase, imagining a lovely woman from a previous era gracefully coming down . . . perhaps to meet a beau. "So you grew up in this house, George?"

"Yes. Some of my earliest memories were in this house. Then, after my parents died, this was my home."

"Did you ever slide down this banister?"

"As a matter of fact, I did." He nodded with a faraway look.

She was surprised. It was hard to imagine serious George ever doing something with that kind of abandon. "Well, I'll bet you haven't done it lately," she teased.

"No, no . . . not lately."

Willow looked at the framed black-and-white photographs on the stairway wall. "Are these family pictures?"

"Yes. My grandmother loved to take photographs."

"These are so good." Willow stared at a photo of a young man leaning against an old pickup. "Who is this?"

"Alex," George said. "Shortly before Vietnam."

"Oh." She nodded. "He was handsome." She pointed to an adorable freckle-faced boy cuddling up with a big tiger-striped cat. "Is that you, George?"

"And my cat, Buddy."

"You had a cat?"

"Uh-huh. The only one I ever liked. But he was a Maine Coon. They're not a typical cat."

"Buddy." She studied the animal's sweet face. "It almost looks like he was smiling."

"Buddy had an excellent disposition. My grandfather always said he was more like a dog than a cat."

"He looks very sweet."

"Best ever. Maine Coons are not your ordinary cat. Besides their superior physical traits, like three layers of fur, long fluffy tails, and oversized feet, they're extremely intelligent. And they're such good mousers the Puritans brought them to America to protect the grain aboard the ships."

"Interesting." Willow was surprised to hear him speaking so favorably about felines—who would've guessed?

Now George led her through a set of sliding-glass pocket doors into a large living room with gleaming wood floors.

"I see what you mean by updates." Willow smiled at the modern-style sofa and coffee table and chairs, arranged on a yellow shag area rug. "Mid-Century meets Edwardian. Very interesting."

"My grandmother picked these pieces out in the sixties. I think she said they were Danish Modern."

"Your grandmother had good taste."

"Even though it doesn't match the era of the house?"

"Well, I doubt that many people would be terribly comfortable with the Victorian furnishings that were in vogue a hundred years ago."

"Maybe not. The kitchen is this way." George led her through a large dining room. Although it had dark panels and a crystal chandelier, the dining pieces were pale, sleek, and Mid-Century. All were in excellent condition.

"These furnishings are probably quite valuable," she told George.

"I suppose." He pushed open a set of swinging doors. "The kitchen."

Willow looked around the spacious room, surprised to see that it looked like something from the eighties. Oak cabinets, blue Formica countertops, white vinyl flooring, and white appliances. "Interesting."

"I know." George sighed. "It doesn't quite fit the house. My grandmother had it redone shortly after I graduated college. Circa 1985."

"Not exactly a fabulous time for style."

"Yes, this is one room I'd like to see changed back to its original form."

"What was it like before this?" She began to unload her food items.

"I never saw the original kitchen. It had been remodeled in the 1950s before I was born," he explained. "I was disappointed when Grandma changed it."

"But didn't you say that's where you got the pieces for your kitchen?" Willow started to poke around the cabinets and drawers, looking for the utensils she needed.

"Yes. I suppose that was the upside."

"And these appliances work okay?" She opened a door to one of the spotlessly clean double ovens.

"As far as I know. They're not much to look at, but they were the best money could buy back then."

Willow tested the burner on the gas stovetop, pleased to see that it flamed nicely. "Looks good." She glanced at George and suspected by his furrowed brow that he felt uneasy about having her here. "If there's anything you need to do, or if you'd like to go relax, I'm sure I can find my way around this kitchen. And dinner should be ready in about thirty minutes."

"Well, I did want to get some things from my grandfather's workshop down in the basement. An electric screwdriver will be helpful to get the cabinets back together tomorrow." He frowned slightly. "I guess you can just make yourself at home."

Relieved to have George occupied with something else, Willow began to pull out the things she needed and set to work. She felt like she was in a time warp, but it was fun to imagine what George's grandmother might've been like. Obviously, she hadn't been a woman intimidated by change. Too bad George hadn't inherited that characteristic. And yet it was charming to think of how, as a little boy, George must've loved his grandmother's fifties-style kitchen. So much that he'd recreated it in his own house.

Willow felt like she was "playing house" as she arranged the Danish-style place settings, silverware, and placemats on the dining table. She'd considered serving dinner in the kitchen, but that eighties-style interior with the awful fluorescent overhead light was so sterile and plastic—she just couldn't bear it. Finding brass candlestick holders and candles in the buffet drawer, she decided to go all out. Hopefully George wouldn't mind. She was about to call him to the table when she heard footsteps.

"Oh my." He stared at the dining table. "This looks nice."

"You said to make myself at home."

George looked uneasy as he hurried over to pull out her chair. "I haven't eaten in this room in years," he muttered as he went around to the other side and slowly sat.

"I hope you don't mind."

"No . . . no. It just feels a bit strange." Then, as if to add to the strangeness, George folded his hands and bowed his head.

"Are you praying?" she whispered.

He looked up with embarrassment. "I, uh, I guess it was just a conditioned response. You see, the only times I ate in here were with my grandparents, and my grandfather always asked a blessing."

"Then by all means." She smiled.

"Well, I, uh . . . okay." He stiffly bowed his head again. "For that which we are about to receive, may the Lord make us truly grateful."

"Amen," Willow said quietly.

"That certainly felt odd." George reached for his napkin. "And to be honest, it felt insincere."

"Was that the blessing your grandfather used?"

"Yes. I never really understood it though. If we were asking for the Lord to make us grateful, well, what's the point?"

"Meaning you should be grateful without the Lord's help?" She passed him the salad bowl.

"I guess so." He shrugged as he served himself. "Not that it matters now."

"Because you don't believe in God?"

"That's right." George smiled. "This looks delicious, Willow. Thank you."

Although Willow would've liked to pursue the subject of God and faith further, she knew it was making him uncomfortable. So she attempted to make light conversation as they dined. More than anything she wanted George to simply relax and enjoy a pleasant evening. But for some reason it felt like pulling teeth to get a natural conversation out of him.

"When did your grandparents pass?" she asked as George helped himself to more salad.

"Oh, it's been about fifteen years. They died within a year of each other," he said absently.

"So this house has remained empty since then?"

He nodded. "I considered selling it, but it's been in my family so long."

"And it's a beautiful house." She gazed around the dark paneled dining room. "Do you ever wish these walls could talk?"

He frowned. "Not particularly."

"Do you have unhappy memories here?"

"No, not at all. Some of my happiest memories were in this house."

"Have you ever considered living here?"

"No . . . it's too big."

"Are there any other family members who would want to live here? I know your brother was killed in Vietnam. But aunts or uncles, cousins?"

"My grandfather's only brother was killed in World War I and he wasn't married, no children. And my mother was an only child. She grew up here and would've inherited everything."

"I see."

"So I suppose I feel some sort of responsibility to this house."

"Like it owns you—instead of the other way around?"

He nodded with a perplexed expression. "It does feel a bit like that."

Willow didn't know what to say. She was tempted to urge him to sell the old house—to be free of its hold and to allow another family to come here and love it. Yet, she had a feeling he wouldn't appreciate that sort of advice. "Well, it's a lovely old home," she said. "But honestly, that kitchen." She laughed. "It's so wrong."

He smiled. "I know. I've always felt like it was a mistake."

"You're so smart about woodworking and all that," she said. "I'm surprised you haven't torn into it and restored it to something that matches the rest of this house."

"Maybe I will." He pursed his lips. "Although I don't really know what it should look like. I don't think a hundred-year-old stove would be too practical."

"I know what I'd do to it."

"You do?" He looked genuinely interested.

"I'd get some nice, tall wooden cabinets and maybe some open shelves too. Then I'd have soapstone countertops, and if money was no object, I'd get Wolf appliances. You know—those big oversized ranges and fridges. They have a sort of timeless look and that kitchen is big enough for something like that." She paused to think. "For the floors, I'd use some kind of stone. Maybe even a checkerboard."

"Interesting." He nodded. "Those are good ideas. Maybe if I actually take this on, I'll have to get you to help with the design."

"Well, I certainly owe you for the way you've helped with Josie's apartment."

George pointed to his empty plate. "That was a pretty nice thank-you."

"Did you really like it?"

He nodded. "I don't go out for dinner much. And as you probably guessed, I'm not much of a cook. But I do enjoy a good meal occasionally. I must admit it feels rather special to have a meal here." He looked around the room with a happy expression. "I'd forgotten how much I love this place."

"It's a lovely home." She gathered their dishes.

"To be honest, I don't look around much when I come up here. I just check on things, do the basic maintenance, make sure no one's broken in . . . then leave."

"Well, the house feels a bit sad to me," she admitted. "Like it's lonely."

"I know." He nodded with a furrowed brow and she immediately regretted her negativity.

"I have vanilla bean ice cream and raspberries for dessert." She stacked the dishes. "How does that sound?"

"Good." He smiled. "Need any help?"

178

"No. You just relax." As she went into the kitchen, she felt hopeful. Almost as if she'd made some kind of breakthrough with George. Was it possible he was warming up to her? Or was there some sort of magic in his childhood home . . . something to help him let his guard down? Whatever it was, it felt like progress.

sixteen

As Willow surveyed Josie's apartment, she could hardly believe the progress they'd made during the past week. She knew they'd never have gotten this far without George's help. Besides putting the cabinets back together, he'd brought over a sander and gone to work refinishing the oak floors. And then he'd helped Josie to lay checkerboard tiles in the kitchen and bathroom. Of course, the two of them had butted heads a fair amount—George was a perfectionist and Josie, well, she just wanted to get it done. But by the end of the week, the little apartment was finished and Josie was actually smiling. Willow couldn't remember ever seeing Josie this happy. It was almost scary.

"What kind of furniture are you planning to put in here?" George asked Willow and Josie as he set his tools by the door.

"Just odds and ends," Willow told him.

"Well, if you have any missing pieces, I've got a lot of miscellaneous things in my grandparents' attic. My grandmother never threw anything away."

"Seriously?" Josie's eyes lit up.

George frowned at the lime-green living room walls. "Although I'm not sure anything would go with the, uh, interesting colors you selected."

"Collin calls this my crayon box," Josie told him.

George smiled as he picked up his electric screwdriver.

"Well, if you really have things you'd like to get rid of, there might be ways that Josie could adapt them to fit in her crayon box," Willow suggested. "A little paint and fabric can go a long way in transforming a piece."

"So when can I come look in your attic?" Josie said.

George rubbed his chin, almost as if having second thoughts. "Well, how about if you make out a list of the sorts of things you need," he told Josie. "Then I'll poke around and see what I can find. It's pretty crowded in the attic. More of a one-man show."

"Cool." Josie did a little spin on her gleaming living room floor. "Don't you just love it?"

"I think it's very charming, honey," Willow told her. "Okay, I'd like to give George a lift home with his tools. If you need help getting that bed frame put together, let me know and I'll come—"

"I can do it myself." Josie put her hands on her hips with a confident nod. "I've actually gotten to be quite handy, Mom. Or hadn't you noticed?"

"I've noticed." Willow picked up George's toolbox. "Ready to go?"

His nod looked weary as he went out the door.

Willow nudged Josie. "How about you run into my apartment and get that container of leftover linguini? I want to send it home with George."

After everything was loaded into Willow's car, George sat quietly in the passenger seat, his tool box in his lap.

"I hope we haven't worn you out too badly," Willow said as she drove.

"No, no. Not at all. I was just feeling a bit disappointed that we're finished."

"Really?" Willow laughed.

"Although I am a bit stiff and sore," he admitted. "Might need a good hot soak in the tub tonight."

"I hear you. Even though I like to convince myself that today's fifties are yesterday's thirties, I don't remember wearing out as quickly."

"Probably good to pace yourself."

"Probably." She sighed. "George, I don't know how I'll ever thank you for all your help on Josie's apartment. Did you see how happy she looked?"

"In her little crayon box." George chuckled.

"It is definitely bright. But it's cheerful too. And I think she needs cheerful more than ever right now."

"I hope it helps to make her happy."

Willow parked in front of his house then helped him to carry his things in, finally setting the package of leftovers on his kitchen counter. "I thought you might enjoy this for dinner, George. Just a small token of my appreciation."

As Willow drove home, she tried to think of a special way that she could show George their appreciation. Something more than just food. She'd actually offered to pay him for his work, but he'd refused, saying it was just "friends helping friends." And, although she liked that philosophy, she wasn't sure of the best way to return the favor.

She was just walking past the gallery when she noticed a

182

poster on the window. It was to promote a hot-air-balloon festival a few miles out of town. She stopped and stared at the poster—that was it! She would surprise George with a hot-air-balloon ride. Perfect! Before long, she'd called the number and made a reservation for two o'clock on Sunday.

* * *

Although George had intended to enjoy an afternoon of some well-deserved R & R the next day, he felt surprisingly energetic after finishing his Saturday morning chores. So despite his plan to lounge in his hammock with a book, he found himself walking up the hill to his grandparents' house.

He hadn't been up there since the night Willow had made dinner. That had been a most unusual evening. In some ways unsettling . . . but also enjoyable. George didn't really know how to describe it, but it had left him with a desire to make some changes in the house. Particularly in that kitchen. He'd never liked the eighties remodel, but seeing it through Willow's eyes had made him actually hate it. And her suggestions had made sense.

After George did some basic measurements of the kitchen, made some notes, and pondered it a bit, he decided to go up to the attic. But once he got up there, he felt instantly overwhelmed. And claustrophobic. Maybe this wasn't such a good idea. After all, he didn't even have any clear goals in mind here. As much as he'd like the entire space cleared out, he realized there were some family heirlooms and valuable antiques mixed in the mishmash.

He stared absently at the dust particles coming in from

the high window, sparkling in the sunlight. Did he want to thin things out up here in order to help Josie? Or was it because he intended to sell the house? In that case, shouldn't he simply clear the whole place out? But what if he didn't want to sell? After all, he really did love this house. Maybe he actually wanted to live here someday. Yet that sounded ridiculous. The place was far too big for him. He backed out of the attic, closed the door. Perhaps he would think about this later. Right now his hammock was calling.

* * *

George missed Willow but didn't plan to call or visit. Not for a while. Although he'd enjoyed working on Josie's apartment—especially when Collin was around to help—the noise and mess and bickering had taken its toll on him. Quite frankly, George didn't know how Willow could stand it. Yes, he felt sorry for Josie. She had definitely gone through some difficult things—she'd made no secret of it while he'd been working there. But the girl was also her own worst enemy.

So when Willow showed up at his house on Sunday afternoon, George wasn't sure how he felt about it. Yes, he was glad to see her . . . but also on his guard. He stopped sweeping his front porch as she got out of her car and strolled up to his house. Admittedly, she looked pretty in a blue-and-white sundress and sandals. He wondered if she was on her way home from church. He knew she attended an odd little church, where services were held in a barn on the edge of town. Although she'd invited him a couple of times, he always had a handy excuse.

"I have a surprise for you," she announced as she came onto his porch.

"What do you mean?" He didn't see a bakery bag or anything else.

"No questions asked," she said. "Just lock up your house and come with me."

"Well, I don't know." He set his broom aside.

"Please, George. You're going to love this. And there's no time to waste."

"But I, uh, I—"

"No excuses." She smiled brightly. "Just trust me, okay? This is my way of thanking you for all your wonderful help last week."

George sighed then turned to lock his front door. Maybe her surprise would involve food. George hadn't had lunch yet. "Okay," he told her. "I trust you."

"Wonderful." She led him to her car and they were on their way. But as she drove out of town, he grew suspicious.

"Where are we going?"

"Remember—no questions." Now she began to tell him how much Josie liked her apartment. "You should see her crayon box now. I took her to the thrift store where she picked out some crazy, colorful pieces. It's a bit like going to the circus, but she loves it."

"That's nice." George frowned out the window. They were about ten minutes from town now, going down an old country road through farmland. Where on earth was she taking him? "What is that?" He pointed to something colorful looming above some treetops.

"You'll see," she said mysteriously. She turned off the road, parking in a field where dozens of other cars were already parked. "Come on."

With her arm linked in his, she led him down a trail that passed through a grove of trees and into an open field where lots of hot-air balloons were in various stages of inflating. "My goodness," he exclaimed. "What a surprise!"

"Isn't it fabulous!" she said. "I've always wanted to come to one of these festivals."

"It's very beautiful." George looked over the rainbow of hot-air balloons. "Will they be going up?"

"Yes. Liftoff is at two." She continued to lead him, moving past a number of bright balloons where balloonists were in various stages of preparation. George would've liked to stop and look at what they were doing, but Willow continued to nudge him along. Perhaps she knew of a good vantage spot where they could watch the colorful liftoff. Maybe there would even be a concessions stand. George thought he could actually go for a hotdog about now.

"Let's get a closer look at that one." Willow led him over to a large red-and-yellow-striped balloon that was fully inflated. "Let's see what it's like in the basket."

"Oh, he probably doesn't want us in there," George said.

"You don't mind, do you?" she asked the young man who was fiddling with some ropes. "I'm Willow and this is my friend George."

"And I'm Rod. Feel free to check out my airship. I call her Molly." He opened a little gate. "Come aboard. I'm happy to answer any questions you might have."

Willow tugged George into the basket. "Look at that." She pointed up. "You can see the *inside* of the balloon."

George peered up to see the striped interior illuminated by

the sunlight overhead. "Is that a propane heater?" he asked Rod.

"That's right." Rod stepped inside to demonstrate how it worked. "See how the hot air goes straight up through the envelope?"

"The envelope?" George asked.

"That's what we call the opening to the balloon." Rod cranked the flame higher.

"Don't you worry about it catching on fire?" George frowned with concern as Rod tampered with the propane.

"Nah. It's easy to control."

"How do you control the balloon once it's in the air?" George asked.

Rod chuckled. "That's pretty much up to the wind."

"Make way." Rod nudged George and Willow back as a man and two young boys entered the basket. Rod welcomed them, explaining the balloon basics as they all stood crowded into the small basket. George was about to say "excuse me" and ask to get past the newcomers when Rod closed the gated entryway and yelled instructions to the ground crew. "Anchors aweigh!" he said, and suddenly the balloon began to lift.

"Wait a minute!" George felt his stomach lurching. "We're still on here."

"Up, up, and away," Willow sang out happily. "This is your big surprise, George. We're going for a balloon ride."

"I'm not going." George grasped the edge, leaning over to see, and he stared down in complete shock. They had to be at least twenty feet up and quickly climbing higher. "Let me out of this crazy thing!" he yelled wildly.

Rod just laughed. "You'll be okay, George. Just enjoy the ride."

"What's wrong with that man?" the smaller boy asked.

"He's scared." The older boy snickered.

As the dad quieted his sons, George felt his knees turn to jelly and his stomach go upside down—similar to the sensation of being in an elevator.

"Isn't this wonderful," Willow chirped at him. "Look how beautiful it is with the other balloons lifting off."

George continued to cling to the basket railing. Closing his eyes, he felt clammy and shaky and sick . . . on the verge of throwing up. This was too much! Way too much!

"Are you okay?" Willow looked at him with concern. "You're so pale, George."

"I—I'm sick." He opened his eyes, wondering if she'd planned this whole thing—*intentionally*.

"I'm sorry." She put her hand over his. "Take some deep breaths. Try to relax, George. You're perfectly safe. This will be fun. You'll see."

"I—I don't like heights," he whispered. "I—I can't do this."

"Here." Rod helped George to sit down on an upside-down bucket then handed him a bottle of water. "Take some slow sips and some deep breaths."

George's hand trembled as he opened the bottle, gingerly sipping and trying to breathe. What if he threw up all over the place? Or worse yet, what if he had a heart attack up here? How long would it take to get down and to get help? As he sat on the bucket, slowly sipping and trying to breathe, he could hear the others commenting on how amazing and beautiful the view was up here. The boys were taking turns snapping photos with their dad's phone, acting as if it were perfectly normal to be floating up in the air like this. Didn't they know that this balloon could get punctured or go up in flames—and that they would all plummet to the ground?

"Don't you want to see it?" Willow asked George. He simply shook his head no, and she returned to the railing to look down.

After several minutes of trying to compose himself, George began to feel silly. What was wrong with him? He forced himself to stand, but his legs felt like noodles. Using the rail of the basket to support himself, he took a deep breath, then looked down. They were so far up that a fresh wave of panic swept over him. Without saying a word, he returned to the bucket and sat down. Leaning over he held his head in his hands and longed for this torture to end.

"How you doing, George?" Rod asked lightly.

"Just great," George growled. "How long does this ride last?"

"Well, this is the deluxe ride. We're due to land on the Warner High School football field at three o'clock."

George groaned. He glanced at the boys who now were more interested in looking at their dad's phone than the sights down below. He was tempted to ask them to call 911 and ask for an ambulance to meet them at the high school. He felt nearly certain that if he didn't suffer a heart attack, he would probably have a stroke. His blood pressure had to be sky-high.

To distract himself from his intense phobia, George watched as the two boys sat down on the floor next to him in order to play a video game on their dad's phone. As much as he disliked electronic devices, he felt some appreciation for the stupid thing now. He watched the boys as they played, grateful for this odd bit of companionship.

Willow and Rod and the dad continued to chatter away about sights below and the direction of the prevailing wind—but George just sat on his bucket and wished this horrible ordeal would soon be over. Maybe he didn't even care if they dumped his lifeless body onto the football field for curious onlookers to see. At least he would be done with this.

Willow and Rod checked on him off and on during what felt like the longest hour of his life. The dad nagged at his sons to stand up and enjoy the trip, finally taking his phone away so that they had nothing better to do than look down at the landscape below them. And finally, finally . . . Rod turned down the propane flame and the balloon began to go down.

Of course, this motion of going down so quickly filled George with fresh nausea. So much so that as soon as they thumped onto the ground, George leaped to his feet and burst out of the gate—even though Rod tried to stop him. George didn't realize that the basket had hopped up a few feet until he tumbled onto the ground and rolled into a crumpled heap.

"Oh, George," Willow exclaimed as she went to join him. "Are you all right?"

"I don't know," he said sharply.

"Did you break anything?"

"I don't think so." He pushed himself up with a dark scowl.

"You weren't supposed to get off that quickly." She helped him to his feet. "You could've been hurt."

"It's a wonder I didn't leap from that stupid thing while we were still in the sky," he sputtered. "I've never had such a terrible experience in my life."

"I'm sorry—"

"Goodbye, Willow," he snapped. Then, without another word, he stormed off toward home.

A fine way to thank someone! George should've known better than to trust that woman. Willow West was just plain crazy. And George had had enough!

seventeen

illow felt terrible about George's disappointing balloon ride and wouldn't be surprised if he never spoke to her again. She knew the prudent thing would be for her to leave him alone—and yet she felt like she still owed him a thank-you gesture. It's just that she had no idea what that would be. Perhaps the best thing she could do for him would be to do nothing. But that was just not her style.

Willow knew that she didn't fully understand George, but she suspected that he was trapped in a life that he didn't particularly love. Oh, George thought he liked the calm, quiet, predictable existence that he'd carved out for himself. But she'd had glimpses of another George. A man who was hungry for more—a man who regretted letting life pass him by. How to tap into that? She just wasn't sure.

After a week had passed by—without crossing paths with George—Willow felt concerned. She imagined him holed up in his little house, afraid to step out and engage with anyone. Was it possible the balloon ride had seriously set him back?

And if so, wouldn't that be her fault? And if it was her fault, shouldn't she do something to remedy it?

Willow read the biweekly newspaper, glancing at the local shelter's pet ad, just like she did every Friday. Her interest was twofold. She loved animals and liked the idea of them being rescued into a good home. But she also hoped to run across a pet that would suit her lifestyle. She wasn't sure if it would be a dog or cat. Or perhaps even a bird. But she was open to a pet and, one day when life wasn't too hectic, she planned to visit the shelter to find one. However, she knew that a single trip to the shelter would result in adopting a pet, and she wanted to be sure she was truly ready.

The photo in this week's pet ad made her heart beat faster. She stared in wonder at the tiger-striped cat with big eyes and a friendly expression. As she read further, she learned it was a four-year-old Maine Coon cat named Baxter, whose elderly owner had recently passed on. Without stopping to think, she grabbed her purse and keys, hopped into her car, and drove straight to the shelter. She hoped against hope that the cat was still there.

"We've had numerous calls about Baxter," the woman at the front desk informed her. "But you're the first one to show up."

"May I see him?"

"Certainly." The woman led Willow back. "If I didn't already have three cats, I'd take him myself."

"I've heard that Maine Coon cats are special," Willow said.

"This one is. He's got personality and intelligence." The woman opened a cage. "Meet Baxter."

"Hello, Baxter." Willow reached in to pet the cat. "How

are you doing?" He rubbed his head against her hand and then she reached in and scooped him up. "You're a heavy fellow." She looked at his oversized paws. "And big feet too."

"Those are characteristic of a Maine Coon cat." She pointed out a few more things that made these cats special.

"Well, I'd like to adopt this guy," Willow told her. "I thought I was getting him for a friend, but now that we've met I'm tempted to keep him myself."

"As long as he gets a good home."

Before long, after purchasing numerous cat items and paying the adoption fees, Willow and Baxter were on their way home. But instead of taking him up to her apartment, like she wanted to do, she knew the kinder thing would be to take him to George. Oh, she knew George well enough to know he would protest—and perhaps even outright refuse her gift. But she had to at least try. George was lonely. A lovely cat like Baxter could make a huge difference in his sad little life. So, as much as she wanted to keep Baxter for herself, she felt like George deserved him more. The question now was how to convince him.

Willow parked in front of George's house and, after giving herself a quick pep talk, got Baxter's cat carrier out of the car and marched up to the door. As she rang the doorbell, she almost hoped that he wouldn't answer and then she could leave the cat and cat things, along with a note, on the porch. But then George opened the door.

"Good morning," she said. "I'm sorry to disturb you, but I'm making a special delivery. May I come in?"

George blinked, but let her inside.

"I know you probably think I'm a menace and a nuisance, George, but I found something that I feel certain you need."

194

"What is *that*?" George pointed to the cardboard carrier box.

"This is Baxter." She set the box on the floor, knelt down, and gently removed the cat, holding him close to her for a moment. "To be honest, I fell so in love with Baxter that I wanted to keep him for myself, but I knew that Baxter was really meant for you, George." She held the cat out. "He is four years old and his master has passed away. Baxter needs a good home."

George's eyes grew wide as she placed the cat in his arms.

She quickly relayed the information the woman at the shelter had given her, about how it was important that Baxter remain indoors for at least two weeks and a few other helpful tips. "Please excuse me for a moment." And before George could speak, Willow rushed out. She gathered up the miscellaneous cat items she'd purchased from the shelter, carried them back into the house, and set them down on the coffee table.

"What am I supposed to do with this stuff?" George set the cat down on the floor with a disgusted expression. "You can't just—"

"I'm sorry, but I've got an art show to prepare for. It's Final Friday again."

"But you can't leave—"

"Like I said, I have a show."

"You know what you are, Willow West?" George shook a fist in the air. "You are a camel's nose."

"What?" Willow stared at him in shock. "That's a fine thing to say!"

"Have you ever heard the parable about the camel in the tent?"

She frowned. "Seriously, are you about to tell me a story?"

"As a matter of fact, yes." He smiled smugly, folding his arms in front of his chest. "The setting is a cold night on the Sahara desert. An Arab traveler is snug in his tent and his camel is outside shivering."

"Really, George, are you—"

"The camel says to his master, 'I'm so cold, please, let me slip my nose into your tent to get warm.' Well, the master agrees and lets his nose inside. Then the camel asks if he might slip his head in as well, and then he asks for his shoulders. And before long the whole camel is inside the tent and there's no room for the master and—"

"So, you're saying that I'm a camel's nose?" Willow sniffed indignantly. "I get it, George, I can take a hint."

"Then take back your cat," he demanded.

"Look, George." She waved an angry finger in the air. "If for some reason you decide that you and Baxter are not compatible, just call me. I will gladly come pick him up ASAP." She glared at him. "Thank you very much!" Then without giving him a chance to say one more insulting word, she rushed out the door. As she drove home, she wasn't sure which was more upsetting—George's nasty attitude toward her, or leaving that lovely cat behind. But it sounded as if she would get Baxter back anyway. Well, fine!

* * *

George honestly thought that Willow was more than just eccentric—the woman was certifiably crazy. Who gets a cat for someone—without asking first—then dumps it and leaves? He stared at the feline on the floor. He didn't even like cats. Why on earth would he want to trouble with this

196

one? Pets were messy and dirty and needy and noisy. This was absolutely ridiculous. Willow would have to come right back and take this cat with her.

George went over to his phone, picking up the receiver and preparing to dial, when Baxter rubbed against his legs. Something about that movement felt so familiar . . . just like Buddy used to do. George replaced the receiver, then knelt down to examine the cat more closely. He could hear the animal purring happily. As he stroked the cat's head, he felt stunned to see how much this cat resembled Buddy. It was rather uncanny.

"Baxter?" George spoke quietly. "Do you really want to live with an old curmudgeon like me? I'm so set in my ways. I don't even like cats. Well, most cats." He sat down in his favorite armchair, trying to think clearly. Sometimes it felt like Willow cast some sort of spell over him, making him say things he didn't want to say or do things he never intended to do.

Like that painting. He stared up at the old pickup in the poppies and just shook his head. He'd never wanted an over-sized piece of colorful art on his wall . . . and yet he knew he couldn't take it down. He didn't even want to take it down. And what about that coffee? After a week of grinding his own beans, George knew he'd never go back to the canned variety. How did such things happen?

Baxter jumped up onto George's lap, so gracefully that George couldn't even feel the cat's claws on his legs. Then he looked up at George with amazingly intelligent mossy-green eyes and a sweet, contented expression that looked strangely familiar. George stroked the cat's thick coat. It felt exactly like Buddy's had once felt. George examined the big fuzzy feet, also very familiar. "Are you related to Buddy?" George whispered. Naturally, the cat didn't answer. But as he nestled into George's lap as if they'd always been friends, George knew he'd gotten his answer. Although it made no sense, George felt fairly certain that Baxter would stay.

• • •

As she ran errands and worked in her studio, Willow kept her cell phone handy. She fully expected George to call and demand that she pick up the cat. But no call came. She even checked with the gallery later in the afternoon, but Leslie assured her that George had not called.

"Everything set for Final Friday?" Willow asked Leslie. "Anything else I can help with?"

"I don't think so. The musicians will be here at 6:30. I got a corner cleared for them. Marissa will work the floor. She said Collin plans to help her." Leslie winked. "I think it's just his excuse to be near her. The poor boy is smitten."

"And the refreshments should be delivered by five."

"I'll manage the food table and Joel plans to man the desk."

"Great. That allows me to mingle with the guests." Willow thanked her and was about to leave. "I'll be in my apartment until six . . . so if George Emerson happens to call down here, please, ask him to call me on my cell. It's important."

"So are you guys back on again?" Leslie had a teasing tone. Probably because Willow had confided too much to her, but it had been nice having someone to commiserate with her.

"No, we are not back on again," Willow firmly declared. "I doubt that George will ever forgive me for that fateful balloon ride."

Leslie giggled. "I can still imagine him sitting on that bucket with his green face then tumbling out onto the football field."

"Don't ever repeat that story," Willow warned her, "or I'll never trust you again."

"Don't worry. Mum's the word." She lowered her voice. "But if you're still in the doghouse with George, why do you expect him to call?"

Willow grimaced. "Because I gave him a cat."

"*What?*"

"I know, I know." Willow held up her hands. "Chalk it up to temporary insanity. But I just felt that he needed a cat."

"Buttoned-up Mr. Emerson with a pet?" Leslie looked doubtful.

"Well, the deal was this—if George doesn't want the cat, I do. So if he calls, I want to talk to him. *Understand?*"

Leslie gave a mock salute and Willow went up to her apartment . . . to sit by the phone. When George never called, she knew she should be grateful. Maybe the cat had actually won him over, although that was unlikely. Instead of feeling relieved, she felt disappointed—and concerned. Hopefully she'd made herself clear with George. If he did not want the cat, she did. Surely, he wouldn't try to return it to the shelter. She could just imagine him marching over there with the cat carrier in hand, demanding that they take the cat back.

But there wasn't time to worry about that now. Willow needed to get ready for tonight's showing. She was just putting on the finishing touches when she heard someone knocking on her door. She hurried to get it, certain that it would be George and Baxter, but it was Josie standing there with a cup in hand. "I'm making mac-n-cheese and all out of milk. Can I borrow some?"

Willow nodded. "Help yourself." She wanted to remind Josie that she'd been given a food "budget," and that maybe it was time for her to start a serious job hunt. But she knew that could lead to an unwanted conflict.

"What are you all dolled up for?" Josie asked as she opened the fridge. "Big date with George tonight?"

"No." Willow hadn't told Josie about the failed balloon ride.

"Where's he been anyway?" Josie filled her cup. "I miss seeing him around."

"I think he's been busy, honey."

"So why are you all gussied up in your gypsy outfit?"

Willow glanced down at her bohemian dress. "I suppose I do look like a gypsy," she admitted. "We're having a showing in the gallery. Naturally, I need to look artsy and dramatic. Think this works?"

"I guess so." Josie's brows arched. "Will there be food at your little shindig?"

"Mostly cheese and crackers." Willow hoped Josie didn't want to come. She could just imagine her raggedy daughter coming down in her uniform of ratty, paint-splattered jeans and torn rocker T-shirt—and making a scene. Even so, Willow knew she needed to handle this carefully and honestly. "There will also be live music. Just a small folk trio, so it shouldn't be too loud."

"Food *and* music?" Josie nodded. "I guess I'll come."

Willow forced what she hoped was a believable smile. "That would be great, honey. Just so you know, people tend to dress up a little for these shows. Not formally, I mean, but nice."

"Nice?" Josie scowled. "What's that supposed to mean? Are you saying I don't dress nice enough to come to my mother's hoity-toity art show?"

"Well, do you have anything that's not worn, torn, or stained?" Willow braced herself.

Josie's scowl grew darker. "As a matter of fact, I don't."

"Really?" Willow studied her ragtag daughter. "I'd offer you something of mine, but I'm afraid you'd be insulted."

Josie brightened slightly. "I don't know. What do you have?"

Willow tried to hide her shock. "Why don't we go see?"

Josie set down her milk and followed Willow into her bedroom, flopping down on her bed. "Show me what you got."

Willow went into her walk-in closet and looked around. "I know you're skinnier than me, Josie, but there might be something you could cinch in or belt or something." She dug around until she found a faded denim sundress that she knew was too small for her, but she'd always liked it. "How about this?" She held it up and Josie wrinkled her nose.

"I don't think so."

"It actually looks much better on," Willow told her.

"What else do you have?" Josie came into the closet and began to look around. "How about this?" She held up one of Willow's favorite tops. "Boho chic?"

"That would look good on you."

"I have a pair of jeans that aren't too bad." Josie held the top up in front of the mirror. "Whaddya think?"

"I think you'd look lovely." Willow touched Josie's stringy hair, which, as usual, needed a good shampoo. "How about a pair of sandals? You still wear an eight?"

"Yeah."

Willow held up a pair of woven leather platform sandals that she no longer felt comfortable in due to the height. "You can have these if you want."

"Really? These are cool, Mom. Thanks." She pointed to the sundress still lying on the bed. "Maybe I'll take that too. Just in case."

"Great. Now I better get down there," Willow told her. "But there's no hurry for you. Things don't usually get going until around seven. You could even grab a shower if you like."

"As in hint-hint?" Josie's tone was sharp, but her grin was sassy.

"Just saying." Willow slid her feet into her own sandals, a low-heeled pair, comfortable enough to get her through the night, but blinged out with rhinestones. "See you later, honey."

As Willow went down to the gallery, she prayed a silent prayer for Josie . . . that she would start finding her place in this town—and in the world at large. Willow was actually encouraged that Josie was interested in socializing. She just hoped her unpredictable daughter wouldn't make a scene. And knowing that Collin would be there didn't exactly foster confidence.

eighteen

By Friday evening, George and Baxter were the best of friends. But now George felt foolish and petty for treating Willow so badly this morning. Had he really called her a "camel's nose"? Oh my.

"I guess I should try to fix things with her," he told Baxter as he dried the last of his dinner dishes. He considered calling Willow with an apology and proper thank-you, but he remembered that she'd mentioned tonight's Final Friday gallery show. George hung up the damp dish towel, then leaned down to pet Baxter. "What do you think, fellow . . . would you miss me for an hour or so?"

Baxter just rubbed against his legs, almost as if to confirm he would be fine on his own. Then George changed into a fresh shirt and put on a tie and jacket. "Do you like classical music?" he asked Baxter as he turned on his radio—tuned, as usual, to the classical channel. "Let Mozart keep you company for a bit."

George gave Baxter a kitty treat then headed out the door. While strolling to town, he rehearsed his apology. He knew he'd have to keep it short and sweet in case the gallery was busy, and since it was past seven, he expected it would be. After his apology, George planned to reassure her that Baxter was settling in just fine and promised to be a wonderful addition to George's simple household. And then he would go.

Strains of music floated out the open door of the Willow West gallery. As he'd expected, the place was crowded. George felt a rush of nerves as he went inside. Not for the first time, he wondered, how did this woman manage to continually push him out of his comfort zone?

"Hello, Mr. Emerson." Marissa looked happy to see him. "Welcome to the show. We have some really great pieces tonight. And refreshments in the back."

Collin came over to say hello as well. Like Marissa, he was so warm and congenial that George hoped Willow hadn't told him about last weekend's balloon ride fiasco.

"How's your job at the bookstore going?" George asked Collin.

"Really great. I'm already full-time."

"Good for you." George scanned the crowd in search of Willow, spying her on the far side of the gallery.

"You should come in next week and say hello," Collin told him. "We're having a little competition of getting customers signed up in the Book Nook Club."

"What's that?"

"It's a promotion that includes discount coupons and special invitations to Book Nook events."

George nodded. "Well, I'll be sure to come by."

"Hello, Mr. Emerson." Josie, looking much nicer than George had ever seen her, came over to join them. She had a plastic cup of red wine in one hand and cheese in the other. "Cool gathering, huh?"

"Yes, it's very nice."

"Free wine too." She giggled.

"Looks like it's time to cut you off," Collin said a bit sharply.

"Says who, Junior?" Josie narrowed her eyes at him as she popped the cheese into her mouth.

"I'll just go let Leslie know that you've had enough," Collin said firmly.

"Butt out," she said a bit too loudly.

"I think it's time for you to go," Collin said quietly. "I don't think you're planning on purchasing any—"

"Who died and made you the bouncer?" she snarled at him.

"Hey, you guys." Marissa's eyes grew wide. "Maybe you should take it outside."

"Don't tell me where to take it," Josie shot back at her.

"Excuse me," George said in his no-nonsense voice. "I don't want to interrupt this family exchange." He looked at Josie. "But I never got to see your apartment after it was all put back together. Any chance you'd show it to me tonight?"

Josie still looked like she wanted to punch her son in the face, but to George's relief she turned to him and nodded. "Sure. I've seen enough of this art. Come on up and I'll show you what I've been working on this week."

George smiled at Collin and Marissa, then, without another word, took Josie by the arm and led her out. "You're looking quite nice tonight," he told her once they were outside.

"Thank you very much." She tossed her empty cup into a nearby trash bin. "Right this way, Mr. Emerson. Come and have the grand tour of my crazy crayon box."

George tried not to wince as they entered the wildly color-ful apartment. "You certainly have livened it up even more," he said as she showed him the lime-green living room. Be-tween the bright prints on the floor pillows and throw rugs and wall hangings, there wasn't a spot in the room where an eye could rest peacefully.

"Mom helped me make the slipcover for the sofa. But I'd still like a couple more chairs. In case I ever have friends over."

"I might have something you can use," George told her. "I did a bit of looking in my attic, but I didn't get too far."

"And I still need a table and chairs for in here." As she turned on the kitchen light, George resisted the urge to blink. "I'd like something I could paint."

"Of course."

"Come and see the shower curtain in my bathroom," she called out. "It was inspired by you."

"I can't wait," he murmured.

She turned on the bathroom light and George peered in to see a tropical-looking ocean scene. "That's *my* Mediter-ranean," she told him.

"Very nice." He nodded with approval. It was actually the least jarring part of her apartment so far.

"And now you have to see my bedroom. Mom dug out this really cool tie-dyed quilt that she made when she was in college."

George prepared himself for more eye pain as she turned on the overhead light. But to his relief, although it was mul-tiple shades of purples, it wasn't too bad. "Very nice," he said.

"I just need a couple of nightstands and lamps."

"Well, maybe you'd like to come over to browse around in my grandparents' attic," he said as they returned to the living room. "Unless it's a family heirloom, I'm happy to part with most anything up there."

"Cool." She pointed to the couch. "Have a seat if you want."

"I don't know." He sighed as he sat down. He still hadn't done what he'd come here for, but the gallery had been so busy. And Willow hadn't even cast a glance his way. Not that he could blame her.

"Are you sad, Mr. Emerson?"

He pursed his lips. "No. Just preoccupied, I suppose."

"You were disappointed in me and Collin, weren't you?"

He considered this. "Well, to be honest, it was a bit disturbing."

"I honestly don't know why we fight so much. I think Collin just plain hates me."

"I don't know about that." George wondered how much to say. "But it almost looks like sibling rivalry to me."

"We are *not* siblings."

"Not actually. But Willow is like a mother to both of you."

"Maybe . . . but don't you think Collin should show me more respect? After all, I am his mother."

"Do you always show your mother respect?"

Her smile looked sheepish.

"And to be fair to Collin, he's not really known you as his mother. It's a lot to expect him to treat you like that now."

"I know. And I don't even want him to. I just wish he didn't always pick fights with me."

"Fights are usually a two-way street."

"So you're saying I'm partly to blame?"

207

"What do you think?" He looked evenly at her.

"You were an English teacher, right?"

"That's right."

"Well, you talk more like a shrink."

George smiled with amusement.

"But I suppose you could be right."

They both sat quietly for a bit. The only sound was the strains of music drifting up through the floorboards. Finally George spoke. "Josie, what are your plans? For your future? What do you intend to do with your life?"

She shrugged. "I don't know."

"Well, it seems to me that Willow is giving you a great opportunity to take full ownership over your life. You could get some kind of training or go to college or—"

"I do not want to go to college," she declared hotly.

"Why not?"

Her brow creased. "The truth?"

"That's usually the best route."

"I'm stupid."

"Stupid?" He frowned. "You're not stupid to me, Josie. If anything, you're rather sharp and witty. You certainly have a fast tongue."

She grinned. "Smart mouth, you mean."

"Whatever you want to call it. I doubt that you're stupid." He pointed to the bright room. "And you appear to have some artistic talent. Admittedly, it's not my taste, but I'm sure there are people who like this sort of thing. Have you ever considered following your mother's example?"

She tilted her head to one side. "You really think I could do that?"

"Like I said, I'm no judge on this sort of thing. But your

mother could probably advise you. She's certainly succeeded in the art world."

"Wow, that would be cool if I could make a living doing art."

"Although I've heard that some artists have to get a day job to support their art—initially."

"That'd be okay." Josie stood, pacing across the floor with a hopeful expression. "I could handle doing a boring day job if I had something else going on." She turned to look at George. "You said you've got a lot of junk in your grand-parents' attic, right? Stuff you want to get rid of. Except for the family heirlooms." She pointed to a little table that was busily painted in a colorful checkerboard and stripes and dots. "What if I did more things like this with old pieces of junk—do you think I could sell it?"

George wanted to say that he'd never pay good money for something like that, but instead he nodded. "I'll bet there are folks out there who'd purchase something like that." *Some crazy folks*, he was thinking. "After all, I'm sure that, like beauty, art is in the eyes of the beholder."

"Mr. Emerson, you're like a mentor to me. Did you know that?"

George wanted to protest this, but didn't want to crush her. "Well, that's nice." He slowly stood. "And we'll have to schedule a time for you to come go through the attic. But I left my cat at home alone and I feel I should get back to him." He quickly explained that it was Baxter's first day in a strange home.

"Oh, yeah," she said. "You better make sure he's okay. I had a kitten once, when I was little. Her name was Bingo and she went kind of nutty every time we left her home alone. She tore up so much stuff that I finally had to give her away."

"Right." George thanked her for her apartment tour, said goodbye, and—worried that Baxter might've gone "nutty" in his absence—hurried toward home. To his relief, Baxter was just fine and nothing in his house was damaged. But he still needed to apologize and thank Willow. Maybe tomorrow.

⸻ •❖• ⸻

It wasn't until the art show was ending that Willow finally got to speak to Collin and Marissa. "Did I see Mr. Emerson here tonight?" she asked.

"Yes," Collin told her, "but he left with Josie."

"Really?" She tried not to look too surprised.

"After Josie and Collin got into a fight," Marissa clarified.

"You got in a fight with Josie?" Willow asked Collin.

"She had too much to drink. I just wanted her to go easy."

"Oh dear."

"But Mr. Emerson did a great intervention," Marissa told her. "He asked to see Josie's apartment. They left and he never came back."

"I see." Willow tried to act like this was a perfectly natural explanation. But the truth was, her head was whirling. Collin and Josie had gotten into a fight? George had intervened? Then spent the evening with Josie? It sounded crazy. "Did Mr. Emerson mention a cat?"

"A cat?" Marissa frowned.

"I didn't hear anything about a cat," Collin told her. "Whose cat?"

"Never mind."

"Well, if you don't need us, I told Marissa I'd get her a coffee at Common Grounds. They've got music there too."

She thanked them for their help and, still feeling confused about George's strange visit to the gallery tonight, she went to help Leslie clean up the refreshment table. She seriously doubted that George was still in Josie's apartment at this late hour, but she was tempted to go up there and ask Josie for her take on the evening.

By the time Willow locked up the gallery, she was too tired to engage with Josie. No telling how that could go. She went quietly up the stairs to her apartment. Her questions about George and Baxter and Josie could wait until morning. But, as she got ready for bed, she felt aggravated. Why had George shown up like that tonight? And then gone off with Josie and not come back? What about Baxter? Had George come by to inform her that he didn't want the cat? Had he possibly given the cat to Josie? Willow hoped not. Josie could barely take care of herself. She did not need a cat.

Willow knew that these obsessive thoughts were not conducive to a good night's rest. So, in an effort to relax and quiet her mind, she tuned her radio to a classical station, turned the volume down low, and drifted off to sleep.

nineteen

By the next morning, Willow was determined to put all troublesome thoughts concerning George and Baxter behind her. In fact, she was ready to put George Emerson behind her. Her distraction was to spend the day in her studio. And since it was supposed to hit triple digits today, the basement-level studio sounded like the perfect place to be. Plus, with the interest some of her pottery had received last night, including two sales, she felt inspired to work with clay today. She was just using a wire to cut a large vase from the wheel when she heard someone calling her name.

"Down here," she yelled, pausing to see who it was.

George appeared out of the shadows with a sheepish expression. "Sorry to interrupt you while you're working," he told her. "But Leslie told me you were down here."

"Hello, George." She kept her voice cool as she continued to remove the vase then carefully set it on a drying board. She turned to look at him. "What can I do for you?"

"First of all, you can accept my sincere apology," he said.

"Apology for what?" She wiped her hands on a rag and waited.

"For a couple of things." He sighed. "First of all, for the way I behaved on the hot-air-balloon ride. I realize now that you thought I would enjoy it, but—"

"Oh, George, it was thoughtless of me. I can see that now. I should've known that you don't like surprises. I just felt that once you were on it, you would see how much fun it could be. But I had no idea you had a fear of heights."

"Yes, well, I've heard that we should face our fears in order to get past them."

"Maybe so, but it should be your choice. Not forced upon you." She smiled. "And you're right, I am like a camel's nose. I'm too pushy. I need to back off. I understand that. So if you accept my apology, I'll accept yours."

He nodded. "Accepted. But I have another one to make. I treated you abominably yesterday when you brought Baxter to me. I'm sorry."

"To be fair, that was similar to the balloon ride. I am a camel's nose. I pushed too hard and sprung it on you without warning."

"It's true that you caught me off guard by not asking first. But it's also true that if you'd asked me first—if you'd given me the option to adopt a cat—I would've firmly told you *no thank you*. Because I did not want a cat. Not in the least."

"Well then. I'm happy to take him off your hands. I think he is a wonderful cat and I'm glad to—"

"But I *do* want him." George looked worried. "You're right. Baxter is a wonderful cat. And he is quite comfortably at home with me. We are well suited to each other."

"Oh."

"That's why I need to apologize. Not only was I horribly

rude to you, Willow, but it turned out you were right. I sincerely thank you for bringing me Baxter."

Willow felt her resolve to distance herself from George melting. "So you really do like him? He looked like such a fabulous cat. I honestly wanted to keep him."

"I can understand that. But I feel that he's very happy with me. I'm such a homebody now that I'm retired. And you're always on the go or working in the gallery. I think Baxter could be lonely with your lifestyle."

She nodded. "You're probably right." She pointed to the stools at her work bench. "Want to sit? I just made a pot of coffee, if you're interested."

While he sat down, she washed her hands then returned with two mugs of aromatic coffee. "So I heard that Collin and Josie got into it at the gallery last night. And I heard that you intervened. Is that right?"

"Yes. I was worried it was about to get ugly. So I put on my teacher hat and asked Josie to show me her apartment."

"Thank you very much."

"As it turned out, Josie and I had a rather nice little visit."

"Really?" Willow had a hard time imagining that.

"It seems I'm destined to become her mentor." George shook his head with a puzzled expression.

"What on earth?" She set down her coffee mug with a clunk.

George explained the plan they'd cooked up. "She feels that she can do her decorative painting technique on some of my old pieces of junk. I promised her she could dig around my attic. As long as she doesn't go for family heirlooms, I don't particularly care. I need to clear that space out. And quite frankly, the attic makes me feel claustrophobic. So she'll be doing me a favor to get rid of a few things."

"How interesting."

"Josie thinks she might be able to sell her painted pieces as art." He frowned doubtfully.

"That's actually a very good idea. I think she could. Especially if she's willing to take some advice and do things right. If her pieces are done well enough, I wouldn't mind having them in my gallery."

George brightened. "That would make her very happy, Willow." He pointed to the vase she'd just thrown. "Did you make that?"

"I did."

He got up to examine it more closely. "You're talented."

"You really like it?"

"It's very handsome. I can't even imagine how it would feel to make something like that."

"Have you ever tried it?"

"No, no. I wouldn't even know where to start." He shoved his hands in his pockets with a furrowed brow.

"It's easier than you think, George." She went over to her workbench, explaining the basics of pottery as she slapped a piece of clay into a ball then planted it on the center of her electric wheel. "It's kind of a messy business, but it's a clean mess." She dipped her hands in water, sat down on the bench, and began shaping the clay, quickly pulling it up into a column then opening it. "See."

"Fascinating."

Willow looked up to see what appeared to be a wistful expression on George's face. "Want to give it a try?" she asked.

"Oh, no . . . not right now. I don't have time." He checked

his watch. "I don't want to leave Baxter home alone for too long, you know, since he's probably still getting used to his new environment."

"Maybe some other day." She reached for a rag, wiping off her hands. "It's actually a lot of fun, and many people find it quite therapeutic. But I understand your concerns for Baxter. How is he settling in?"

George's face lit up as he described Baxter's unusual intelligence. "I must admit I wasn't too thrilled when he decided to sleep on my bed. But Baxter was surprisingly considerate. He politely curled up on the other side. Almost as if he'd been trained."

"What a cat."

"Yes. Thank you again for bringing him to me."

"Give him my best regards." Willow couldn't help but chuckle to herself as George left her studio. It looked like Baxter had fallen into a fine-feathered nest. And it appeared that her friendship with George had been restored once again.

◆◆◆

George didn't consider himself a particularly intuitive person, but he could tell that something was wrong with Collin when he went to visit the bookstore on Monday morning. "You just fill out this form." Collin pointed to the computer with a somber expression. "That way you'll get our newsletter with offers and coupons emailed directly to you."

"But I don't have email."

Collin frowned. "Not at all?"

"Not at all." George frowned. "So without email, I can't

participate in this? You can't simply mail your newsletter to my house via the US Postal Service?"

"The newsletter's electronic," he said curtly.

"Oh, well, I guess I'll have to pass on it." George studied Collin closely. "Are you all right, Collin? You don't act quite yourself today."

Collin shrugged.

"Of course, it's none of my business." George smiled stiffly. "I suppose I'll just browse around a bit." He waited to see if Collin wanted to assist him, but seeing his young friend's disinterest, George continued on his own. He felt distracted as he wound his way down the aisles, finally finding himself standing in front of a shelf of self-help books.

George had never been a fan of self-help books. In fact, he wasn't sure he'd ever read a single one. But a certain title, face-out in the center of the shelf, caught his eye. *Getting the Upper Hand over Obsessive Compulsions*. He wasn't sure if it was something about the cover's bright design or the title itself, but he felt compelled to pick it up and, when he read the back cover's cheesy sales copy, it was as if the words were speaking directly to him.

He attempted to replace the book on the shelf, but something inside of him wouldn't let it go. And so he marched to the register and purchased it. As the cashier gave him back a penny, George figured it was probably a complete waste of $14.99. "Here you go." She handed him the bag with a smile. "Hope you enjoy it."

George just nodded. Did anyone enjoy reading a self-help book about obsessive-compulsive behavior? And if they did enjoy it, did they admit it to anyone? "Thank you." He took his package and headed for the door but was stopped by a hand on his shoulder.

"Mr. Emerson?" Collin sounded urgent and his eyes looked troubled. "Will you be home this afternoon? Any chance I can talk to you during my lunch hour? I mean, if you're not too busy."

"I'm not too busy, Collin." He smiled. "Feel free to pop on over if you like. You can meet my new cat, Baxter."

Collin solemnly thanked him, promising to come at noon. As George left, he wondered if this might be related to Collin's mother. Josie had a knack for bringing out the worst in her son, but George had hoped his little talk with her might've helped some. Still it was an odd and awkward relationship between mother and son. And George felt sorry for Collin. Such a sensible young man with such a flibbertigibbet for a mother. As he waited to cross the street, George checked his watch. He had just enough time to get a bag of kitty litter and make it home before Collin came to visit.

George had just freshened Baxter's litter box when Collin arrived. He introduced Collin to Baxter then offered him lunch. "I usually just have a peanut butter and honey sandwich, apple, and milk," he admitted as he washed his hands. "If that suits you."

Collin shrugged. "I guess so. I'm not too hungry."

"Go ahead and take a seat." George nodded to the dinette by the window. "While I fix our lunch you can tell me what's troubling you."

After a long silence, Collin spoke. "It's Marissa. She broke up with me."

George sighed as he spread peanut butter. "I'm sorry to hear that. Marissa seems like a very nice girl."

"I thought so too," Collin said glumly.

George wasn't sure how to proceed. He was no expert on things of the heart. "Did you two have a disagreement of some sort?"

"No, no, nothing like that. It was all very civilized."

"Oh?" George cut the first sandwich in half.

"It all started after we left the gallery show on Friday night. Marissa and I went to Common Grounds as planned. And everything was perfectly fine . . . until this guy came in. Then she started to act pretty weird."

"Weird?" George cored the apple, sliced it into neat eighths, and placed four pieces on each plate.

"Weird as in sort of flirty and silly—not how she normally acts. But it was all toward this guy named Marcus Schnell. He used to go to Warner."

"I remember that boy. Didn't he graduate a year or two ago?"

"Yes. He just finished his first year of college at Oregon State, but he's home for the summer. Anyway, I guess he and Marissa had been friends in high school. More specifically, Marissa had crushed on him since she was fifteen. But they never dated or anything."

"I see." George set their plates and paper napkins on the table then went to get the milk glasses. No sense in telling Collin that Marcus had been a good student, well liked by everyone.

"For some reason, Marcus was being extra friendly to Marissa, and she just ate it up. I felt pretty much invisible."

George returned with their milk and sat down, waiting for Collin to continue and wondering what he could possibly say to encourage this young man.

"Anyway, Marissa ignored my texts on Saturday. Then she called me on Sunday morning to say she was breaking up with me. Naturally, I asked if it was because of Marcus. She admitted that she went out with him on Saturday night. So just like that I'm yesterday's news. End of story." Collin had real tears in his eyes.

"That must've been very hard." George took a bite of his sandwich, slowly chewing and wishing he had some words of comfort.

"What do I do, Mr. Emerson?" Collin used the paper napkin to blot his tears.

George swallowed, then took a sip of milk.

"Do you know how it feels to get your heart broken?" Collin looked desperately at him. "Have you ever been through anything like this?"

"Not exactly like your situation, Collin. But I did get my heart broken . . . when I lost a girl . . . the love of my life." George felt surprised that he'd actually admitted this to anyone. He hadn't spoken of it for decades.

"What happened?" Collin's eyes grew wide.

George thought hard. Was he really ready to tell this story? But seeing Collin's pain, the tears in his eyes, George began. "Well, you see, I fell in love with a girl in college. Laura Vincent. She was beautiful . . . inside and out. I'd admired her from afar for a whole year before I got up the nerve to ask her to get a coffee with me. I couldn't believe it when she accepted. It was autumn. My senior year. Laura was a junior. We were both serious students and we dated steadily for the whole year. We had a few ups and downs, just little misunderstandings, but we were both in love. I asked Laura to marry me a few weeks before my graduation."

"And she said no?"

George sighed. "She said yes. Our plan was to be engaged for a year—until I got my master's degree and she graduated with her bachelor's. Then we'd get married."

"What went wrong?"

"Laura was killed in a car wreck." George felt the old lump in his throat. "Just three days before my graduation."

"Oh . . . I'm sorry."

"This isn't a story I usually tell," George explained. "But considering your circumstances, it seemed appropriate. My circumstances were different . . . but my heart was broken just the same."

"How did you get over it?"

George considered this. *Had* he gotten over it? Certainly, it wasn't something he thought about on a daily basis anymore. But how long had it taken to reach that place? "Well, it was certainly painful. I didn't even attend my own graduation. But my grandparents tried their best to help, and they encouraged me to continue with school and to get my master's. After that, well, I moved back to Warner and went to work teaching." He sighed. "Time passes . . . the pain lessens . . . you move on." But George felt hypocritical. Had he moved on? Really?

"As horrible as I feel about Marissa, I'm guessing you must've felt worse, Mr. Emerson. I can't even imagine how that would feel."

"I don't know if you can measure pain. It's probably relative . . . different for everyone." George attempted a smile. "The thing is, Collin, you have to keep going. And that gives me an idea. What about aiming for something higher than our community college for your first year? How about a more academic school?"

Collin frowned. "The main reason I settled for community college was because of Marissa. Now it sounds like the stupidest idea ever. But it's probably too late to get in anywhere else. Maybe I'll just skip school altogether this year. I can just work at the bookstore and—"

"What if I looked into a college for you?" George offered. "I'm an alumnus of Whitfield College. I just read in the newsletter that they have a new president, and he's an old friend of mine. Of course, I can't make any promises, but I could certainly ask."

"That'd be great."

"It's a small liberal arts college," George explained. "Some might think it old-fashioned, but I liked it."

"Sounds good to me." Collin picked up his sandwich and bit into it.

While they ate, George told Collin more about the college, and by the time they finished, Collin actually appeared somewhat encouraged.

"Thank you, Mr. Emerson. It means a lot to me that you shared that story."

"Like I said, it's not something I like to talk about much."

"I understand." Collin nodded. "I don't think I want to talk to anyone else about Marissa either. Except I know Nana will ask me about it . . . eventually. Or maybe Marissa will mention it since she's working for her."

"No harm in simply saying that you and Marissa parted ways."

"That's true."

"Perhaps you can mention your interest in going to Whitfield. Your grandmother will probably appreciate that. She was concerned about your educational goals."

"I know." Collin's brow creased. "When do you plan to call your friend? The one who's the president of the college?"

"No time like the present." George went to his phone and, after dialing for information, was soon connected to the college. While he waited to be transferred to the president's office, Collin stood nearby with an anxious expression. "I'll probably just have to leave a message," George quietly told him. But to his surprise, he was soon speaking with his old friend. After catching up a bit, George told Martin about Collin. "He has a strong interest in English and is probably one of the best students I've taught." He paused to listen then turned to Collin. "He wants you to email your transcript. Can you do that?"

"Of course." Collin nodded as he pulled out his cell phone. "I'll do it right now." He waited while George relayed the email address to him.

As George continued to visit with his friend, Collin punched things into his cell phone, then gave George a thumbs-up signal, mouthing, "It's sent."

"It looks as if my young friend has just sent you his transcript." George tried to hide his amazement that this could all be handled so quickly and efficiently. The wonders of modern technology!

Martin assured him he'd go over the transcript as soon as possible. George thanked him and hung up. He turned to Collin. "Martin and his wife are about to go on vacation, so he promised to get on this right now."

"I hope my grades are good enough." Collin looked uneasy as he pocketed his phone and glanced at his watch. "I need to get back to work now. But thanks for everything. Especially for calling your friend like that."

"I'll let you know what I hear," George promised.

"That'd be great." Then Collin frowned. "I'll understand if it doesn't work out. It's just nice that you tried. I appreciate it." He said goodbye to George and headed out the door.

Less than an hour later, Martin called back. He assured George that Collin's transcript was top-notch. "Based on your hearty recommendation, I'm happy to accept him."

"That's wonderful!"

"As you must know, we don't normally handle applicants like this, but enrollment was slightly low and I feel Collin will be a great addition to our student body. Feel free to give him the good news, George. My assistant will handle everything else via email. She'll help Collin to connect with the registrar and all that."

George thanked him profusely. "You have a great vacation, Martin. I hope to be in touch with you this fall."

"Maybe you can pay us a visit."

"I'd like that." George thanked Martin again. After he hung up he was so excited that he decided to walk back to the bookstore to share the good news with Collin in person.

He found Collin straightening a sales table. "You won't believe it," George told him. "But you've been accepted."

"Are you serious?" Collin's eyes were wide. "Just like that?"

"Well, Mr. Howard explained to me that he just happened to be in his office today. We were lucky to catch him there tying up some loose ends. Anyway, he did a quick review of your transcript and was suitably impressed." George paused to catch his breath. "He and his wife will head off to Canada for a cross-country train trip tomorrow, and he won't be back in his office until late July. So it was pretty good timing."

Collin's face lit up in a big smile. "Thanks so much, Mr.

Emerson. This is the best news ever. I never dreamed you'd get results this quickly. It didn't seem possible."

George nodded. "I was a bit taken aback too."

"How about if you tell my grandmother the good news? I'm sure she'll be relieved—and happy."

As George strolled through town, he felt a real sense of accomplishment. Not only had he helped to cheer up Collin, but Willow ought to be pleased as well.

twenty

Willow didn't know what to say after George shared his "big news." She wasn't usually speechless, but at the moment she was afraid to speak—afraid she'd say something regrettable. She went back behind the counter, relieved that she was the only one working in the gallery this afternoon, as she attempted to wrap her head around what George had just told her.

"Isn't this great?" George asked with enthusiasm.

"Let me get this clear," she began slowly. "Collin plans to go to Whitfield College? This fall?"

"That's right. I thought you'd be pleased."

"But how on earth did this happen? And why didn't anyone tell me?"

"I just saw Collin at the bookstore. He asked me to come over here and tell you for him."

"But why did he keep this a secret from me?"

"It wasn't meant to be a secret, Willow. More like an unexpected surprise. It all happened rather quickly." George briefly explained about Marissa and Collin's breakup, and about his friend's recent appointment as president of George's alma mater.

"I'm sorry to appear dense," she said. "But this is not making sense."

"You see, Collin was in a bad way," George said slowly. "He was completely brokenhearted over Marissa breaking up—"

"Collin never said a word to me about any of this. Neither did Marissa. But you're saying that Collin went to *you* with his troubles?"

"Is there anything wrong with that?" George looked offended, but Willow wasn't sure she cared. After all, she was offended herself.

"No, there's nothing wrong with that." She shook her head. "But I do feel a bit left out. Collin usually communicates with me." At least he used to communicate. But then Josie entered the picture. And there was Marissa. "Did Collin and Marissa really break up?"

"Yes. That's why Collin was suddenly so interested in this college. And he's so happy about it, he wanted me to tell you he'd been accepted."

"And he is accepted? Just like that? How on earth does that happen?"

George told her about someone named Martin who just happened to be in his office before going to Canada with his wife.

"I still don't get it." Her irritation was growing.

"You see, Martin Howard is my friend, and he's the president of the college. After I spoke to him and after he reviewed Collin's transcript, he accepted him as a student, to be enrolled for this fall. Does *that* make sense?" George looked perturbed.

"What about tuition? This is a private college. I can only assume it will be rather expensive. Shouldn't someone have spoken to me about the cost? And Collin is still a minor. Wouldn't they need a guardian's consent?"

"The full application is probably on its way right now. Collin and I simply assumed you'd be happy about this new development. I remember how distraught you were the first day I met you—you were so worried that Collin was settling for a community college and—"

"Yes, but you helped me to see that was a sensible plan."

"Perhaps it was sensible then. But only because Marissa was going there. After Collin and Marissa fell apart, well, it no longer sounded like the best plan." George frowned. "Are you saying that tuition expenses might be prohibitive?"

"I don't know what I'm saying, George. Except that I question your involvement in this. It feels like you've stepped over a line. And I resent being left out of this major life decision for my grandson. Collin is my responsibility, and you had no right to do all this behind my back."

Suddenly the tables had turned and George appeared to be speechless. Although Willow felt a bit sorry for her strong words, she knew they were true. She did resent this intrusion. It was wrong. And to spring it on her like this—that was wrong too. She heard the door buzzer, signaling they were no longer alone. "I have a customer to attend to," she said.

"You've made your feelings quite plain," George said quietly. "I'll let you sort this out with Collin. I'm sure that nothing has been set into motion that cannot be stopped." And without another word, he left.

• • •

George spent the next few days vacillating between conflicting feelings of self-pity and guilt. Mostly he felt confused. He wasn't completely sure what had happened that day . . . or why it had all turned so sour. But one thing he knew for certain—from now on, he would refrain from "helping" anyone.

As a result, when Josie called, asking if she could start clearing out his attic, he'd made an excuse . . . saying it wasn't a good time for him. He detected the disappointment in her voice, but really, what could he do? The irony of the whole debacle was that George had prided himself on being an uninvolved and non-intrusive sort of fellow. So how had he gotten himself so entangled in the Wild West family?

"Hello, George," Lorna called over the fence. "How are you and Baxter doing on this fine Fourth of July?"

George paused from grooming Baxter's thick coat and, setting down the wire brush, went over to greet Lorna. "We're all right," he told her. "Did you have a good visit at your sister's?"

"Yes. We had a lovely time. I just got home. My goodness, the traffic was something else. I completely forgot this was a holiday." She pointed to Baxter as he rubbed against George's ankles. "You're letting him roam outside now?"

"I think he's settled in enough, although I don't let him out here by himself. He just enjoyed a nice sunbath then rolled in the dirt."

"So any big plans for Independence Day?"

He shrugged. "Only to enjoy my independence."

She chuckled. "So no big dates with your friend Willow?"

"No, no." George shoved his hands into his pockets and looked down.

229

"When was the last time you saw the fireworks show over the lake?" she asked.

He thought for a moment. "Probably not since I was a teen."

"You gotta be kidding!" She pushed her dark glasses to the top of her head to stare at him with a shocked expression. "I'm going with some friends. We plan to take a picnic dinner up there. You could join us if you like."

George considered this. "I don't know. Baxter might be lonely without me."

"You said he's settled in," she reminded him. "Come on, George. The lake is so beautiful with the fireworks reflecting on it. And my friend Cathy is bringing most of the food and she is a fabulous cook. She's making ribs and potato salad and all sorts of good stuff."

"That's tempting." George mentally compared that to the soup and sandwich he had planned for his dinner.

"Then say you'll come." She smiled brightly. "And don't worry, George, this isn't a date. It'll just be you and me and my friends, sharing some good food, a few laughs, and the fireworks show together."

"All right," George agreed. "I'll come."

"Great. Be ready to leave by six. I'll bring an extra camp chair for you."

Before George could change his mind, she told him she needed to go make a fruit salad to take with them. It was set. George was going to the fireworks show with Lorna and her friends. Interesting.

⬥ ⬥ ⬥

Willow felt badly for the way she'd treated George the other day. Especially after Collin expressed sincere enthusiasm for his acceptance at the small private college. When Willow asked him about Marissa, he hadn't said much. But she could tell he was deeply wounded. And she knew that George's "intrusion" had been good for Collin. For that reason alone, she'd wanted to straighten things out with George, but it had turned into a crazy-busy week at the gallery.

For starters, Marissa had quit—with no notice. At first Willow had assumed it was related to the breakup with Collin, but she later heard it was because Marissa had decided to go on a backpacking trip with her new boyfriend. Meanwhile, Joel had just left on vacation, so now it was up to her and Leslie to run the gallery. And since summer traffic had picked up, they'd barely had time to breathe. But because today was a holiday—and it was just her and Collin at the gallery because Leslie had the day off and Collin had kindly offered to help out—Willow decided to close shop early.

"I have an idea," she told him as they locked up. "What if we have a little Fourth of July party up on the terrace tonight? Leslie told me that we can probably see some fireworks up there."

"Sounds okay," he said in his usual unenthused way.

"I thought perhaps we could invite George to join us."

He brightened slightly. "He might like that. He acts kind of lonely to me."

"How about you call him while I figure out what we need from the store." Then on her way to her apartment, Willow met Josie in the stairwell and explained their plan.

"Cool." Josie nodded. "I've been wanting to talk to him about that attic of his. He sounded so eager to get it cleared out, but every time I call him, he's too busy."

"Mr. Emerson can't come," Collin announced as he came up the stairs.

"Can't come?" Willow asked. "Or won't come?" Was he still mad at her? Was this her punishment?

"He said he has other plans." Collin unlocked his door.

"What kind of plans?" Josie demanded.

"He's going to the lake to see the fireworks with some friends," Collin glumly informed them.

"I didn't think he had any friends," Josie said sharply.

"Apparently, he does," Collin shot back at her. "He said they're having some sort of big picnic with ribs and potato salad and chocolate cake."

"Interestingly cliché." Willow wondered if George had made the whole thing up. His clever way to keep them all at bay.

"I wanna see the fireworks too, Mom," Josie pleaded in a childlike tone. "Let's go to the lake."

"I suppose we could go." Willow would've preferred a quieter evening up on the terrace. She imagined herself up there with some quiet jazz music, the fireworks glowing in the distance. She looked at Collin. "What do you think? Would you go?"

"I guess." His enthusiasm was underwhelming.

"We'll get takeout food on our way," Josie suggested.

"I vote for KFC," Collin declared with more enthusiasm.

So it was settled. The West family would spend the evening at the lake. But Willow seriously doubted that George would be up there. Unless she was mistaken, George was home with his cat . . . by himself . . . and completely content. To her surprise, she felt envious.

It didn't take long to gather a few things and swing by

KFC. It was just past seven by the time they transported their takeout picnic and quilts toward the lake. Taking in a deep breath of fresh air, Willow felt glad they'd come. The lake looked beautiful in the shadowy light, and the park was slowly filling with people of all ages. Children and dogs were romping about. Some groups, like them, were enjoying picnics on the grass or at the park tables. Others were out in rowboats and kayaks. The scene was so picturesque that Willow was tempted to take some photos on her phone, but she didn't want to spoil the magic of the moment. Instead, she just soaked it in.

"How about there?" Collin pointed to a vacant patch of grass near the edge of the lake and soon they were settled in. So far, he and Josie hadn't exchanged any serious hostilities. To be fair, they hadn't exchanged any words at all. But it still felt like an improvement. Just in case, Willow sat between them on the ground. She knew that if she paid more attention to Josie, it would go better for everyone. Willow justified this by reminding herself that Collin had received her sole attention for fourteen years, but Josie had only had Willow's attention for a few turbulent teen years. It was no wonder that she felt somewhat cheated.

"What a beautiful evening." Willow bundled up her trash. "I'm so happy we came." She leaned back on her elbows with a contented sigh.

"I'll go dump our trash," Collin offered. "And walk around some." He took the bags and drink cups and left.

"He's probably on the lookout for Marissa," Josie said after he was gone.

"That could be." Willow sat up and glanced around. "He doesn't say much, but I can tell he's still hurting."

"The first heartbreak is rough."

Willow studied Josie's profile. "When was your first heartbreak?"

"I was a lot younger than Collin," Josie admitted. "You probably don't even remember."

The truth was Willow didn't quite remember. "Then it couldn't be Zeke." Although Zeke was Collin's father, Josie had lost contact with him after Zeke dumped her and moved away. "I do remember a boy you liked a lot—it was the first year when you came to live with Asher and me. I think his name was Nathan. He seemed like a nice young man."

Josie turned to her with surprise. "Yes. It was Nathan. I was only fourteen, but I was head over heels for that boy. And he was nice. Well, until he dumped me for Mattie Harris." Josie scowled. "I still hate that girl. I hope she's gotten fat and ugly by now."

Willow suppressed the urge to chuckle. She wanted to point out that Josie's hatred toward Mattie was hurting Josie more than Mattie, but she suspected that wouldn't be too well received. "So, at least you know how Collin might be feeling."

"Yeah, I've been trying to cut him some slack."

"Good for you." Willow noticed that Collin was on his way back now. To her relief, he didn't look too gloomy. Hopefully he hadn't seen Marissa with her new beau.

"Mr. Emerson is over there." Collin jerked his thumb over his shoulder. "He's with a bunch of women."

"Are you kidding?" Josie stood up, peering in that direction.

"Don't stare, honey." Willow tried to act nonchalant. So

what if George was here with a bunch of women? Why should it concern her?

"They're over by the dock," Collin told Josie.

"I'm gonna go say hello." Josie took off now.

"I'm sure Mr. Emerson will enjoy that," Collin said sarcastically as he sat down.

"How many women were with him?" Willow asked.

"I didn't count them. But I guess it was about six or so. He introduced me to one of them. She's his neighbor. It looked like he was with her."

"That must be Lorna Atwood. She lives right next door to him." Willow wanted to ask if George was *with her* as if on a date, but didn't want to appear overly interested. Really, it was nice that George had gotten out this evening. As she lay back on the quilt, she hoped he'd enjoy tonight's display. Hopefully he didn't have a phobia of fireworks or loud noises. At least he'd have a lot of women around to comfort him.

twenty-one

The weekend following the Fourth was busier than ever at the gallery, so much so that Willow actually asked Josie to help out a little. To her surprise, Josie arrived with clean hair and decent clothes and, for the most part, minded her manners. Still, it wasn't ideal.

"I'd rather be an artist than work in a gallery," Josie said as she helped Willow to close on Sunday evening.

"I couldn't agree more." Willow sighed as she locked the door. "Fortunately, we're closed tomorrow. Then Joel is back on Tuesday. And I have a couple of applicants to interview."

"Good. Because I need to get back to my art projects."

Although Josie still hadn't managed to connect with George and peruse his attic, she'd unearthed a few stray items in Willow's studio to keep her busy. So far, she'd decorated a small stepladder and an apple crate, and she was about to start on a pair of wooden stools.

"I'd like to get back to my projects too," Willow said as they trudged upstairs. She'd bisque-fired her most recent pottery creations, and although she'd glazed them, she hadn't found the time or energy for their final firing. Maybe tomorrow.

As she went into her apartment, she thought about George. She still hadn't spoken to him. Not since their disagreement over Collin's college plans. Although it was undeniable that George had overstepped a bit, Willow also had to admit that she'd been unkind and unreasonable. She owed him a sincere apology.

As she changed into more comfortable clothes, she wondered about taking George some sort of gift to help with her apology. She remembered how he'd complimented her on her pottery and thought about the tall vase that was waiting for its last firing. She'd glazed it with a turquoise blue that would look lovely in George's bungalow. Especially if it was full of sunflowers. As tired as she was, she decided to go down to the basement to load and fire up the kiln.

Of course, it took longer than she expected. But at least she had an automatic timer on this kiln so she wouldn't need to babysit it like she used to do. Even so, she stayed down there for a while, sweeping up and cleaning paintbrushes that Josie had left behind. And leaving her a reminder note to take better care of them. She paused to look at Josie's stepladder. It was actually quite nice. Josie had listened to Willow's suggestions, taking care to be sure that all surfaces were painted. Josie's eye for color was definitely interesting. And Willow knew that if the right customers came into the gallery, these pieces could sell. At the very least, they were helping Josie to build confidence and would look fun in her apartment.

Finally, satisfied that the kiln was at the right temperature and that the timer was working properly, Willow said a little prayer for good results, then turned off the lights and went up to her apartment. Hopefully there would be no kiln mishaps and George's tall turquoise vase would look beautiful tomorrow. She was just going into her apartment when Collin popped his head out the door. "You missed Mr. Emerson, Nana."

"What?"

"He came by here about an hour ago. He said he was just on a walk and had stopped in to say hi."

"Oh, that's nice." She pushed hair away from her damp forehead. "How was he?"

"He acted just fine. Said he really enjoyed the fireworks the other night." Collin frowned. "Do you think he's dating his neighbor now?"

"I don't know."

"I thought he liked you."

Willow gave a weary smile. "Well, George and I are sort of like oil and water, Collin. We're so different that I don't—"

"But I thought opposites were supposed to attract."

"Maybe briefly. But given time, they can rub each other wrong." She unlocked her door. "But I do plan to speak to him soon. I owe him a bit of an apology."

"Yeah, that'd probably be good."

She said good night, then went into her apartment. She hadn't mentioned the details of her unfortunate conversation with George, but it was almost like Collin knew. Perhaps George had told him.

George felt discouraged as he got ready for bed. It had taken a lot of nerve to go knock on Willow's door tonight. He knew the gallery was closed and, according to Collin, Willow was home. But when she didn't answer, George felt certain

238

it was because she didn't want to see him. He imagined her inside her apartment, peering through the little peephole in her door, still seething over George's recent intrusion. She was finished with him. And he'd honestly believed that he was finished with her as well. But then time passed . . . and George's thoughts often drifted to her.

He knew it made no sense, but he missed her. And he felt badly about the other night when he hadn't bothered to go over to say hello at the fireworks display. Both Collin and Josie had told George that she was there. But George had remained stubbornly in his borrowed lawn chair, surrounded by Lorna's lady friends. Admittedly, it had been somewhat amusing to be the only male in the company of those women. At least at first. But as the evening wore on, their gossipy chatter had grown increasingly tiresome. So much so that George had wanted to cover his ears and run. Oddly enough, Lorna had proved the least aggravating and most interesting of the group. At least she could talk about her recent trip with her sister. They'd gone to Yosemite National Park and a few other places. Finally the fireworks started, and although he hadn't appreciated the loud booms, George had preferred that noise to the women's grating voices. By the time it was over, he'd been eager to get home. He'd missed Baxter.

"I guess it's just going to be you and me," he told Baxter as he put his toothbrush in its holder. As usual, Baxter was perched on the toilet tank, watching with intelligent feline interest . . . and perhaps an expression of sympathy in his jade-green eyes. "A couple of bachelors living the quiet life." He went out to the living room to turn off the light, pausing to look at the painting above his couch. It was funny. He remembered how jarring that painting had been initially.

Oh, he'd been drawn to the subject matter because of Alex's old pickup. But the oversized and colorful painting had felt intrusive at first. Yet now, he was used to it. And if someone removed it from his wall, he would most certainly miss it. In fact, he'd be upset to see it gone. Interesting.

Perhaps it was possible to adjust oneself to new things after all. And perhaps it was possible to pursue a relationship with someone as strange as Willow West. Except she acted like she wanted nothing to do with him now. Who could blame her? George knew he was by no means typical. He was standoffish and stuck in his ways and, according to some people, downright peculiar. But being a fan of Ralph Waldo Emerson, George had excused his atypical lifestyle as "individuality." He marched to his own drummer. If it made people uncomfortable, they could simply keep their distance.

Willow enjoyed sleeping in on Monday morning. She took her coffee out to the terrace, taking time to water her plants and do a little garden maintenance. She loved being out here in the cool of the morning. At the west edge of her terrace she'd planted dozens of sunflowers as a sort of screen. Already they were blooming profusely. They would look perfect in George's turquoise-blue vase, which she hoped had made it safely through last night's firing.

As an experienced potter, she knew about the surprises that sometimes came with the opening of a kiln. Occasionally a pot would have an air bubble that resulted in an explosion that ruined the other pieces. Or the timer could malfunction, and the items could be under- or overcooked. Glazes could run or drip or crack or flake. You never knew what you'd get. But that was actually one of the things she loved about pottery. You had to expect the unexpected. Sort of like life.

As she got her second cup of coffee, she made a mental to-do list for the day. She wanted to offer Josie an enticing payment in exchange for some good janitorial maintenance in the gallery. She needed to make appointments with the job applicants and hopefully make a decision by the end of the day. She also wanted to work in her studio. And she really wanted to go to the new tai chi class that Lulu from church had just started. She'd even told Lulu that if she had the class late in the afternoon, she'd come. So Lulu had scheduled it at four.

Besides all that, Willow needed to take her peace offering to George. Naturally that was at the bottom of her list. Although it was somewhat encouraging that George had come by last night, after all was said and done, she wasn't sure if it had been to see Collin or her. And she didn't want to ask Collin. Still, she was determined to take him the vase . . . if it hadn't exploded. And if the vase was ruined, she might take that as God's hint to back off from George. For all she knew, George would probably be grateful.

It was midafternoon by the time Willow accomplished almost everything on her to-do list. To her pleasant surprise, the contents of the kiln had fired perfectly, and the turquoise vase was gorgeous. It was even more gorgeous filled with sunflowers of varying shades—everything from bright yellow to a rich russet. Willow's plan was to drop off the peace offering then continue on to tai chi class. The perfect excuse not to linger and make a nuisance of herself. She'd even written a short apology note just in case George was out.

Dressed in her black yoga pants, a neon green tank top,

and flip-flops, Willow drove over to George's house, hoping that she could just leave her gift by his front door. But she was barely on the porch when the door opened and George, dressed casually in khaki pants and a blue shirt, stepped outside. He even had on sandals. With socks, of course, but still, they were sandals! Willow tried not to stare.

"Hello." George's smile looked genuine.

"This is for you." She held the vase out to him and immediately launched into her somewhat rehearsed and lengthy apology. "I want to say I'm sorry for the way I acted after you helped Collin to get into Whitfield College. I was very unkind and most ungracious. Instead of being grateful, like I should've been, I took offense for feeling left out. But Collin is so pleased about his college plans, I not only owe you an apology, but a great deal of gratitude. Please, accept my peace offering."

George blinked as she handed him the vase. "Thank you. This is very nice."

"The flowers are from my terrace, and I made the vase," she said quickly. "Remember? You saw me take it off the wheel when you visited my studio."

"It's really beautiful, Willow. You shouldn't have gone to so much trouble."

"I wanted to . . . it's my little peace offering."

"Well, I feel like I owe you an apology too. Do you have time to come inside? You can say hello to Baxter."

"Just for a few minutes. I need to be at tai chi at four." She followed him in.

"Tai chi?" George said as he placed the vase in the center of his wooden coffee table. "I've heard that's a good form of exercise, but I really don't know anything about it."

"A friend of mine is teaching a class." She knelt to pet Baxter, scratching the top of his head and his chin while he purred. She stood and looked at George. "Hey, you should come with me. It'd be fun."

"Oh, I don't know." George suddenly looked uneasy.

"Really, George. You'd probably like it. It's supposed to be relaxing—as much for the mind as the body. And it's good for older people." She grinned. "Not that we're old. We're not. Come on," she urged. "We'll be tai chi buddies."

"Maybe next time," he said with a promising smile. "I—uh—I'm not really ready for this today."

"But this is the first class, George. So everyone is a beginner. If you wait to come, you'll have to catch up." She poked him in the chest. "Besides, you're dressed casually. You look ready to me."

"Well, I—"

"Come on, George. What's the worst that could happen? If you don't like it, you never have to go again. But if you don't go today, I bet you'll never go." She glanced at his wall clock. "It starts in fifteen minutes." She tugged on his arm. "Tell Baxter goodbye and come."

To her surprise, George quit protesting and came. As she drove over to the church, which was actually a restored barn, she chatted to George about her latest happenings, telling him about Josie's progress as an artist and how Collin appeared to be recovering from his heartache.

"The tai chi class is here?" George frowned as she pulled into the gravel parking lot. "I thought this was your church."

"Well, it's a lot of things. Kind of an activity center and everything." She parked and hopped out. "Come on, George, we don't want to be late." But as they hurried across the

243

parking area, she felt a stab of concern. What if the class was women only? Or what if George resented her pushiness? Had she been a camel's nose again? But how else did one get George Emerson out of his rut?

To Willow's relief, George wasn't the only male in the class. Lulu's dad, Donald, was there. He was probably close to eighty but in great shape and took a real interest in George. The class was surprisingly soothing and, although the motions were slow and not overly physical, Willow felt like she'd had a bit of a workout when the class ended. But a good sort of workout. And she really appreciated how Lulu incorporated God into the meditative part of the exercises. "That was wonderful," she told Lulu afterward. "Thank you."

"Do you think your friend liked it?" Lulu asked quietly. George was in the back of the room talking to Donald. "I couldn't tell by his expression."

"Hard to say," Willow told her. "But I'll find out."

"It would be nice if he kept coming. Dad was worried he'd be the only fellow."

As Willow drove George home, she asked what he thought of tai chi. "I realize I sort of kidnapped you," she confessed. "I hope it wasn't too torturous."

"It was okay. As you know, I don't believe in God, so I didn't particularly appreciate Lulu's references to faith and Bible verses and such. But I must admit that the mental and physical part was good." He sighed. "And I do feel more relaxed. It's too bad she couldn't just leave her religious propaganda out of it. I doubt that was how tai chi was meant to be practiced."

Willow felt sad to hear him talk like this. She was familiar with George's claims of atheism and knew his beliefs differed from hers, but somehow she perceived him in a different sort of light. He had a kind and generous spirit. He seemed vulnerable . . . like a wounded wayfarer on his own faith journey. One that she hoped would eventually lead him to God. But hearing him going on like this about the tai chi class was disheartening. Almost like a setback. Maybe it had been a mistake to take him with her today.

twenty-two

Willow wasn't quite ready to give up on this conversation about God and faith with George. Even if it felt uncomfortable, it was important. Besides, she genuinely cared about George. "I'm curious," she said slowly as she drove through town. "I know you don't believe in God, George, but you mentioned your grandparents were churchgoing people. It makes me curious as to how you arrived at your atheist philosophy."

"Time . . . and life. It just makes sense to me."

"It's ironic. I grew up in a family that never darkened a church door. I was a wild, crazy girl who never had faith of any kind. For most of my life too. But I eventually hit a place where I needed a higher power in my life. And when I discovered that God was really real, well, I grabbed on tight and I've been holding on ever since."

"Interesting." George sounded more bored than intrigued. But Willow was not dissuaded. Not yet anyway.

"I'm wondering about something." She parked in front of his house. "I've decided it takes a lot of faith to be an atheist. Even more faith than it takes to be a believer."

246

"I don't understand."

"Well, you're putting your trust in your own belief that God does not exist." She turned off the ignition and looked at him. "What if you get to the end of your life and find out you're wrong—you discover that God is real, but you've banked all your bets on the conviction that he's not real. What then?"

"What about you?" George countered. "Haven't you banked all your bets on the possibility that God *is* real? What if he's not?"

She considered this. "Well, at least I'd be able to say that I lived a good life. That I was happy and at peace. That I tried to love everyone and practiced forgiveness. I didn't live in fear. And I fully appreciated the beauty around me and utilized my natural talents. So if by chance God wasn't real, at least I'd have enjoyed a rich and full life. Can you make that same claim?"

George didn't respond, but his brow was furrowed.

"So you see, my belief wouldn't have hurt me. What about yours?"

He continued to stare straight ahead in stony silence.

"But, George, if God is real—like I believe he is—I will be exceedingly thankful that I did believe in him. Not only because of a satisfying earthly life, but because I'd like to continue a loving relationship with God throughout eternity."

"That's a very long time." George sighed.

"It would be a much, much longer time if you had to spend eternity *without* God. I can't imagine being separated from God's love for even a day."

"Here's the truth, Willow." He turned to her with a very

somber expression. "If I believed in God, I would have to believe that he is a hateful, selfish, mean God."

"But he's not. He's loving and gracious and kind and—"

"I must disagree. If God does exist, which I cannot accept, then the only explanation would be that God must hate me."

"How can God hate you?" She frowned. "God is love. He loves all his creation, George. He loves you."

"No . . ." He turned away, reaching for the door handle. "If you're right and God is real, he's had it out for George Emerson. He's gone to great lengths to torture me. And for that reason, it is easier and less painful for me to not believe in God." George got out of her car.

Willow refused to allow the conversation to end like this. "Wait," she called out. Running to catch up, she followed him into the house. "You can't leave me hanging like that. You owe me an explanation, George. What did you mean? What makes you so certain that God hates you?" She sat down on his sofa and waited.

George slowly sat in the easy chair across from her with a very perplexed expression. "Do you really want to hear this, Willow?"

"Of course, I do. And just so you know, I have no plans for the evening. I have all the time in the world."

"Well, I plan to keep this as brief as possible." He folded his arms in front of him. "First of all, there were my parents. They took my brother and me to church every Sunday. The same church my grandparents belonged to. My mother was kind and good and quite serious about her faith, but my father . . . well, he was a good guy when he wasn't drinking. He'd been drinking the night he and my mother were killed in the car accident. I was six at the time and my grandparents told me that God needed my parents, that was why he took them up to heaven. But I missed them—especially my mother. I missed them so much that it seemed mean and selfish of God to take my parents from me."

"That must've been terribly hard."

He nodded. "Then my grandparents, as you know, took Alex and me in. And they continued taking us to church and time passed and I had nearly stopped questioning God about taking my parents. Then Alex went to Vietnam. I was ten when he died."

Willow felt another wave of sadness. "Oh, George, how horrible for you."

He nodded again. "So now God had taken all of my immediate family. I had two questions. One, did God hate me so much that he wanted them but not me? Was I not good enough? Or, two, did he hate me so much that he would take the people I loved from me?"

"I can understand that—especially from a child's perspective."

"I became pretty closed up after Alex died. For the next few years and into adolescence, I learned to keep my feelings to myself. Otherwise, my grandparents would either preach at me or send me to the reverend for counseling. Simply out of concern."

Baxter jumped onto George's lap and, as he petted his cat, he continued. "I didn't start to open up again until college. During my senior year I dated a girl who took her faith very seriously. I loved her so much that I began to attend her church and my heart toward God softened. We became engaged." George pursed his lips. "Then she died." He shook his head glumly, but his eyes were misty. "After that,

I knew that if God existed—although I no longer believed he existed—then he must really hate me. It was quite clear. Everyone I loved dearly had died. Even my best friend, you remember him, Greg Walters . . . he died too. From cancer. Not long after my grandparents both passed away. That felt like the final blow."

"Oh, George." Willow felt tears trickle down her cheeks. "I had no idea you'd been through so much pain. So much loss. No wonder you believe the way you do."

"So can you still tell me that God is real?" He looked at her with sad eyes.

She wiped her tears with her hands. "All I can say is that there are a lot of horrible things in this world, George. You can't deny there are atrocities like the Holocaust and terrible wars and famines and natural disasters and serial killers and all sorts of other horrors. But just because those things exist doesn't mean that God doesn't. That's like saying the sun doesn't exist because it gets dark at night. Or that because there is evil means there isn't good."

He barely nodded. "That's true."

"We live in a beautiful world, but it's got some flaws. We're human so we've got flaws too. And God doesn't control us, George. He gave us free will. And our choices—or someone else's choices—come with consequences. But I honestly believe the bad things can help us to turn to God. We get to a place where we realize we're not enough. We know we can't do this on our own. We are forced to admit we need God. And then we cry out for his help. That's what happened to me. When Asher got sick and I knew I was losing him . . . that was when I found my own faith. I needed God—I cried out to him. And he answered. He didn't let me down."

"Well, he let me down."

She nodded. "I'm sure it must feel like that to you. But your story isn't done, George. You might be living like it's done. I know how you've frozen yourself into some sort of safety capsule, like you're living all alone in a time warp, but your story isn't finished yet. I believe you've got a lot more living and experiencing to do." She stood. "But I didn't mean to preach at you. I hope I haven't said too much."

She could see he was in pain and hated to think it was because of her. Willow went over to his chair and, after giving Baxter a good stroke, she wrapped her arms around George and just held him for a long moment. "For some reason God has put you on my heart, George, and I can't help but think that means he's trying to show you how much he loves you. He must love you very much." Then without belaboring her point further, she stood up straight, smiled down on him, and quietly departed, praying for him all the way home.

———◆◆◆———

Willow was barely out the door when George broke into tears. Not just trickling-down-the-cheeks tears, but a full-blown sobbing and wailing that was so loud that even Baxter was startled. He hopped down to the floor, looking up at George with a curious expression of concern. George wasn't completely sure what had triggered this reaction in him, but as he continued to cry and sob like a little child, he hoped this wasn't going to become a permanent condition. And he hoped Lorna couldn't hear him. Fortunately his windows were closed.

He went to the bathroom to splash cold water on his face, then actually blew his nose with a hand towel, which was so out of character, but he continued to cry. Was this a side effect of the tai chi class? Or the result of opening old wounds and revisiting old hurts? Or was it that hug from Willow that had unhinged him like this? And what she'd said about how much God must love him?

George honestly did not know what had triggered this strange reaction. But what he did know was that he needed to get control of himself. Perhaps, for the sake of his own emotional health, he should give up tai chi for good. And maybe he should return to his avoidance of Willow West at all cost. He needed to get control again—even if that meant locking his doors and locking everyone and everything out.

George's hands shook as he poured himself a glass of milk. Milk always had a calming effect on him. But he could barely swallow against his sobs. He set the glass down and leaned over, and gripping the counter's edge, he attempted a slow, deep breath. Somehow he needed to get control again. He couldn't let this emotional outburst get the upper hand. He continued to try a few more deep breaths, but finally, feeling miserable and hopeless and weak, George stumbled off to his bedroom, fell into bed, and even though it wasn't yet seven o'clock, cried himself to sleep.

———•••———

Although Willow felt terrible about George's painful story and a bit guilty for having left him in such a desperate way, she knew that the only thing she could really do for him, at the moment, was simply pray. So as she carried a tall glass of iced tea out to her terrace, she did pray. Quite specifically, she asked God to make himself real to George. What more was there to say? She had too much respect for God

252

to go on and on—as if God were dense and couldn't understand what she'd just asked. She knew that God was big enough and smart enough to do something to get George's attention—and she believed that he would. And so, she left it in God's hands.

But as she lay back in her comfortable lounge chair, sipping her green tea, she wondered at what she'd just heard. She'd suspected that George had faced sorrows in his life, but she'd never guessed there'd been so many. In some ways, it was no surprise that the poor guy had reached the conclusion that God did not exist. It was simply less painful. Or so he thought. Hopefully God would prove him wrong.

As Willow looked at the beauty around her—the little world she'd created up on a neglected rooftop that had smelled of tar and cat urine—she thought about God's beautiful world. The oceans and mountains and forests and meadows . . . right here in Oregon where George had spent his entire life. She wondered that George hadn't observed the beauty around him, that he hadn't questioned how such a place could've simply evolved. But it was possible that his pain had blinded him. It certainly had trapped him. Poor guy.

• • •

George woke with a start and tried to get his bearings. It was dark and stuffy and warm—and although he was fully dressed, he was in his bed. He sat up and shook his head, trying to remember the dream. It had been an amazingly good dream. So much so that George felt disappointed to be awake. As he got out of bed and turned on the bedside light, he was surprised to see that it was past midnight. He rubbed his hair. Had he really been asleep for more than five hours?

Baxter looked up from where he was still curled up on the other side of the bed, gazing curiously at George—as if to ask why he was getting up at this time of night.

George felt hot and dry and rumpled as he padded, barefoot, to the kitchen and poured himself a glass of orange juice. As he sipped the cool, sweet drink, he tried to remember the dream. He'd been in a beautiful place—light and bright and unlike anything he'd ever seen before. He'd felt a sense of peace and calm . . . and a sort of weightlessness . . . like all his troubles had evaporated. As he set the empty glass down he remembered something. His mother had been there. She'd been smiling happily and stroking his hair like she used to when he was just a boy. It had been such a good, happy feeling. He wished he could get it back.

As he opened some windows to let some cool air into the house, George tried hard to hold on to the pleasant dream. But it was like trying to hold on to the gentle summer breeze wafting in—it just slid right past him. Feeling a rumble inside of him, George returned to the kitchen to make himself a peanut butter and honey sandwich. But before sitting down to eat it, George realized that he felt like something was missing in his dark, quiet house. Something that he wanted, but he wasn't sure what it was.

Leaving his sandwich behind, George went into the living room and opened the cabinet that stored all the old vinyl LP records. Perhaps it was music that he needed. He remembered telling Willow that, once he retired, he planned to listen to music again. And yet he hadn't. George looked over the two rows of albums that had once belonged to Alex and, seeing one that looked far more dog-eared than the others, he pulled it out. It was Simon and Garfunkel's *Bridge Over Troubled*

Water. He stared at the two guys on the cover—they looked like they'd been pulled straight out of the seventies . . . and yet they looked like someone he could know right now. He slid out the vinyl record, placed it on the old turntable and, hoping that everything still worked, turned it on.

The first song was "Bridge Over Troubled Water" and, although George knew that he must've heard this song before, he didn't really remember it. It was like hearing it for the first time. The lyrics were so amazing that he had to sit down just to listen. The words sounded like they'd been written just for him. Despite the warmth of the summer evening, George felt goose bumps from head to toe. Although he feared he was hallucinating or about to suffer some fatal condition like a stroke or heart attack, it felt as if the words to that song were being sung by a higher power. God, perhaps?

He listened to the song three more times then turned the whole thing off and, just sitting on the sofa with his hands dangling between his knees, he shook his head. What had just happened? Was it possible that God Almighty—if he did exist—could speak to George through Simon and Garfunkel?

Still feeling slightly delirious, but hungry, George went back to the kitchen and ate his sandwich, washing it down with milk. Then he took a long shower and, feeling bone-tired and wrung out, he returned to bed . . . in the hopes that the beautiful dream would return and continue.

twenty-three

Every time Willow thought of George during the next few days, she simply shot up a brief but earnest prayer. She'd consider checking on him, but then something would distract her. Collin needed help filling out the rest of the college paperwork, as well as some morale boosting over his recent breakup. And Josie wanted company down in the studio while working on painting projects. So Willow threw herself into pottery and actually produced some nice gallery pieces. Besides that, Willow had to train the new girl who was working in the gallery. Haley was smart enough, but she lacked confidence. To make matters worse, Joel hadn't scheduled himself for many hours and Leslie had taken off several vacation days. By the weekend, Willow felt the need for a vacation herself. Fortunately, the gallery would be closed on Monday. And Leslie would be back on Tuesday.

Although Willow did miss George, which was a bit like missing a toothache, she reminded herself that his life was not nearly as jam-packed and busy as hers. He had a sweet cat to care for . . . and a hammock to lie in. If he'd wanted to spend time with her, he certainly knew where to find her.

By Sunday morning, though, her curiosity got the best of her. Especially since Josie appeared concerned as well. "Every time I call his phone, he never answers," Josie had complained the previous evening. So Willow decided to stroll over and say a friendly hello. Hopefully he wouldn't mind the intrusion. She suspected that she'd pushed him too hard during their last encounter—he probably was simply establishing his boundaries by placing some time and space between them. And that was fine. If he still wasn't ready to talk to her, she would simply continue on her stroll.

When she got to George's house, Willow tried ringing his doorbell and knocking loudly, but he didn't come to the door. Now she was feeling concerned. So much so that she went around to peek over his fence, only to see the hammock empty.

"George isn't home," the neighbor called out as Willow came back around. "He's been gone all week."

"*Gone?*" Willow shaded her eyes to see Lorna watering a pot of petunias. "On vacation? Did he take Baxter with him?"

"I don't mean gone as in gone-gone. Not like a vacation." Lorna dropped her hose and walked over to the edge of her lawn. "But he goes out each morning—quite early. And he takes Baxter with him. Totes him along in a carrier case. Stays gone all day."

"Really? But you don't know where they go?"

"I asked George about it, but he just said he was taking care of business. Very mysterious." Lorna chuckled. "But then you know how George likes to keep to himself. Strange fellow, but likeable, and he's a good neighbor."

Willow simply nodded. But, as she left, she had a good

guess where George might be spending his days. She turned down the street that led up the hill to where the Rockwell Mansion was situated. That had to be where George and Baxter were holed up. She was curious as to why and hoped he wouldn't resent her checking on him, but friends popped in on friends.

The big, old house looked just the same on the outside—somewhat neglected, lonely, and rather sad. The place had such a look of abandonment that Willow doubted that George really was inside. But she rang the doorbell and waited. When no one answered, she tried again, then tested the door to find that it was unlocked, which felt rather un-George-like. Was something wrong?

"George?" she called out as she tentatively went in. "Are you here?" She looked around the elegant foyer, surprised to see it now filled with all sorts of old furnishings, cardboard boxes, and general clutter. With no order or appearance of a plan, it looked as if someone had blown up a storage unit.

She peeked in the living room, only to see more pieces of furniture and clutter piled all around. George must've gotten over his attic anxiety. She called out again, but he still didn't answer. He was probably in the attic, hopefully not trapped and buried in debris. She went up the stairs, pausing briefly to admire the family photographs along the stairway wall. His grandmother had a good eye for photography. These photos were real treasures, and Willow felt relieved he hadn't removed them. But she did wonder what he was up to. Had he decided to sell his family home after all? Although it made sense to do so, she felt sad to think of him letting it go. She knew he loved the old house . . . or at least the memories.

"George?" she called from the third floor. Then she spotted an open door and a steep wooden stairway that had to lead to the attic. She was about to holler again when she saw George, dusty and dirty with cobwebs in his hair, coming down with an old rocking horse in his arms.

"Willow!" he exclaimed. "What are you doing here?"

"Sorry, I just let myself in. But I was worried about you," she confessed. "I stopped by your house and Lorna said you were—"

"How did she know I was up here?" He dusted his hands off on his equally dusty trousers.

"She just said you were gone, that you go out each day and take Baxter with you. I sort of guessed the rest."

"Oh." He nodded a bit stiffly. "Well, how have you been?"

"Very busy." As she followed him and the rocking horse down the two flights of stairs, she gave a brief description of her overly full week. "Looks as if you've been rather occupied too."

He set down the toy. "Yes. I decided it was time to get busy and clean this place up. It's way overdue."

"So do you plan to sell the house?"

He rubbed a hand through his uncharacteristically messy hair. "I'm not sure yet. I just want to thin out some of the junk. I've set aside a pile for Josie. I planned to call her in a day or two to come look through the items."

"Do you need any help with this?" She tried not to grimace. "It looks a bit overwhelming."

He sighed. "I've actually considered calling a dump truck to haul it all away."

"No." She firmly shook her head. "There are obviously a lot of great things here, George. But it looks like too much for just one person. You know that Josie was eager to help.

And I'll bet Collin would help too. He's got Monday and Tuesday off."

George frowned at the crowded foyer. "The trouble is, I honestly don't know what to do with all this stuff. I try to sort it out, but then I get frustrated." His expression looked frantic. "I just wish it would all go away."

"You should have an estate sale, George. Maybe you could use the proceeds for fixing up that kitchen and—"

"I can't do that. I'm no salesman. It's been hard enough bringing this stuff down. I can't organize a sale. I have no idea how to price this junk."

"It's not all junk," she protested. "I'm sure there are some valuable items here."

"I removed the valuables years ago," he said. "My grandmother's jewelry and important papers and all that sort of thing. I worried the house could be burglarized. Although that never happened."

"Even so, you don't want to throw away items that you could sell instead. I worked at an antique sale back in college, so I know a thing or two about what's valuable and what's not." She held up a finger. "And I have a good friend, maybe you know her—Betty Harris. She used to have an antique shop here in town. She's retired now, but I bet we could recruit her help."

"I don't know . . . doesn't sound worth it to me." George looked so overwhelmed that Willow's heart went out to him.

"You need help, George. It's too much for one person. Let Josie and Collin and me help. We can recruit a few others too." She glanced toward the packed living room. "We should start by selecting what pieces you'd want to keep."

"I don't want any of it! Not a single stick."

"Nothing?" This was worse than she thought. George was losing it.

He waved both hands. "I just want it to all go away."

Willow felt worried. It was as if something in George had snapped—or was about to snap. "George," she said slowly. "Do you believe that I'm your friend?"

He nodded somberly.

"Then, can you trust me?"

He shrugged. "I think so."

"How about if you let me organize your estate sale? I've been a businesswoman for more than twenty years. I can handle this for you."

He looked close to tears now. "It's too much to ask."

"I'm your friend, George." Willow spotted Baxter cowering between an old trunk and a rocking chair. "I think you and Baxter should go home. You take a nice, long shower, and let me start working on this in an organized manner. I'll get Josie and Collin over here to help with the heavy stuff."

"I can't just leave you—"

"Just take a break, George. Come back whenever you feel like it."

"I guess I could use a break." He removed a grimy handkerchief to wipe his brow. Then he handed her the keys, loaded Baxter into his cat carrier, and left. Of course, as soon as he was gone, Willow wondered . . . Had she bitten off more than she could chew? But she was used to challenges. In fact, she rather enjoyed them. It was something that had often frustrated Asher. But after a few years, they learned to give each other their space and their freedom. In the end, it had strengthened their marriage. Perhaps helping George like this would strengthen their friendship.

—•••—

First Willow called Josie, asking her to come lend a hand. "And you can collect some treasures while you're here. George has made a nice little pile for you to choose from." Then she called Collin, explaining how overwhelmed George was right now. "I know you work until two today, but if you feel like helping afterward, I could really use your muscle." After he agreed, she asked him to drive her car over so they could load some things into it.

Next Willow slowly strolled through the maze of boxes and furniture, going from room to room and trying to put together a plan for an estate sale. Finding a tablet and pen in what appeared to have been a den—although it was so cluttered it was hard to tell—she began to make notes. Then she called her friend Betty and explained the situation.

"An estate sale at the Rockwell Mansion?" Betty said with enthusiasm. "How exciting. When do you think you'll have it?"

"Well, I'm up here right now trying to organize, but it's a bit chaotic. I've enlisted my kids to help. Hopefully for the next couple of days."

"My granddaughter, Savannah, is staying with me this summer—and complaining of boredom. Perhaps she and I could come over to help. I know I'd love to get a peek at the place. I might even be in the market for a few things myself."

Willow arranged for them to come on Tuesday afternoon. "That'll give us a chance to bring some order to the place. It's on the verge of dangerous right now."

"When do you expect to be ready for the sale?" Betty asked.

"To be honest, I can't devote a whole lot of time to this project," Willow told her. "I'd sort of like to have the sale as soon as possible."

"Next weekend?" Betty asked. "There are a number of sales in town. You could probably piggyback on the traffic. If you like, I could get you an ad in the newspaper and onto Craigslist and whatnot."

"That'd be wonderful, Betty. And good motivation for us to get it all ready in time." Willow glanced around the foyer, wondering if next weekend was too soon. Then she remembered the desperation on George's face. Perhaps sooner was better.

As she began to sift and sort and move things about, she wondered if George was going to regret his decision to get rid of everything. Surely some of these things had sentimental value. She went into the living room, spying the Danish Modern furniture pushed way to the back of the room. George had appeared to like those pieces, even if they didn't quite go with all the dark floors and woodwork and heavy drapes. If this house was lightened up some, they might possibly work well in it.

Willow made an executive decision. As George's "trusted friend," she would attempt to save the items that looked like they might still work in this house . . . as well as anything, like the family photos, that had sentimental value. She would find a large room where they could all be safely stored. Then if George didn't want them, they wouldn't be difficult to be rid of. In fact, Willow would happily purchase the Danish Modern pieces from him. She still had one apartment to restore and furnish as a rental.

By Sunday evening, after just one relatively short squabble,

Collin and Josie had managed to get the rest of the attic emptied, and the "blueprint" that Willow had created for the estate sale was slowly shaping up. Although there was still much to be done, the place was beginning to show signs of order, and Willow knew it was quitting time.

"How about pizza?" Willow asked after Collin and Josie set a bureau in the large downstairs master bedroom where they were putting all the bedroom pieces.

"Sounds good to me." Josie went over to the corner where George had started setting items aside for her. "Do I really get to keep all these?" she asked Willow.

"George said they were for you. You can take some now and more tomorrow."

"Cool." Josie picked up a small wooden chair. "I can't wait to hit this with paint."

"Does Mr. Emerson really want to get rid of everything?" Collin asked as Willow locked the front door.

"He said he does. But I think he's stressed. I want us to go over everything carefully," she told them. "If you see something that you think he might regret letting go, we'll just set it in the conservatory for now."

By the next morning, George felt guilty for having allowed Willow to take over for him at his grandparents' house. But it was almost as if he had no choice. It felt as if someone had pulled the plug on him. Even as he ate a bowl of cold cereal, the simple weight of lifting his spoon felt exhausting. After he rinsed his bowl, leaving it unwashed in the sink, he sat down in his easy chair and, with Baxter snuggled in his lap, fell promptly asleep. He didn't wake up until eleven.

As he puttered around his house, forcing himself to wash his breakfast things, George wondered if he was seriously ill . . . possibly dying. His last annual checkup hadn't been quite a year ago, but there had been no concerns. The doctor had proclaimed George in "excellent health." Even so, George called to schedule another checkup for as soon as possible. After the phone call, he felt exhausted again. So he went outside to his hammock. He picked up his self-help book and read, for what must've been the fourth time, the first chapter—then took another nap.

When George woke up, he considered calling Willow to see how things were going. But the truth was, he did not want to know. If she had changed her mind—realizing it was too much to take on—he didn't even care. He would simply call in some sort of removal service to clear it all out. Maybe they'd do it in exchange for everything that needed to be taken away.

By the time George went to bed on Monday night, he told himself that he'd check on Willow the next day. After all, it was irresponsible of him to just abandon the process that he'd begun. Except that every step of the way had been excruciatingly painful. Seeing old pieces of his life—his brother's life, his mother's life, his grandparents' lives, and even the ancestors that he'd never known—it had all taken its toll on him. As if it had drained him completely and now he was bone-dry and a summer wind could come along and just blow him away. He truly believed his only escape, the only way to survive this ordeal, was to get every last thing out of that house. Like an exorcism of sorts. But he hadn't the strength to do it.

On Tuesday morning, George didn't feel any different.

He still felt drained and hopeless. In fact, it was almost as if he was now shackled to his house. To step out of his little bungalow would surely invite calamity. Perhaps his heart would give out completely. He picked up the phone several times throughout the day, thinking he would call Willow and ask how it was going. But then he would set the receiver back down again. It was just too much. Too hard. Too painful. Perhaps tomorrow would be better.

twenty-four

Although Willow was somewhat relieved that George continued to keep a low profile while they sifted and sorted through several generations of accumulation, she felt a bit of concern as well. It didn't seem like him to just let this all go and not even show up and inquire how it was going. She'd known he was stressed and tired, but he'd had three days to recuperate by now. As she carried a cardboard box of smelly old clothes out to the Dumpster that Betty had suggested was necessary for those items that no one in their right mind could honestly want, Willow considered calling George and inviting him to come see their progress. Really, he should be relieved and impressed to see what they'd accomplished in just a few days.

Betty's granddaughter, Savannah, was a real godsend. Energetic and smart about antiques and collectibles, the nineteen-year-old girl had even managed to turn Collin's head with her good-natured teasing and flirting. Or at least she'd distracted him from his disturbing obsession over Marissa. Savannah had spent most of Monday and Tuesday here. Willow wondered if it was due to Collin. But he was working at the bookstore on Wednesday and Savannah still showed up.

"I want to have my own resale business someday," she told Willow as they cleaned and priced miscellaneous kitchen items, setting them out on tables and counters for the sale. "If I thought I was closer to setting up my own shop, I'd probably want to keep a lot of this stuff. But I have to finish school first." She held up a seventies Corning Ware casserole. "Besides, I know that you can find this stuff at estate sales all over the country—and who knows what will be hot by then?"

"You're a wise young woman."

"But I did have some good finds," Savannah reminded her. "You're sure that Mr. Emerson won't mind?"

"He said he wanted everything gone," Willow told her. "And for the work you've done, it sounds like a fair payment. But just to be safe, I plan to check with him this evening."

"Well, I'm glad you're saving a few things for him." Savannah set an old Crock-Pot on the kitchen table. "Just in case he changes his mind. All that Scandinavian furniture you stashed in the conservatory is so cool. I'd love to keep that myself. Well, if I had a place to store it."

"Where do these go?" Josie came into the kitchen with a box of the photographs from the stairway wall. "Just so you know, the conservatory is pretty full."

"Put them in my SUV," Willow told her. "I'm hoping George will want to hang some in his bungalow. He's got a lot of bare walls." Willow had already stashed some of the more personal items from George's and Alex's childhood bedrooms in the attic, including an old violin they'd found in George's room and a guitar in Alex's. Then, worried that some treasures could've still been missed, she'd asked Collin to carefully go through both rooms, salvaging any items that he felt that George might want saved. From what she could see, Collin had done an excellent job too. Several interesting boxes were stored in the attic with "save for George" written on them. All in all, they were in good shape for the estate sale, which would run Friday through the weekend. But first, Willow wanted to speak to George.

After Savannah and Josie left, and Willow was turning off the lights and locking the doors, she decided it was time to pay George a little visit. She felt slightly irked that he'd remained away for this long. And slightly guilty that she hadn't attempted to call him before now. Anyway, it was time to talk. She would use the delivery of the photographs as her excuse to invade his space.

George looked somewhat pale as he opened his front door. Willow studied him for a moment, then, while carrying the box of photos inside, she inquired about his health.

"The truth is I've been a little under the weather," he said quietly.

She set down the box and turned to look more closely at him. He really did have a wan look about him. "Have you been to the doctor?"

"I have an appointment on Friday afternoon."

"Oh?" She pushed a loose strand of hair away from her forehead.

He looked down at the box. "What's that?"

"Those old black-and-white photos that your grand-mother took. You know, from the stairway." She pulled out a photo of Alex and George. "I thought you might like these here in your bungalow."

He took the photo from her, gazing at it with a hard-to-read expression. "Thank you." He set it on the coffee table next to the vase and some rather wilted-looking sunflowers.

"I think these are ready to toss." She picked up the vase, carrying it to the kitchen where she tossed the flowers into the trash, but she was surprised to see the sink full of dirty dishes. Without commenting on this, she rinsed the vase and set it aside.

"I—uh—I've gotten behind on my daily chores," George said with obvious embarrassment.

"Well, you're not feeling well." She resisted the urge to touch his forehead. "I'm glad you're going to the doctor." She gave him a weak smile. "I also wanted to let you know that we're almost ready for the estate sale. Now, don't worry, you don't need to lift a finger. It's all organized and I've got people set up to help and—"

"I'll gladly pay them."

"That's not necessary, George. But I do want to be sure you're on board with the way you can recompense them." She quickly explained how Savannah and Betty had picked out a few things for compensation and George readily agreed. "Josie is delighted with the pieces you saved for her. And Collin has set aside a bunch of Audubon and nature books that he'd like to keep. But if you don't agree—"

"He's welcome to any of the books," George said quickly. "I already have all the books I want here." He nodded to his cabinet.

"So you're really certain that you want the house completely cleared out?" she asked.

He simply nodded.

Willow wanted to ask him if he was dying, but couldn't

270

think of a polite way to say it. "Do you think you'll sell the house?"

He shrugged. "I really don't know."

"If you were to sell it," she said tentatively, "do you think it would be worthwhile to freshen it up some? Perhaps some lighter paint? Remove some of the old, dark wallpaper? After spending so much time there these past few days, I think there are some ways the place could really be brought back to life. And I'm sure you'd get a better price for it."

"It is very dark, isn't it?" He frowned. "My grandmother used to always say that very thing. But my grandfather grew up in the house and didn't see the need to change anything."

"I have a designer friend—a customer at the gallery," Willow said. "Donna's got excellent taste. She might be able to give you some suggestions. I could give her a call if you like."

"Sure. That's a good idea." George sat down on the sofa with a deep sigh.

"Well, I can see you're not feeling too well." Willow bent down to give Baxter a couple of good strokes. "Baxter, you take good care of your master now." She glanced up at George. "Is there anything I can do to help? Wash your dishes or—"

"No, no, you've done enough, Willow." He waved a hand. "I think I just need to rest some . . . for the time being. I'll see what the doctor says on Friday."

"Let me know how that goes." She went to the door. "And don't worry about the estate sale." She smiled. "Maybe we'll make enough to cover the expenses for some renovations at your grandparents' house."

George looked doubtful. "Just getting things cleared out is worth a lot."

Willow told him to take it easy then let herself out. But as she drove home, she felt concerned. George did not look well. And having seen Asher going downhill after his pancreatic cancer diagnosis, Willow wondered if she was about to go through something like that again. Could she take it? She felt unsure. And yet . . . George was so alone.

twenty-five

Willow didn't get a chance to talk to George again until Friday evening. Instead of just popping in on him, she decided to call. That would probably be less stressful for him. "How was your doctor's appointment?" she asked gently.

"I'm not sure," he said in a weary tone. "He didn't find anything specifically wrong with me, but he took a lot of blood tests and whatnot. I suppose I won't hear about the results for a week or so."

"How are you feeling?" she asked.

"About the same." He let out a low sigh that reminded her of Eeyore.

"I was thinking of sending Josie over to give you a hand."

"No need for that."

"Well, she might like to. Anyway, I wanted to let you know the estate sale went very well today. I honestly think you'll make enough to cover some of the renovations at the house. Also, I spoke to my friend Donna—the designer I told you about. She would absolutely love to get her hands on your house. She wants to pop in tomorrow to look around. During the sale. Do you mind?"

"No, no . . . that's probably a good plan. It's sensible to have some improvements made. I'm afraid I've been negligent."

"Not really. The house is in good, solid shape, George. You've maintained it well. It simply needs some updates to bring it into the current millennium."

"Well, I did like your suggestions for the kitchen renovation. Perhaps you could tell your friend Donna your ideas. And I agree it needs some lightening up in the other rooms. Perhaps you could communicate that to Donna for me. If it's not too much trouble."

"Not at all," she assured him. "I'm happy to help."

"You're a good friend." He sounded weary . . . and sad.

"Well, I won't keep you. I hope you're eating healthy and taking good care of yourself."

"The doctor suggested some vitamin supplements. I picked them up on my way home."

"Well, let me know if you need anything. And take care to get better," she said brightly. But as she hung up, she wondered. Was George seriously ill? She wanted to be a good friend to him . . . but it scared her too. What if whatever he had was terminal? It was painful to help someone who was dying. She wasn't sure she could take it again. But she was helping him with his house. And it hadn't been easy neglecting the gallery this week. At least she had a full crew of employees now—and sales were picking up. And Savannah, who had shown excellent people skills at the estate sale, had even expressed interest in some part-time work at the gallery. Naturally, it had made Josie a bit jealous.

But like Willow had reassured her, Josie was an artist, not a salesperson.

• • •

On Saturday morning as they drove over to the estate sale, Willow tried to convince Josie that the best way to help George might be to pay him a visit. "He sounded very down last night," Willow explained. "And he might even need help with his housework."

"Is he really sick?" Josie frowned. "Like contagious?"

"I'm not sure what's wrong exactly, but he's definitely not himself. I doubt that it's contagious. But I thought maybe you could pick him up some chicken stock at the natural food store. It's made the old-fashioned way and is supposed to be really good for whatever ails you." She parked her car then handed Josie some money. "You go ahead and heat up the stock and insist he have some."

"You really think he'll do what I say?" Josie looked doubtful as they got out of the car. "He can be pretty stubborn."

"If he's feeling as bad as he sounds, I think it's worth a try."

"Okay." Josie pocketed the cash.

"Try to cheer him up," Willow said as she unlocked the front door of the Rockwell house. "You know, he's got a bunch of really good old movies. Maybe you could ask to watch some with him."

"That's a lot to expect, Mom. It's not like I'm a miracle worker."

Willow smiled. "Just do your best." As Willow went inside the house, she wondered about George's recent disconnect with this place. It was as if he'd handed it over to her

275

to manage. But if he was seriously ill, that probably made sense. He might be concerned about wrapping up his affairs. Of course, the thought of this simply filled her with fresh dread. But customers began to trickle in and, since she was the only one there to assist them, she had little time to fret about George.

Betty and Savannah arrived by ten, so Willow busied herself with tidying things up and rearranging. It was impressive how many things had already been sold. Hopefully they'd have the place nearly cleared out by the end of this sale—and hopefully with enough money to make a good dint in the cost of the improvements needed. Willow had already started to list her ideas for George's house in a little notebook.

When her designer friend arrived, Willow was ready for her. She started by giving her a full tour of the house. "The kitchen is the biggest challenge." She explained her vision for it. "And beyond that it'll mostly be painting—light neutral tones to brighten and freshen the place up."

"What about the woodwork? Will we be painting that?"

Willow considered this. "I think some of the worn pieces— like baseboard and window trim—might look fresher with some paint. But I think the stair banister and the doors and a few other carved pieces should remain natural wood."

"A lot of people are painting all the woodwork in these old homes. It really gives them a more contemporary look."

"I know." Willow ran her hand over the dining room doors. "But I think these are too beautiful to cover."

"So are you in charge of this project?" Donna removed her glasses to peer curiously at Willow.

"Well, yes." Willow felt uncertain. Perhaps she'd been mistaken to ask Donna to consult on this.

"Are you and Mr. Emerson, uh, involved?"

"We are very good friends," Willow said. "He asked me to handle this for him. He's been a little under the weather."

"So, if I agreed to take this on, I'd report to you? Does this mean you'll oversee everything? The bathrooms, the finishing choices, the furnishings, everything?"

Willow frowned. "To be honest, I'm not sure that George is ready to redo everything in here, Donna. I'm afraid we could be jumping the gun. I only asked you up here as a friend . . . to talk about ideas."

"It sounds like you already have your ideas." Donna looked disappointed. "This house could be so beautiful—done right. If you just want to do it piecemeal, well, at least it will be an improvement. But nothing like it could be."

"I know." Willow nodded. "But, you see, George is very easily overwhelmed. And like I said, he's not feeling too well right now. I think the best plan might be to proceed slowly."

"Well, you're a friend." Donna smiled. "So how about if I give you the number of my favorite contractor. Cliff Grant has more than twenty years' experience in this town." She elbowed Willow. "And he's single."

"And he's good at kitchen remodels?"

"The best. Anyway, you get the wheels rolling, and if George decides to take it to the next level, you give me a call. Okay?"

Willow smiled. "Yes. That sounds perfect. Thank you."

"I've heard that George Emerson is a bit of a character." Donna winked. "He's been sitting on this gorgeous property for years. I'm impressed that you've gotten him to budge on it at all, Willow. Good luck."

Willow thanked her, and then, feeling overwhelmed, she

put Cliff Grant's number in her phone while she walked Donna to the front door. Even though George had asked her to handle these improvements, Willow felt uneasy. Yet as she looked at the big old house, which was steadily emptying— and she knew the profits from sales were adding up—she felt eager to see this place taken to the next stage. Perhaps it would be just what George needed to begin feeling better. Maybe he'd wanted to do it himself, but had become overwhelmed while emptying the attic. To be honest, she felt her interest in working on the Rockwell Mansion was somewhat selfish too. It would be just plain fun! As an artist, Willow had always entertained an interest in interior design. She'd taken charge of all the improvements in their Sausalito home—and it had been a pure delight. Plus, knowing that the gallery was in good shape . . . well, why not?

So Willow went out in the front yard and called the contractor, explaining the project and asking for him to stop by at his convenience. But like Donna, when he heard it was the Rockwell Mansion, he was eager to come see it. "How about Monday morning?" he asked.

"That'd be great. Hopefully, we'll have everything cleared out by then." She explained about the estate sale, and he reassured her he could see past that. As she hung up, she decided that he sounded like a very nice man. And if he was as good as Donna had insinuated, this should be a piece of cake.

* * *

By late in the day Saturday, Willow could hardly believe how cleared out the Rockwell house had become. "It almost seems a waste of time to have the sale tomorrow," she told Savannah as they were closing it down.

"But some people said they're coming back," Savannah said. "They expect everything to be half off."

"Oh, that's right." Willow turned off the lights. "I forgot that your grandmother put that in the ad."

"So I plan to be here," Savannah assured her. "Collin said he was coming over to help too. Don't tell him, but I'm going to ask him to go out with me afterward."

Willow smiled. "Good for you." She waved as Savannah got onto her bike, thanking her again for her help. Even though Savannah had been "paid" in the form of some collectibles, Willow felt like the girl's contribution was probably worth more than the secondhand items she'd chosen. But she appeared to be enjoying herself. Not only that, she'd impressed Willow enough to secure a part-time job in the gallery this summer. Hopefully it wouldn't go south the way it had with Marissa.

Willow wasn't going to worry about that. Right now, she was more concerned about George. She hadn't heard anything from Josie and hoped that didn't mean that George had rejected her offer to help. Willow planned to drop by on her way home. If George had refused Josie's assistance, Willow wasn't opposed to forcing her way in and taking over. But when she got there, she was surprised to see that Josie was lounging on the sofa and George and Baxter were in his chair—watching a black-and-white movie on the old-fashioned television. And the house was a wreck.

"Sorry to barge in." Willow tried not to stare at George's wrinkled and stained shirt—or the pile of junk food wrappers splayed across the coffee table. "I just wanted to see how you're doing."

George shrugged, but remained slouched in his chair. "I think I'm better. We're watching *Bright Eyes*."

Willow blinked at the old-fashioned TV. "Is that Shirley Temple?"

"Shhh!" Josie scowled at them.

"She'd never seen Shirley Temple before," George whispered. "This is our third one. Do you want to sit down? It's barely begun."

"No, no, that's okay." Willow remained by the door. "I'm tired and in need of a good long shower."

Josie shushed them again, so Willow gave a little finger wave and slipped out. But as she went out to her car, she felt dumbfounded. Not that Josie and George were watching Shirley Temple films together. That was rather sweet. But seeing George in those dirty clothes with messes all over the place . . . well, that was pretty concerning. Especially since she'd sent her daughter over there to help out. To be fair, Josie would never earn a Good Housekeeping Seal. Still, it was somewhat disturbing. It was almost as if George had simply given up.

But why?

- - -

Willow was just sweeping the worn wood floors in the spacious Rockwell living room when she heard someone at the front door. "It's me—Cliff Grant," a man called out. "The door was open so—"

"Yes, yes, please come in." Willow hurried to the foyer and introduced herself. As she shook his hand, she felt pleasantly surprised to see that Cliff Grant was quite good-looking— tall, dark, and handsome. And hadn't Donna mentioned that he was single? Willow guessed that he was probably in his forties—not that age differences had ever concerned her much.

"This is quite a place." He gazed around the foyer.

"I really appreciate you coming on such short notice."

"No problem." He gave the banister a firm shake, but it didn't budge. "I've never been inside before, but I've always admired this house."

"They call it the Rockwell *Mansion*," she said. "But it's not the largest house on the hill anymore. I think it's just a little over four thousand square feet."

He ran a hand along the wood wainscoting by the stairs. "Do you know when it was built?"

"Late 1800s." She led him to the living room. "By the same family that started the Rockwell lumber mill."

He looked at the dark wallpaper. "This looks almost as old as the house."

"Yes, it's pretty bad. We're thinking it should be removed and the walls painted. And this baseboard too. And the wood floors need refinishing." She explained her idea to preserve some of the original woodwork and doors, and he agreed it was a good plan, making notes as she led him to the dining room.

"I don't like seeing the original character stripped from some of these old beauties," he told her. "I understand the need for livability, but history should be respected. By the way, is this on the historic register?"

"No, although I'm sure it could be."

"Well, that's actually a relief when it comes to renovating. Less hoops for everyone to jump through."

"Even though it's not registered, it seems wise not to do the sorts of changes that would prohibit that in the future. Just one more reason to give it a light touch."

"Yes, I've seen old homes that have been modernized to

create great rooms, and then they're listed for sale and the buyer wants everything back to the historic blueprint."

She briefly described her vision for brightening up the dining room, then led him to the kitchen—where Cliff broke into laughter. "What the heck happened in here?"

She explained about George's grandmother. "Apparently she wanted to lighten up and modernize the whole house, but her husband put his foot down. Except for in here. Mrs. Rockwell really went to town in this room."

He picked up the blue wall phone. "Hello? The eighties are calling—they want their kitchen back."

Willow chuckled. "I guess her husband was right to rein her in."

Cliff opened a cupboard door, letting it close with a bang. "I have a cabinet guy who can make something that's both functional and respectful of the era."

"That sounds wonderful." Willow explained her ideas for tall cabinets and soapstone or marble countertops. "And I think some sort of stone floor would be nice."

"Nicer than this vinyl." Cliff made more notes then turned to her. "So are you handling all the design decisions? Or hiring Donna for that?"

"Well, we don't want to go all out at first," she explained. "George Emerson is the owner and he's, well, rather frugal. But I have an art background and some design experience, so he's entrusted me with the decisions."

Cliff looked more closely at her now. "I don't mean to be nosy, but are you and George a couple?"

"No, no, we're just good friends. I'm helping him with the house."

"And I assume you own that new art gallery in town?"

"Yes. That's mine."

"Nice." He nodded with appreciation. "Show me more of this place."

She gave him the full tour, telling him generally what needed to be done, and he continued to take notes. Finally they were back in the foyer. "I'll work up an estimate for you," he told her. "In the meantime, you can select your cabinets and finishes and paint colors and all that. And it would help my painters if you came in here and actually marked, with painter's tape, which wood surfaces you want left alone. Be very specific so there's no chance for confusion."

"Right. I can do that." She pointed to some leftover piles of stuff. "And we'll get all this cleared out—"

"I can have my demolition guys haul that out when they demo the kitchen. They'll send anything worth recycling to the Habitat thrift store."

"That's wonderful." She opened the doors to the conservatory. "This is the only room that probably doesn't need anything done. All the glass in here is in fabulous shape. As far as I can see it's never leaked. I'm using the space to store furnishings that I think can be reused after the house is updated."

"Looks like a nice space."

She closed the doors then led him to the second and third floors. "As you can see, it's mostly about paint up here. The wood floors are in good shape."

"Any updates in the bathrooms?" he asked.

"I know the tile and fixtures are old-fashioned, but they're handsome and seem to work. For now, I think we just lighten the rooms with paint."

She led him back down, wrapping up the tour.

"How about the exterior?" he asked as they went outside.

"Well, I'm not sure," she confessed. "I do think the trim could use some paint. It looks like it's crackling in spots." As they went around the perimeter of the house, Cliff tested the bricks and a few other things, finally deciding that the wood trim was probably the only thing that really needed help right now. Willow expressed relief, admitting that George would probably be overwhelmed when he saw the bid.

"We'll just stick to the basics," he assured her. "I can probably get back to you in a couple of days." He smiled. "Want me to drop it by your gallery?"

"Thank you." She shook his hand again. "Any idea of when you can start?"

He scratched his head. "Well, if I thought the place was going to get really fixed up—I'd probably ask you about putting it in the Tour of Homes. That's the second week of August. It'd be amazing to have a house like this on the tour."

Willow was surprised. "You could have it done that soon?"

"Well, you're not doing a whole lot here. I could probably move some things around in my schedule—I mean if we were going to include this on the tour. But the place would have to be really fixed up."

"What do you mean by *really fixed up*?"

"You know, like a showplace. Furnishings and everything. I've never had a house of this caliber on the tour before. And I'd gladly pull out all the stops just to have my name on it."

"What if I got it all staged and looking great?" Willow asked. "I could bring in art from my gallery, save back some interesting furnishings. And maybe a few other tricks to make it sparkle and shine."

"Well, if you can do that, I'll put it into full gear to get it done on time." He frowned. "As long as my cabinet guy comes through. You better go talk to him ASAP." He pulled a business card from his wallet and handed it to her. "If Ross knows it's the Rockwell Mansion, and that it would be on the tour, he might make it happen."

"This is exciting," she told him. "I'll do my best . . . if you will."

"And if you folks are considering selling this place, it'd be a great opportunity to show it off." He nodded toward the yard. "But the outdoor space should be spiffed up some too."

Willow promised to discuss it with George, and Cliff promised to get back to her within twenty-four hours. This was all going much faster than she'd anticipated. But it would be worth the effort. The question was, how would George react? As she dialed George's phone number, she prepared her speech.

It took a few minutes to convey the information, but to her relief—as well as her concern—George still sounded rather detached from the whole thing. "I trust you, Willow. Whatever it takes to get it fixed up and ready to sell. That's fine. I appreciate the help."

"But it might take more than the estate-sale money to cover the expenses. I don't have the bid yet. I asked him to keep it minimal."

"I have the funds needed for renovations," he assured her in a somewhat flat tone. "And I want to pay you for your time too, Willow. This isn't charity."

"I understand, but I'm actually enjoying this, George. And I agree with the contractor—it'd be fun to have your house on the Tour of Homes. And it could help if you decide to sell it."

"Well, I suppose that's a prudent plan. The house has sat idle for too long. As you mentioned, it's been *sad*."

Willow felt a bit guilty. She had called it sad. And now it appeared George was sad too. "How are you doing?" she asked quietly.

"I, uh, I'm not sure."

"I suppose you haven't heard back from the doctor yet?"

"No, nothing yet. He said the end of the week."

"Well, don't worry about your house, George. It's getting the best help possible. I think you're going to be impressed."

"Yes . . . I'm sure."

She talked a bit longer, but George sounded tired . . . or bored . . . or maybe just plain sick. She told him to take it easy, then hung up. Poor George.

twenty-six

Willow got thoroughly into the thick of renovations at the Rockwell Mansion. Not only did she love making the design decisions and putting together a plan with Ross, the cabinet maker, she was not opposed to rolling up her sleeves and helping with the manual labor. By the end of the week, she'd successfully removed wallpaper from the living room and foyer. "If I were to have a second career, I think it would be something like this," she told Cliff as she turned off the steam machine. "It's so fun watching this house coming back to life." She pointed to the bare wall. "Even without paint, it looks so much lighter and brighter. Like the house is getting happier."

He chuckled. "That'd be a good slogan for your new restoration company. *Making homes happier.*"

She nodded. "I like it."

"I just stopped by to check on a couple of things. Are you taking a lunch break today?" He looked at his watch. "It's past one."

She dropped a sheet of soggy wallpaper into the garbage pail. "Come to think of it, I am hungry."

"Want to join me?" He smiled pleasantly. "We can discuss some kitchen decisions."

"A business lunch?" She frowned down at her stained overalls and flip-flops. "I'm not exactly dressed for success."

He chuckled. "It won't matter at the place where I'm taking you. It's come as you are. All the construction dudes eat there."

"Sounds like my kind of place."

Cliff's pickup was one of those where Willow almost needed a stepladder to get into the cab. Fortunately, Cliff gave her a hand. As he drove he told her that he'd just met with Ross. "He's off to a great start, but he wanted to double-check on a few things." He handed her a short list. She'd just finished reading through it when he parked in front of Dot's Diner. "This is the place," he announced. He hurried around to open her door and help her down. "They've got the best burgers in town."

He was just leading her into the fifties-style restaurant when Willow noticed George across the street—staring directly at her. She waved to him, but without responding, he simply turned and hurried away. Although she felt slighted, she was glad to see him out and about. Hopefully that meant he was feeling better. But it was disheartening that he'd ignored her.

⁘

George didn't know why he felt so angry as he walked home from the doctor's office. He really should've been feeling happy that the doctor had given him such a clean bill of health. Especially since George had felt certain that he was dying. "Stress can make you feel very unwell," the doctor

had told him. "I recommend you find some activities to al-
leviate your stress."

"Such as?" He'd attempted to conceal his irritation at the
doctor's suggestion. After all, George was retired. He had a
hammock and a cat. Why should he be "stressed"?

"Yoga. Reading. Music. Walks. Gardening. Whatever helps
you to relax and enjoy life." He'd smiled as if to say, *That's
it . . . next appointment, please.* So George had felt miffed
as he'd exited the medical office. Then to see Willow being
helped out of the big black pickup with a contractor's name
on the side of it . . . well, that hadn't helped any.

As George stormed through town he assumed that Cliff
Grant Construction was the company working on his grandparents' house. Even though George had given Willow free
rein there, he now wondered if that was a mistake. Not so
much because of the house. Oddly enough, he didn't feel
too concerned about that. But he did not like the way it had
looked as the tall, dark-haired man had helped Willow out
of that pickup. It looked far too friendly and intimate. And
unless George was mistaken, the man was younger. What
did Willow think she was doing?

By the time George got home, he felt a bit silly for his
earlier anxieties. First of all, the doctor could be right. Perhaps George did need some stress-relieving activities. And
besides that, it was none of his business what Willow did in
her spare time. Or any of her time. They'd made it perfectly
clear they were only friends. Why should he feel so jealous
of the handsome contractor?

George considered the doctor's recommended activities.
Well, George had already tried tai chi—and wasn't sure he
wanted to go again. He read daily and would continue to do

so. As for music . . . well, Simon and Garfunkel had nearly done him in. That left walks, which he'd just done. And gardening. He glanced out the back window to see his grass looked long and shaggy—with dozens of dandelions in full bloom. When had he last mowed? Or weeded? As he went outside, he wondered what his neighbors must think. George would've said something to his renters if they'd allowed their yards to become this overgrown and weedy.

"Hello, George." Lorna came over to the fence just as he wheeled out the mower. "Catching up on yard work today?"

"Uh, yes." He nodded nervously. "I've been, uh, a little under the weather."

"Feeling better?" she asked.

"I, uh, I think so."

"How about I give you a hand?" she offered. "I'll be right—"

"That's okay. I can handle—"

"I insist," she cut him off. "I'll just grab my garden gloves and pop around to the side gate." Before he could stop her, she was on her way. As he went to open the gate, he thought perhaps it wasn't a bad idea to accept her help. The grass was so overgrown it would take a lot of time to get it all raked up. And despite his doctor's proclamation of good health, George still felt weary. It took several pulls to start the mower and then George felt slightly winded. Maybe this was what it was like to be *retired*—first you became tired, and then you got tired all over again!

— • • • —

Willow could hardly believe that it was already Final Friday art walk night again. Hadn't they just had one? Still, it felt rather nice to be cleaned up, dressed up, and ready to greet guests in her gallery. Between Leslie and Joel and Haley and Savannah, they were well staffed. Not only that, but both Collin and Josie had mentioned their plans to make a showing. Collin probably just wanted a chance to see Savannah. And Josie hoped to garner some interest in the three pieces of folk art, which was what Willow was calling Josie's creations, that were now on display. Hopefully Josie would heed Willow's advice to "go easy" tonight. "No one wants a pushy salesperson," Willow had warned her. "Especially on an art walk evening. Just have fun and talk about the art process if someone asks. If they're interested, they'll make the next move."

Willow's only plan tonight was to enjoy herself—and her guests. Thanks to Haley's boyfriend, Nick, a classical guitarist, the music was covered. Leslie had arranged for the refreshments. Everything and everyone was in place as Willow entered the gallery. The music was light and airy, the aroma of a blood-orange candle was clean and sweet, and the food table looked inviting.

"You've all done a fabulous job," she told her crew shortly before the gallery was officially opened. "Thank you so much. It's very reassuring to know the gallery is in such good hands."

Willow welcomed tonight's featured artist, an older woman named Belle whose oil landscapes were an old-world sort of gorgeous. "Thank you for joining us tonight," she told Belle. "It's a perfect summer evening. Hopefully we'll get lots of traffic. Enjoy yourself."

It wasn't long before the gallery began to fill with people. Some were obviously just there for the eats, but some were valued customers, and others were just vacationing in the area. To Willow's relief, Josie, dressed in another one of Willow's hand-me-downs, acted fairly laid-back. And Collin, trying to appear nonchalant while remaining near Savannah, was in good spirits. All was well.

Willow was just introducing a customer to Belle when she noticed a tall man with dark hair enter the gallery. She blinked, but tried not to look surprised to see that it was Cliff Grant. She finished her introduction then went over to greet him. "I didn't know you were a patron of the arts."

"I'm sure there's a lot you don't know about me," he said with a twinkle in his eye.

"Yes, I'm sure you're right." She smiled warmly. "Thank you for coming. Would you like me to show you around?"

"That'd be great. If you're not too busy."

She linked her arm in his and proceeded to give him the "two-bits" tour. She was just introducing him to Josie and showing him the stepladder Josie had recently finished when Willow noticed another familiar figure entering the gallery. To her pleasant surprise, it was George, dressed in his old buttoned-up way—suit and tie and every hair in place. Willow couldn't help but smile. Sure, he was an odd duck, but he was a likeable odd duck. She was about to wave to him when he abruptly turned around and exited the gallery.

"What's with George?" Josie asked with a frown.

"I don't know." Willow just shook her head. Trying to put George and his strange ways to the back of her mind, Willow continued to take Cliff on his little tour. She was actually impressed with how much he knew about art in general. She hadn't expected that.

"My older sister is an artist," he confessed as he helped himself to the food table.

"What sort of art?" Willow set a canapé on a cocktail napkin.

"She did a little bit of everything. But now she sticks with watercolors."

"Is she good?"

"Of course she's good. She's my sister." Cliff grinned. "But she's good enough to have her work in a gallery on the coast."

"Maybe she'd like to have some pieces in here. If she's ever in town, tell her to stop by."

"She's planning to come during the Tour of Homes week. Maybe I can get you two together then."

"That reminds me," Willow said. "I've had an idea. I plan to close my gallery during the tour and—"

"Close your gallery?" He looked concerned. "Just for the Tour of Homes?"

"I want to bring most of the art over to the house for those four days," she continued. "My employees will help me display items throughout the house, as well as be on hand to help give tours."

"That's an excellent idea." He held up his plastic cup like a toast. "You're a sharp businesswoman, Willow."

"Well, it just sounded like a fun way to mix things up."

"Hey, there's our designer friend, Donna." Cliff waved to where Donna and her husband, Lyle, were just coming in. Before long the four of them were visiting and Cliff mentioned the plan to include the Rockwell Mansion in the Tour of Homes.

"You're kidding." Donna looked offended as she turned to Willow. "You never said a word about that to me."

"It was my idea," Cliff clarified. "I sort of talked her into it."

"What will you do for furnishings?" Donna demanded.

So Willow explained her plan to utilize the furnishings she'd set aside and then to bring her art to the house.

"That's all good, but it's a huge house. I can't imagine you'll be able to fully outfit it."

Willow shrugged. "I'll just have to do my best. Some rooms might be a bit bare, but at least they'll have nice art."

"Tell you what." Donna held up a finger. "You let me help with the staging—in exchange for getting my name in the credits—and I'll bring you the missing pieces."

"Really? You'd do that?"

"Absolutely. I'd love to have my name associated with that house."

Willow explained her hopes to utilize some of the modern pieces. "I have some ideas on how to make it feel like a mix of contemporary and traditional. Do you think you could work with that?"

"That sounds interesting. Let's meet in my office next week to talk about it," Donna said. "I think this could be quite fun."

Willow nodded. "Yes, that's what I want it to be—fun. And somewhat unexpected, but without insulting the house." Even as she said this, Willow couldn't help but wonder . . . what if she insulted the house's owner? Perhaps she already had.

* * *

George felt lost as he walked back home. Not literally lost, since he obviously knew his way. But he felt lost inside . . . as if he had no idea of where he was going . . . or why. Lost and confused. And it was doubly frustrating because he'd really made an attempt to regain his old self this evening. After getting his yard back into shape yesterday, he'd spent most of today catching up on his housework. Then he'd decided to clean himself up and pay Willow a visit. But she'd been with that man again. Cliff Grant.

George had mentioned that name to Lorna yesterday. Just in passing while they'd worked on the yard together. He'd casually said that Cliff Grant was doing some work for him on a family piece of property. He didn't reveal anything about the property since he had no intention of telling Lorna all the details of his life. But when her eyes lit up at the name, George gently pressed her for more information. "I hope he's a good contractor . . . trustworthy and all. You never can tell."

"I don't know about his work ethics, but Cliff Grant's a real looker, that's for sure." Lorna leaned on her bamboo rake handle with a dreamy expression in her eyes—reminiscent of certain girls from George's teaching days whenever a good-looking jock passed by. Not terribly mature. "And he's one of our town's most eligible bachelors."

Hadn't people once referred to George as "an eligible bachelor"? Not lately, of course. Perhaps never again. The bloom was most definitely off that rose by now. "What do you mean—*most* eligible bachelor?" George asked Lorna.

"It simply means that men like him are in high demand. In a town where single women greatly outnumber single men, a man like Cliff Grant is quite a catch." Lorna pursed her unnaturally pink lips—the color reminded George of a plastic yard flamingo. "Quite a catch."

"Do you know him personally?"

"I've never actually met him, but I've seen him around town. I sure wouldn't mind meeting him. My friend Gayla went to school with him. She says that he's been divorced a couple of times and always has a new girlfriend. So apparently he's looking around. If he's Gayla's age, he must be pushing fifty, but I think he looks a lot younger." She patted her platinum hair and looked hopefully at George. "Any chance you could arrange an introduction? Say, how about we visit your family's property together and just happen to bump—"

"No, no. Sorry, that's not possible." George bent down to start his mower again, loudly revving the engine and setting his focus on keeping the mow-lines of his lawn perfectly uniform. But her comments had concerned him so much that his lawn appeared to have been mown by a drunkard. Not only that, but it had motivated him to clean himself up, put on a suit, and pay Willow a visit at the gallery. Only to discover it was too late. Judging by the way she'd looked at that suave Cliff Grant, the way their arms had been entwined . . . George knew it was too late. And now he felt worse than ever. He felt like completely giving up. What was the use?

twenty-seven

The next morning, George jumped in alarm to hear his doorbell ring—not just once, but again and again. Shocked to see that it was past eleven and embarrassed to still be in his pajamas, he didn't know what to do. Whoever was on his porch, now pounding on his door, could easily peek through the window and see him crouched by the bookshelf. Poor Baxter had scampered off when George jumped in surprise, but short of slinking down to the floor and crawling behind his chair, George had no place to escape as the pounding and doorbell ringing continued. Who on earth was it? George picked up the newspaper, attempting to shield himself with it.

"George Emerson!" a female voice called out. "I know you're in there. Let me in before I break the door down!"

He peered over the top of his newspaper to see that it was Josie, now pounding on the window next to the door. Relieved that it wasn't someone else, George reluctantly opened the door. "What do you want?" he growled.

"I want to know what the heck is wrong with you." She pushed past him.

"The only thing wrong with me is people who burst in like—"

"Why did you come to the gallery last night, then not even say hello?" she demanded as she flopped down onto his sofa like she owned the place. "I saw you there. Mom did too. You walked in then walked out. Just like that." She shook her finger at him. "Bad manners if you ask me."

"And you should be the expert." He glared at her.

"Seriously, George, what's up?"

"I simply changed my mind." George sat down in his chair, gathering up and neatly folding his newspaper as if the rest of the room wasn't in complete disarray. Not that Josie would care. She wasn't big on tidiness either.

"I don't believe you." She leaned forward, peering at him with a skeptical scowl. "Something is bugging you, George. My mom is worried. And so am I."

"Willow is worried?" He stopped folding the newspaper.

"Yes. She's gotten it into her head that you might be dying." Josie rolled her eyes. "And now I broke my promise to her. I swore I wouldn't tell you about that."

He blinked. "She thinks I'm dying."

"Well, you've been acting pretty weird. I mean weird for you. And you've been going to the doctor. And, well, she remembers how it went down when Asher died. I mean, her husband was obviously a lot older than you. But I guess the way you're acting has got Mom worried." Her brow creased. "You're not dying, are you, George?"

He shook his head. "Not that I know of."

"You sound disappointed."

He shrugged.

"Do you want to die?" she demanded.

"No, no—not exactly. But I suppose I don't know what I have to live for."

Josie frowned. "What does anyone have?"

"I don't know. Your mother thinks there's plenty to live for. But then she's got her religion. I suppose she has to be like that."

"She wasn't always like that." Josie leaned back, folding her arms behind her head. "And to be fair to my mom, she's not really *that* religious. That's what she says anyway. She says that she loves God and she loves people and that it's *not about religion*. To quote her, 'It's about relationships.'" She rolled her eyes. "At least that's what she tells me whenever I make the mistake and call her religious."

"Yes, she said something similar to that to me." George set aside the newspaper. "But she does go to church fairly regularly."

"Yeah, I went with her and Collin once." She sat back up. "And it really wasn't too bad. It didn't really feel like church to me. Not like I remember church anyway. The pastor dude is pretty cool. Don't tell my mom this, but I actually made a counseling appointment with him. She doesn't know it, but I've been a couple of times and will probably go again. He actually gave me some helpful advice."

"Interesting." He tried to imagine Josie taking advice from a clergyman. Was she pulling his leg?

"So you're really not dying, George?"

He sighed and shook his head again. The truth was he'd actually hoped that he was dying. He'd wanted the doctor to say something like "I'm sorry, you've got six months to a year left, George." And then George had intended to live differently. Oh, he hadn't known exactly what he'd do or how he'd do it, but he'd make some big changes. Maybe he'd volunteer at the soup kitchen or send money to feed orphans in Africa or even join the local square dancing club. But now that he had this obnoxious "clean bill of health" George had seriously considered taking up activities like smoking and drinking and recreational drugs. Maybe he'd get a motorcycle—and a tattoo. Or try skydiving.

George knew, of course, that he wouldn't do any of those things. The problem was he didn't know *what* to do anymore. Nothing brought him any pleasure. Nothing motivated him. Nothing appeared worth living for. And the truth was, he didn't even have anything worth dying for. Maybe he was simply a lost cause.

"Can I give you some advice, George?"

He shrugged. "Why not?"

"Well, you seem really down to me. And I'm thinking you need someone to talk to—like a professional someone. Pastor Hal has a counseling degree and he's really pretty good at it. Maybe you should consider giving him a call." She got up and went over to his telephone table. After checking on her cell phone, she wrote something down on his notepad, then turned to him. "I'm glad to hear you're not dying, George. But it could be you need to do something to get yourself back on track."

"All things are possible."

She smiled sheepishly. "Take it from someone who's been in the pit of despair—you can make a comeback." Then, to his relief, she let herself out. After he locked the door and pulled the blind down on the side window, he sat back down and pondered her words. Was it possible that George Emerson had sunk so low that he was now taking advice from someone like Josie? He looked around his mess of a living room. Maybe so.

—◦◦◦—

For the next week, Willow spent long days in the Rock-well house cleaning, planning, and even helping with some of the painting. Although she called George a time or two to give updates, he continued to maintain an off-putting nonchalance about the renovating. But at least, according to Josie, George was not dying. That was something to be thankful for.

Although George promised to come by to check on the progress, so far he'd not shown his face. Perhaps that was for the best. Willow had no idea how she'd react if George didn't approve of something already in the works. She knew how persnickety he could be. And she really didn't like the idea of him showing up while things were torn up and in process, like these last few days when everything was in flux. But by the end of the week, with most of the painting finished and the kitchen nearly in place, she began to hope that he might pop in.

So it was that on Sunday, with no workers around to get in the way, Willow stopped by the house after church and gave George a call. "I know you appear to have no interest in seeing what's going on up here, but I'd really appreciate it if you stopped by."

"Is something wrong?" he asked.

"No. Something is right. The place is really in good shape. And I think you'd enjoy seeing it."

"I don't know."

"Please, George," she begged. "I'm doing this for you.

The least you could do for me would be to stop by. Just give me fifteen minutes of your time—we'll walk through it and you can—"

"Fine," he said. "I'll leave straightaway."

After she hung up, Willow immediately felt nervous. She walked through room after room, taking an inventory of what had been done, pleased with how light and clean it all looked. The walls were painted in light neutral shades that not only brightened the place but added a depth. Some of the worn woodwork was painted a clean milky white, which set off the recently refinished wood floors that gleamed with warmth and character. And the kitchen—that was the best. The tall Shaker-style cherry cabinets with some glass doors reflected the era of the home but were functional in a modern way. The white marble was classic and clean looking, and the checkerboard floors, with concrete tiles in white and gray, looked both modern and classic. She felt certain George would love it—and she couldn't wait to show him.

She hurried to the front of the house, waiting eagerly in the freshly painted foyer, impatient for George to arrive. Spying him coming up the walk, she opened the tall, oversized door wide and smiled brightly. "Welcome," she said happily.

George frowned as he came up the walk. "Someone painted the trim," he said a bit sharply.

"Yes. Doesn't it look—"

"That trim has always been white," he snapped.

"Yes, but the white looked so stark. Don't you think that charcoal gray sets off the red bricks nicely? It's so classic and brings out the leaded glass—"

"The white trim was just fine."

"But it was dirty and the paint was cracking and—"

"I could've painted it myself. And I would've painted it white." He waved some envelopes at her. "And I assume that's what these bills are for—"

"You told me to have them sent to—"

"These are things I could've done myself," he declared as he stormed through the front door.

"But you said you didn't want to—"

"Oh, no!" He stopped in the foyer with a horrified expression. "No, no, no."

"That old dark wallpaper is gone and the woodwork has been re—"

"This is just terrible."

"But it looks lovely, George. So fresh and clean and—"

"I cannot believe it." He walked on through to the living room. "Oh, no." He shook his head. "Oh, no, no, no."

Willow began to feel sick inside. "George, you knew what we were doing—"

"This is horrible. Just horrible." He continued on through the dining room, muttering complaints about everything. "Everything gone. Everything changed. No, no, no."

"I don't understand," Willow said meekly. "You wanted the house updated. I told you exactly what we were do—"

"Oh, no." George stopped in the kitchen, covering his mouth with his hand. "Did that contractor do this? That Cliff Grant?"

"Well, yes. Cliff has overseen everything. But he's just doing what I asked of him. And the cabinets were made by—"

"It's all wrong." He stomped out, mumbling under his breath. Then, after going quickly through the other first-floor rooms, he marched up the stairs, complaining with each step. "Everything's gone," he finally said. "Everything is changed. It's all gone. All wrong. All changed."

"But that's what you wanted," Willow tried again. "You said you—"

"You should've known I was having a hard time." He looked at her with tear-filled eyes. "I was in a bad way, Willow. In no position to deal with all this." He waved a hand toward an empty bedroom. "Everything is gone."

"I know, but—"

"Never mind. I have to go." And then without giving her a chance to say another word—not that she knew what to say—George ran down the stairs.

After hearing the front door slam, Willow sat down on the top step and cried. Of course, George was absolutely right. She should've recognized that he wasn't himself. Probably in the midst of some sort of midlife crisis or mental breakdown. She should've just backed off . . . given him room to recover. Instead, she'd been a camel's nose. She'd charged along in her usual bossy way, always ready for a challenge, eager to tackle the world, nothing too hard, nothing too big . . . and now this. She'd spoiled everything.

twenty-eight

By Monday morning George was in a bad way again, and he really wanted to talk to someone. Someone beyond a cat. Not that Baxter wasn't a sympathetic listener or a great comfort. But George needed a fellow human to talk to. That in itself was unusual. But why should he be surprised? Nothing about this summer or his "retirement" had been usual. That, he knew, was mostly due to Willow. But she was the last person he wanted to talk to right now.

George paced back and forth in his living room, feeling somewhat like a caged lion—toothless, declawed, and aging, but still full of some sort of pent-up rage that made him feel trapped and slightly frightened. Eventually he noticed a name and phone number by his telephone. He picked up the pad, remembering that Josie had jotted this down. Ironic that he'd take the advice of an unstable woman who'd spent her adult life as a grunge groupie, but just the same, George dialed the number and asked for Pastor Hal. When a friendly male voice answered, George stammered through an explanation of why he'd called, finally saying, "I'm not a part of your congregation, but I'm a friend of the West family. They recommended you as a counselor and—"

"Let's meet for coffee," Pastor Hal said. "How about Common Grounds at ten thirty? Does that work?"

"Sure," George agreed. That would give him just enough time to clean himself up and walk over there.

Just before ten thirty, George stood at the counter of Common Grounds wearing a suit and tie and ordering the "house coffee" as if he were a perfectly normal sort of fellow. At least that was how he hoped he looked. The barista had just served him his coffee when a short, bald man walked in. "Hey, Hal," the barista called out. "You want your regular?"

"Thanks." He grinned. "I'm meeting a guy named George here."

George went over to introduce himself and, after a warm, firm handshake, Hal led them to a table in the back. "So tell me about yourself," Hal said as they sat down. George stammered a bit but explained he was newly retired from teaching and possibly having some adjustment issues. He paused as the barista set down Hal's coffee, some fancy drink with whipped cream on top. "My wife tells me that this coffee is more like dessert in a cup." He chuckled, then took a sip that topped his upper lip with a white mustache. He wiped it with a napkin and smiled. "So you're having a rough summer?"

George wasn't sure he'd said that, but since it was true he nodded.

"And you called a pastor for some counsel?"

George sighed. "Rather ironic, since I consider myself an atheist."

"I think an atheist is simply a seeker who is hoping God will show up."

"I heard someone else say something like that." George wasn't ready to tell Hal about his relationship with Willow. Especially since he didn't understand it himself.

"So are you?"

"Am I what?"

"Hoping that God will show up?"

George folded and refolded his napkin then looked at Hal. "Do you think God could speak through music—more specifically, through Simon and Garfunkel?"

Hal grinned. "You bet I do."

George felt a bit of relief as he told the pastor about listening to "Bridge Over Troubled Water." "It's embarrassing to say, but the song completely unhinged me. I honestly felt like I was having a nervous breakdown, like I'd wake up in a straitjacket or in a padded cell in Crestview."

"That's a wonderful song, George. Every time I hear it, it's like God is singing directly to me."

"You too?" George felt a small wave of relief.

"It's a song about being in pain, being alone, being tired and down . . . and then this amazing friend is going to lay himself down for you—like a bridge over a raging river—just so you can get across. To me that's like Jesus. He laid himself down to get me through all that pain and loneliness . . . to get me safely to the other side." He took a sip of his frothy coffee with a look of deep contentment. George wasn't sure if it was from the "dessert in a cup" or from what he'd just said.

"Do you really believe that?" George studied him closely.

Hal set down his cup firmly. "You bet I do."

George slowly shook his head. "Well, I've always been a follower of Ralph Waldo Emerson. At first I thought it was because of the name . . . because my last name is Emerson.

But the more I read about Ralph Waldo, the more I identified."

"How so?"

"Well, we have many commonalities. He was a teacher.
And he experienced a lot of losses—his father died when
he was a boy, his first wife died at the age of twenty, his
brother . . ."

"Have you had a lot of loss?" Hal's pale gray eyes looked
kind.

George quickly listed his lost loved ones.

"I'm sorry." Hal shook his head. "I'm sure that's taken a
toll on you, George."

"But that wasn't all I liked about Emerson," George said
quickly. He didn't want to talk about his personal pain . . .
didn't want to break down here in public. "I embraced Emerson's general philosophy. Independence, self-reliance, a liter-
ary man in need of no one. A man who shunned religion."
George studied the pastor, curious if he'd offended him, but
not particularly concerned if he had.

"Admittedly, I don't know a lot about your Emerson, but I
have studied him some, and I think he must've been a lonely
man." Hal smiled sadly. "I can appreciate how his anti-God
rhetoric might've been related to the church of his day. I don't
disagree with his opposition to a church that had grown
rigid and judgmental and, in my opinion, not particularly
Christlike. To be honest, I'm sorry to say there's too much
of that in the church today."

George felt his brows arch. "But you're a pastor of a
church."

"That's true. And our church has its problems. But I like to
think we are trying . . . that we are being sincere and honest

and genuine . . . attempting to live in a Christlike manner even if we stumble a bit."

"What do you mean when you say *Christlike*?"

"That's a very good question, George. Not easy to answer, but simply put, I think it means we believe in Jesus and trust him enough to follow him, to imitate his example."

"What does that mean? What kind of example? I went to church as a kid, but I found it confusing. Lots of rules and laws—do this, don't do that. Act like this, not that. Say this, not that. Frankly, it was a relief to let the whole religion thing go."

"That's the problem with religion, George. And the very thing that I'll bet Emerson rejected. As a matter of fact, I do too. Emerson and I agree that religion basically sucks."

"But you're a pastor."

"Just for the record, George, Jesus wasn't a fan of religion either. The religious leaders of his day were bogged down in it, and they were crippling the people with their laws and restrictions. But Jesus only gave us two rules."

"Yes?" George thought this sounded vaguely familiar but couldn't really remember.

Hal held up two fingers. "Number one, Jesus said we need to love God with everything we've got—heart, soul, mind. And number two, he said to love the folks around us as much as we love ourselves."

"That's it?"

"Jesus knew we humans need to keep it simple." Hal sighed. "But he also knew it was humanly impossible to keep those two simple rules—without his help."

"I don't really understand."

"It's kind of like the 'Bridge Over Troubled Water' song,"

Hal said. "We get weary and lonely and down and sad on our own. We need Jesus to transport us across the raging river."

"I think I get the metaphor—but how does Jesus do that on a pragmatic level?"

"By becoming your friend, George. He's eager to have a daily friendship with you. But you have to believe in him, you have to agree to his terms. And that's when everything changes." Hal smiled.

George didn't know what to say, so he just sipped his coffee. This counseling session was not going as he'd imagined. Not that he had much experience with such things. But he'd envisioned this pastor giving him some encouraging words of advice. Sort of like his doctor had done—not that George had followed it.

"I realize I just threw a lot at you," Hal said quietly. "But it was only because you asked, George. I hope I didn't overwhelm you. I know I made it sound simple—and it really is— but it's also something that takes a lifetime to fully understand. And maybe not then. The good news is you only have to take these things one day at a time."

"Well, you have certainly given me a lot to think about," George admitted. "Although I must say I'm surprised to hear a clergyman saying some of the things you just said. And yet I find some of it refreshing." He was still chewing on what Hal had said about relating to Emerson's views on religion. That was very interesting.

"I can see that you're well on your way, George—on your own spiritual journey." Hal's eyes lit up. "Please feel free to call me anytime you want to talk. And not just about spiritual things either. I'm interested in lots of topics—everything from soccer to French cuisine to gardening to literature. In fact, you've given me the urge to do some research on Ralph Waldo Emerson. I don't think I've read any Emerson since college days."

"I have lots of Emerson books if you're interested."

"I most certainly am. And I want you to feel free to come to our Sunday service. I don't care what your beliefs are—you are welcome. I think you'll be surprised to see it's different from what you recall as a child. After talking to you, I'm considering some Simon and Garfunkel music for our next Sunday service." Hal shook George's hand, and George thanked him for meeting impromptu like this.

But as he slowly walked home, George wasn't sure what to think. Although Hal had given him plenty to consider, George still felt stirred up and unsettled inside. Still, it was encouraging to think he might be on his own spiritual journey. At least that meant he was going somewhere.

twenty-nine

Once again, George felt the need to apologize to Willow. How many times would this make for him? Oh, sure, she'd apologized to him as well. But he was usually the one holding his hat in his hands. And after going into fits over his grandparents' house—after he'd given her complete freedom to do as she pleased—well, he knew he was in the wrong.

He also knew that the problem—besides being shocked at the many changes—was the knowledge that Willow had incorporated these "improvements" with the help of the handsome contractor, Cliff Grant. Even his name had a bit of a Hollywood ring to it. Perhaps it wasn't the name he'd been born with. Maybe he'd hoped to be discovered for film but hadn't been. So he'd taken up construction instead. George knew it was silly to make up these stories in his head, but that was what one did when one was jealous. And George knew that he was jealous.

"What should I do?" George asked Baxter on Tuesday morning as they sat in the morning sun together. "Should I try to win her back? Or should I simply apologize and let it go?" Baxter purred with contentment, as if to say, *Forget the whole thing and stay here with me.*

"Yes, I could do that." George gently lifted Baxter out of his lap, setting him on the floor. "That might make us both happy for the time being. But it wouldn't last long." George carried his coffee mug into the kitchen and began to wash up his morning dishes. His recent goal was to return to his old routines, but not in the regimented ways he used to. According to his self-help book, the first chapter anyway, one key to managing OCD was to *rule it instead of letting it rule you.*

Laundry could be done on any day of the week and at any hour of the day. And the grass would survive without being mowed every Saturday morning. It was even okay to let the dishes sit in the sink for an hour or two. But then, especially if flies invaded, George would jump up and compulsively wash and dry, putting them safely away. Wasn't that just good sanitation?

As George dried his dishes, he noticed Lorna outside. Although she was watering her petunias, she didn't have on her usual stay-at-home clothes. Unless he was mistaken, she was dressed for an outing. Probably one involving shopping. That was Lorna's favorite pastime and she wasn't afraid to admit it. Of course, if she knew how off-putting this was to George—or any bachelor who cared about his bank account—she might be more careful of her words. But suddenly, George felt like a shopaholic was just what he needed today. He set down a still-damp bowl, tossed down his dish towel, and hurried out to say hello.

"Oh, hello, George." She waved.

"Looks like you're going somewhere." George tried to

appear nonchalant as he went over to the low hedge that separated their yards, picking off a stray leafy twig that he must've missed during its last trimming.

"Just going to Lampton." She smiled sheepishly. "Sale at the outlet mall."

"Ah, shopping." He nodded. "You're quite the expert at that, aren't you?"

"I'm quite the pro if I do say so myself." Her expression grew curious. "Why do you ask?"

"Well, I'm not much of a shopper. Especially when it comes to clothes." He waved down to his button-down blue shirt and gray trousers. "So much of my wardrobe was for teaching. I don't really have the sorts of clothes that—"

"Why, George Emerson, you're coming with me today," she declared. "That is a fabulous idea. We'll take you shopping for retirement clothes. I don't know why I didn't think of this sooner. Are you ready?"

"I guess so. Let me go check on my cat and a few things, and I'll be right with you."

"This is gonna be fun," she called out as he hurried back to his house.

Not surprisingly, George had second thoughts as he changed into his oxfords. What was he getting himself into—and with Lorna? Was he opening up that proverbial can of worms? And for what reasons?

George didn't really want to admit the motivation behind this madness. Not even to himself. The truth was he hoped to compete with that Cliff Grant fellow. Haunted by images of Cliff's interaction with Willow while dressed in a casual but attractive manner, George felt the urge to make some personal changes. Although Cliff didn't wear a suit and tie, which would hardly be the appropriate apparel for a contractor, he always looked well put together—almost like one of those fellows on the cover of *GQ*. Not that George had ever purchased such a silly magazine, but he'd seen them at the store. And Cliff definitely had that sort of flair and confidence.

As George brushed his teeth and combed his hair, he was willing to wager that one of Cliff's ex-wives or girlfriends had taught him how to dress. Maybe they even shopped for his clothes for him. George wouldn't be surprised. It was shallow—he knew it was—but George thought that if he looked a bit more fashionable . . . perhaps it would make apologizing to Willow easier. And perhaps—if he was really lucky—it might even improve his chances of winning her back. He knew that was a stretch, but improving his appearance couldn't hurt.

"Talk about being stuck between a rock and a hard place," Willow said to her designer friend as the two of them rearranged the furniture in the living room again. It was their third try to get it just right. And with just one more day to get everything set for the Tour of Homes, Willow was trying not to feel overly concerned. But between George's unpredictable behavior and the upcoming deadline, it was difficult not to feel some stress.

"I'll say. That Mr. Emerson is a hard one to figure." Donna stepped back to look at the sofa. "But stick to your guns, Willow. You've got this house on the tour, and you have to honor that commitment. Sort things out with Mr. Emerson afterward." She pointed to the pair of chairs. "Let's anchor those to the other edge of the rug."

"Do you think this Danish Modern is too much for this room?" Willow asked as she set one of the chairs into place. "I mean, I do like it, but maybe—"

"No, no, I actually think it's superb in here. I never would've done something like this myself. But with those more traditional pieces I brought—and this gorgeous carpet, well, I think it totally works. It's just getting everything into the right positions that's the challenge now." She stepped back to look. "How about that?"

"Yes. That's it." Willow gazed over the room with satisfaction. "I personally love this room now. I can't wait to get the art up and everything else in place."

"I'm so glad you decided to slipcover the old upholstery in off-white." Donna pulled a colorful pillow from a box and tossed it onto the sofa. "Really sets these off."

"George was so worked up over the bills, I actually paid for the slipcovers myself," Willow confessed. "But that yellow, green, and orange upholstery was pretty jarring. This is much nicer."

"Well, George should be grateful for how much you've accomplished with such a small budget." Donna continued to arrange the pillows. "Trust me, you could've easily spent many times that much."

"He got me so upset that I canceled the housecleaners I had coming for today."

"Looks like you've got a pretty good crew anyway."

"Thanks to Savannah, Josie, and Collin. They've been hard at it since yesterday." Willow held a large piece of art above the antique console against the back wall. "What do you think of this up here, Donna?"

"Oh, that's fabulous. I love the juxtaposition of the modern art over that bulky walnut piece. And I have a pair of brass lamps that'll be perfect on either end of the console. Is that one of the original Rockwell pieces that you held back?"

"No, this is one that Betty volunteered." Willow set the painting on it for now. "It's sweet how many of my friends are helping me with this. I'd like to have a thank-you party after the tour is over, just to show my appreciation."

"And will you invite Mr. Emerson?"

Willow cringed. "I'm not sure he'd even come." In fact, she sincerely hoped that George would stay away until the whole thing was over and done with. After that, well, she didn't want to think about it right now.

The crew continued to work on the house—both inside and out—and by Wednesday evening, the Rockwell Mansion looked better than ever. At least to Willow. She was fairly certain that George wouldn't agree.

"I'm stunned," Cliff Grant said after she finished giving him the full tour. "This is nothing short of miraculous, Willow. How did you do it?"

"With a lot of help." Willow tweaked the massive bouquet on the dining room table. The flowers were from her terrace garden, artfully arranged in an oversized pottery vase she'd made several weeks ago. "I keep telling everyone that it's taken a village to bring this house back to life."

"Well, you've sure managed to do it. Between the art pieces from your gallery, the mix of various styles of furnishings, and Donna's designer touches, this house looks better than I thought possible. I'm proud to have my name on it." He grinned. "Although, the truth is, I didn't really do much more than organize the crews."

"Speaking of that, I'm in love with the kitchen." She pushed open the door and went into the renovated kitchen where everything was now perfectly in place.

"I like how you've warmed it up with all these copper pieces."

"Those are actually from my kitchen," she admitted. "Mine looks pretty stark at the moment."

"I think this place is going to be a hit." Cliff ran his hand over the sleek marble countertop. "I really appreciate your efforts, Willow." He smiled warmly at her. "You're one hard-working woman."

"Thanks. And thank you for helping."

"I've known a lot of women who prefer to just sit around while the guy does all the work." He reached over to push a stray strand of hair off her forehead. "It's refreshing to meet a woman who knows how to stand on her own two feet. And it's very attractive too."

"Well, thank you." Willow felt uneasy as she turned to adjust a stack of hand-thrown mixing bowls. Was Cliff making a pass at her? Although it was flattering, she had no real interest in any kind of romantic involvement with him. "It's been a long few days," she said with finality. "And I'd like to go home to do some repair work tonight." She held out her hands. "Like a manicure for starters." She laughed as she headed back through the dining room. "Tomorrow I'd like to look more like an art curator than a common laborer."

As she led him out the front door, pausing to lock it, Willow turned to give the house one last look. The porch lights were on, illuminating the handsome arrangement of wicker furnishings that Donna had brought over earlier today. All in all, the front porch looked very inviting.

"This is charming out here." Cliff sat down on the love seat, patting the cushion beside him. "Care to join me?"

Willow didn't want to be rude, but she didn't want to encourage him either. So she sat across from him in one of the chairs. "And comfortable too," she said. "I barely had time to check this out earlier. Donna set it all up." She pointed to the large flower pots. "Those are from her house. Her husband brought them over."

"Very nice."

"And look at the view from here," she said with surprise. "I hadn't really noticed it before. How pretty the town's lights look at this hour. It's really sweet." She was actually tempted to linger.

"And romantic. All we need is some champagne and—"

"Like I said, I really need to get home." She stood. "Tomorrow is a big day." She hurried down the front steps and into her SUV, but as she pulled into the street, she thought she spied a shadowy figure near the oak trees out in front. She slowed down and peered hard. Meanwhile, she noticed lights in her rearview mirror as Cliff's pickup headed the opposite direction. Too late to call out to him for help.

She reached for her phone. The last thing she needed right now was a break-in or vandalism. Especially with all that art inside—and no security system in place. This could easily turn disastrous. Who knew what a silly, restless teenager might do on a warm August night just a couple weeks before school was back in session. After all, she'd been a teen once. She rolled down her window. "Hey," she yelled in her best tough voice. "What're you doing there? Come out and show yourself before I call 911."

To her surprise, George stepped out from the shadows,

holding up his hands as if she were an armed police officer. "It's just me," he said sheepishly.

"George Emerson!" She felt a wide span of emotions— ranging from real horror to huge relief. Why on earth was he lurking in the shadows like that? She got out of the car and walked toward him. Was he here to pull the plug on everything? After all, this was his house, his property—and despite him giving her permission, she had nothing in writing and she knew George was unpredictable. If he wanted, he could put a stop to everything—just like that. And there was nothing she could do about it.

"You gave me a good scare," she declared. "Why are you hiding out here like a criminal?"

"I was just on my usual evening walk," he said curtly. "Any law against that?"

"A walk through the oak trees, here in the shadows?"

"To be honest, I wanted to get a look at my house. You know, before your big festivities tomorrow. But I didn't expect to find you here . . . with your, uh, friend . . . Cliff Grant. You two looked pretty cozy up there on the porch." His tone sharpened. "I didn't want to interrupt."

"You wouldn't have been interrupting anything, George." She matched his sharp tone, then instantly regretted it. What good would it do to initiate a fight with the only man who could slam the brakes on her involvement in the Tour of Homes? "Would you like me to give you the full tour?" she said more gently. "I've actually been wishing you'd come up here."

"Really?" His tone softened too.

"Come on, George." She linked her arm in his. "Come and see your house."

"Humph. Doesn't feel much like *my* house anymore."

"Did it ever feel like *your* house?" Keeping her arm securely around his, she continued up the front path. "Looked to me like you just let the house sit. It felt like an abandoned house, George. It just needed some love." She paused on the porch. "Just look how charming this is." She turned around. "And I never realized you had such a lovely view of the city lights from here. It's actually rather romantic."

"I'm sure you and Cliff Grant must've been enjoying it."

She glanced at George in the porch light. Was he jealous of Cliff? Or perhaps, more likely, he was jealous about his house being in the hands of others. "George," she said. "You look different." She waited as he unlocked the door. Once she saw him in the light of the foyer, she was surprised to see that he looked unusually stylish. "I don't think I've ever seen you in blue jeans. Your hair is different. And you're wearing loafers—*without socks*!"

He just shrugged, like nothing about this was unusual.

"What's going on here?" she asked.

"I just decided to make some changes. Lorna and I went shopping. She helped me out." He turned away, looking around the foyer. "I guess maybe it does look better in here. Without that dark wallpaper." He turned back to her with a sheepish expression. "You know the real reason I came up here tonight?"

"Not really."

"Well, it was true that I did want to see the house without people crawling all over the place. But I was hoping to find you here too." He looked down at his stylish loafers with a long sigh. "So that I could apologize."

"You want to apologize?" She studied him more closely. He actually looked rather handsome with this new makeover.

The short haircut was an improvement over his usually slicked-down dark hair. And the blue-and-white-striped oxford shirt with sleeves rolled up was a nice compromise of his usual buttoned-up style gone casual. The blue jeans, which fit nicely, made him look younger too.

"I'm sorry I threw that fit last time I was up here, Willow." He looked into her eyes. "It was very childish on my part. I hope you'll forgive me."

"Done." She smiled. "I can understand how shocked you were to see how much had changed. I really don't blame you for that. This was your childhood home."

"I suppose I had some regrets about letting you get rid of everything. It was true that I'd been in a bad way when I made that decision and—"

"But I didn't get rid of everything, George. You didn't give me a chance to explain. I saved back a lot of things." She took his arm. "Come on, you'll see." As she led him through the living room, she explained that the Danish Modern pieces were simply slipcovered. "You can take them right back to their original look if you like."

"I think they look better like this." He stood looking all around. "I can't believe this is the same room. It's so light and bright and cheerful." He slowly shook his head. "Maybe this is what my grandmother wanted."

"This room makes me feel happy," she said. "Every time I come in here, I want to smile." She tugged him toward the dining room. "I want you to see everything."

"The dining room feels very welcoming," he told her. "I'm glad you reused my grandmother's furnishings here too." He turned to Willow. "These were some of the things I felt badly about losing. Thank you for saving them."

"Oh, that makes me so glad." She smiled. "Come see the beautiful kitchen. Everyone who's seen it has fallen in love with it, George. Honestly, if you decide to sell this place, this kitchen will seal the deal."

He paused in the doorway, looking all around. "It really is nice. Much nicer than I thought when I first saw it." He looked down at the floors. "I like that."

They continued the tour downstairs and George didn't hide his pleasure. But when they went upstairs, he grew quiet. "This was Alex's room," he said solemnly.

"I know." She nodded. "It looked like very little had changed since the 1970s."

"I removed his record albums and stereo, but everything else was the same." He looked teary. "I used to come up here sometimes . . . when I missed him."

Willow felt his sadness and wasn't sure how to comfort him. "I did ask Collin to help me with this room," she explained. "And with what I assume was your boyhood room."

"To help you?" George removed his handkerchief, dabbing his eyes.

"I asked him to carefully go through things—before we took the furnishings down for the estate sale. I asked him to box up any memorabilia that he thought you might want saved."

"You did?" George's eyes grew wide.

"The boxes are stored in the attic, marked with your name."

"I don't know how to thank you."

"It just seemed—" She was interrupted by someone yelling her name. "That sounds like Cliff Grant," she told George. "Hello?" she called out. "I'm upstairs."

They heard the sound of fast footsteps up the stairs and then Cliff appeared at the top. "What's going on?" he asked breathlessly. "I saw your SUV parked halfway down the street with the headlights on. And then the lights on in the house. I thought maybe—"

"Oh dear." Willow frowned. "I think I left my keys in the ignition too."

"I'm George Emerson." George stuck out his hand. "I assume you're Cliff Grant, the contractor. Thank you for helping with my house."

"George Emerson." Cliff shook his hand. "Pleased to meet you."

"If you guys will excuse me, I better go see to my car." She smiled nervously. "And if you can lock up, I'll just head on home. Bye now." Hoping that the two men would enjoy a congenial conversation, she hurried on out. She felt slightly guilty leaving George like that. She suspected he didn't have the highest regard for Cliff, although she didn't know why. But maybe this would give him a chance to get better acquainted. Or maybe George would challenge Cliff to a duel. She chuckled to herself as she drove home. Was it possible that George Emerson was jealous of Cliff Grant? Wouldn't that be something!

thirty

The next four days passed in a happy blur for Willow. The Tour of Homes was an all-around success. The locals enjoyed the experience of being inside the lovely historic home, and a number of them expressed genuine interest in purchasing it. Willow took down names and numbers to save for George . . . just in case. She was pleased to recommend Donna and Cliff to people planning renovation projects. And Willow was thrilled to sell several pieces of art to customers who hadn't even been in her gallery before. All in all, it was well worth the effort she'd put into it.

But by Sunday afternoon, about an hour before it was time to close down the tour, Willow was exhausted. Since the foot traffic had lessened considerably, she'd sent her helpers home and was about to remove the open-house signs when she heard footsteps in the foyer.

Pasting a smile on her face and preparing to be hospitable, she went to welcome her last-minute guest, only to be pleasantly surprised to see Pastor Hal. "Welcome," she told him. "Where is your sweet wife?"

He grimaced. "Beth will probably throw a fit to hear I came here without her. But she's been visiting our pregnant daughter in Salem. She's supposed to get home tomorrow. And to be honest, although this looks like a handsome house, I'm not up here for the tour. I came to visit with you."

"To visit with me?" She smiled. "How thoughtful." She pointed to the porch. "Want to sit out here? There's a nice breeze."

After they were comfortably settled, Hal jumped right in. "I'm aware that you're a good friend of George Emerson."

"You know George?" She didn't expect this. "Did you know this is his house?"

"No, I had no idea. Nice place, though."

"I've been helping him with it."

"Then you really *are* good friends with him?"

"Well, yes. I like to think I am. But it's been a bit of a roller-coaster ride. I'm afraid that's mostly my fault. I push the poor man far too much. He calls me a 'camel's nose.'"

"A camel's nose?"

She quickly relayed George's parable and Hal just laughed. "That sounds like something George would say."

"So you really do know him?"

"We've met for coffee a few times. And he came to church today."

"*He did?*" Willow couldn't imagine such a thing. "I wish I'd been there. But I had to be here at the house."

"George is the reason I wanted to talk to you. I don't want to overstep my bounds, but he's an unusual fellow. Quite likeable too."

"Very unusual." She nodded. "That's probably what attracted me to him."

"*Attracted* you?" Hal's brows arched.

She waved a hand. "You know, as a friend. I liked George right from the start. But he is an odd duck. There's no denying it." She laughed. "But to be fair, so am I."

"Well, then . . . are you aware of George's feelings for you?"

"Feelings?"

He looked uneasy. "I normally don't get this involved, Willow, but George is a special case. I think it's only fair to warn you that George is in love with you."

She sat up straight. "Oh, Hal, you can't be serious."

"I am serious."

"How can you possibly know something like that? I can't imagine that George would ever say such—"

"He didn't exactly say so. Not in so many words. But it's written all over his face, Willow. Whenever he speaks of you. Trust me, I know what I'm saying. And the only reason I'm giving you this heads-up is because I can't stand to see that sweet man get his heart broken."

"Get his heart broken?" Willow spoke slowly, still trying to take this in.

Hal looked uncomfortable. "I don't like to interfere, Willow. And if Beth knew what I was up to, she'd probably give me what for. But as you know, I do couples' counseling, so this is familiar turf for me. Besides that, I really care about George. He's a special guy."

Willow nodded. "George is special to me too."

"So, please, forgive me if I've overstepped my bounds in telling you. But, as my grandmother used to say, a word to the wise is sufficient." He started to stand.

"But wait." Willow held a hand up. "I'm curious as to why you're so worried. Do you honestly think I'd do anything to hurt George?"

"No, of course not. Not intentionally, anyway. I just feel he's vulnerable. I wanted you to know." He sat back down.

"Can you enlighten me about this?" she asked. "Why is he so vulnerable? Because I feel that I've done everything possible to win his trust—and yet it always blows up in my face."

Hal leaned forward with folded hands. "I think George is afraid to love you."

"Afraid—why?"

"Well, I'm in this deep. I might as well continue." He held up two fingers. "First of all, George is worried that you're smitten by your handsome contractor—and that it's pointless for him to pursue you."

"Well, that's perfectly ridiculous." She released an exasperated sigh. "Cliff Grant is only a friend."

"That's exactly what I thought." He held up the other finger. "This is probably the reason that concerns me most. George is certain that if he loves you, he will lose you. Everyone he's loved, it seems, has died. It's as if he thinks he's cursed."

"Or that God hates him." Willow nodded. "He's told me that before."

"But I think George is shifting his beliefs. Apparently it started with Simon and Garfunkel and—"

"*What?*"

He waved a hand. "Never mind. But, trust me, Willow, George has been going through some pretty major changes lately. He's definitely on a significant spiritual journey."

"That's wonderful. I've been concerned for him." Despite being glad to hear this, Willow still felt bewildered. What did Hal expect her to do? And what if he was wrong about George's feelings toward her?

"It's a relief to hear you've been such a good friend to George. I was very uneasy about bringing this up to you. But I prayed about it and felt God gave me a green light."

"To be honest, George and I haven't had much opportunity to talk these past couple of weeks. Something always interrupts." She wasn't ready to admit that most of their recent conversations had been derailed by silly misunderstandings.

"One reason I wanted to talk to you about this is because I feel a little bit guilty."

"Guilty?"

"Well, I may have said something dumb to George yesterday. We met for coffee and George was speaking so fondly of you. I rather flippantly told him that he should tell you how he feels. It seemed a good idea at the time. I usually encourage people to be up front with their feelings. But then I saw George in church today and, well, he looked so vulnerable. I got to thinking . . . What if he decided to take my advice and you rejected him? How hurt would he be? I really wished I'd kept my advice to myself."

"What makes you so sure I'd reject him?"

His brows arched hopefully. "You wouldn't?"

"I don't know." She shrugged and looked away. "And shouldn't that be between George and me? But I do promise you this, Hal, I wouldn't do anything to hurt him. Not intentionally. More than anything, I've tried to be his friend. I value his friendship. I genuinely like him."

He reached over to grasp her hand. "Oh, Willow, I should've known you'd handle this just right. Even if I didn't have the sense to keep my big mouth shut." He slowly stood. "Thank you for being so understanding."

"Thank you for giving me this little heads-up." She chuckled as she stood.

"You sound amused."

"I guess I am. And here's a confession—I think I started courting Mr. Emerson months ago. But I haven't been doing a very good job of it. I eventually gave up."

He laughed. "You know what I think, Willow?" He grew more serious. "I think you're not the only one courting Mr. Emerson."

She waved a hand. "Believe me, I know all about that. Women seem to line up for that funny guy."

"No, that's not what I mean." His eyes twinkled. "I think God's been courting him too."

George was perplexed.

On Sunday evening, after the Tour of Homes concluded, Willow stopped by to give him a short list of people who'd expressed interest in buying his grandparents' house. But that wasn't why he felt confused, or why he was pacing back and forth in his living room while Willow waited for his answer.

It was because of Willow's suggested new plan. She wanted the two of them to host a thank-you party on Monday night. It was, she said, to show appreciation to everyone who'd helped on his house. It wasn't that he didn't feel grateful, but he did feel concerned. Was this gathering just an excuse for Willow to spend more time with Cliff Grant? If so, he wanted no part of it. No part at all!

He replayed the awkward conversation he'd had with Cliff after Willow had abandoned them the other night. Cliff had insinuated that Willow was his new girlfriend. The braggart had gone on about what a fine woman she was and how he'd been looking for an independent partner with her own business and bank account . . . expressing weariness of those "weak gold diggers" who attached themselves to him, only to sue him for alimony when it turned sour. George had listened with impatient dismay.

"I don't know," George cautiously told Willow. "You want to do this tomorrow? That's so soon. You just finished the Tour of Homes. Aren't you worn out?"

"It's just that I'd like to have this get-together while the house is still intact and looking so pretty. I'm keeping the gallery closed until Wednesday. That gives me Tuesday to get all the art moved back. I asked Betty and Donna to wait until Tuesday as well, so it's Monday or not at all."

"A party is such a lot of work . . . and on such short notice."

"Not for me. The house is already set. I'll keep it simple and handle all the arrangements—and I'll cover for food and drinks."

"Even so." He frowned, struggling for a good excuse. "I just don't understand why you need *me* at the party, Willow. I'm not very social and—"

"All you have to do is show up, George. Just smile at folks and express your gratitude. You have no idea how many people helped you with that project." Now she began listing names—both of people who had been hired to help as well as many who'd simply volunteered.

"Why did people give their time for free?" he asked.

"Because they are my friends," she declared. "And perhaps they want to be your friends too."

"Oh?" He considered this. "I suppose your contractor friend will be there too."

Her mouth twisted to one side. "You don't like Cliff very much, do you?"

He shrugged. "I don't really know him."

"But you don't like him, George, I can tell."

"You want the truth?"

"Yes, of course."

"Well, for starters I've heard he's a womanizer."

"A womanizer?" She laughed. "Who on earth told you that?"

"Lorna's friend Gayla said that Cliff has been married a couple of times and has had several girlfriends."

"That sounds like gossip to me."

He felt unsure. Should he repeat what Cliff had said the other night? Or was that stepping over some invisible line?

"And that's why you don't like him?" She peered curiously at him. "Just because your lady friends are telling tales out of school?"

"There's more." He felt like Willow deserved to know the truth about Cliff. Then if she wanted to proceed with a relationship, at least she'd have her eyes wide open.

"Do tell." She had a smug expression.

"Well, Cliff said a few things . . . the other night when you took off and left me at the house with him."

"What sort of things, George?" She folded her arms in front of her, waiting.

George told her, but once again, she didn't seem to care. In fact, she acted completely nonchalant about the whole thing. "I just thought you should know," he said a bit defensively. "If you're going to be involved with—"

"My involvement with Cliff Grant was purely professional, George. And it was for your sake." She tapped him on the chest. "I put up with Cliff in order to get your house fixed up for *you*."

George relaxed some. "So you're not interested in him—romantically?"

She laughed. "I really don't feel he's my type."

George felt a tiny rush of hope. "What is your type?"

Her smile looked a bit coy. "Wouldn't you like to know."

"I would like to know." He tried to conceal his eagerness.

She pursed her lips. "Well, George, if you really want to know, perhaps you'd like to help me host that thank-you party."

"Is this some sort of blackmail?"

"Does that mean you're coming?"

He shrugged. "I suppose I am."

"Thank you, dear. The party will begin at seven. I hope to see you there a little before that. Say, six forty-five?" Then, to his complete surprise, Willow came over and kissed him on the cheek. And it wasn't just a peck either. It felt like an intentionally warm and passionate kiss. And it left him longing for more.

⬦⬦⬦

George hardly slept on Sunday night. And then, throughout the day on Monday, he couldn't stop thinking about Willow. Had he imagined their conversation to have been more than it was yesterday? Had Willow given him reason to believe he really had a chance with her? After all the times he'd blown it with her? Was she still interested? Surely it was impossible, and yet . . .

By the time he was dressing for the party, George was a bundle of nerves. So much so that he changed his clothes several times before deciding on his old standard of suit and tie. He realized he'd probably be the only one dressed like this, but he didn't care. It simply felt comfortable. And tonight, of all nights, George felt the need to be comfortable.

When it was six thirty sharp, he gave Baxter a kitty treat then told him goodbye and headed out on foot to his grandparents' house. Although the shadows were lengthening, it was still light out as he strolled up the hill. There was a feeling in the air that suggested autumn was around the corner. For a moment, George felt the old rush of nerves to think that it was teachers' in-service week—followed by relief to realize he no longer needed to report in for work.

As he got closer to the house, he was surprised to see it not only lit up inside but also by lanterns along the walkway and strings of lights around the wraparound porch. Very festive and very welcoming. The front door was open and he could hear strains of music—jazz, but the quiet kind. As soon as George went into the foyer, he felt so strangely at home that he felt a mistiness in his eyes. As if this was the place where he belonged but had not been in ages. Maybe ever.

A generous bouquet of fresh flowers was on the entryway table, with several candles flickering around it. The air smelled sweet and spicy and like something else . . . food perhaps.

"George," Willow exclaimed happily, coming from the living room in a flowing dress of shimmering shades of aquatic blue that set off her peachy skin. "You're here! And right on time."

George nodded. "I promised."

She grasped both his hands in hers. "And you look so handsome in your suit and tie." Her turquoise-blue eyes sparkled. "Thank you for coming."

"The house looks beautiful," he said. "All the lights and all. Very nice."

"Thank you."

He stared at her, taking in her softly curling strawberry-blonde hair and creamy skin. "You look beautiful too, Willow."

Her whole face lit up. "Why, thank you, George."

"Is there anything I can do to help?" he asked, suddenly feeling nervous and self-conscious.

"No, I've got caterers in the kitchen, and I think everything is pretty much ready."

"Would you mind if I took a look around the house?" he asked. "I've never seen it looking quite like this. I mean, with candles and everything . . . at this time of the day."

"I'd love you to look around." She linked her arm in his. "I'm actually feeling rather sad to think this is the last night it will look quite like this. I want to soak it in myself." She led him into the living room, which had never, in George's memory, looked so perfectly lovely.

"I wish my grandmother could see this," he murmured as they slowly walked through it. "I think she'd wanted it to be like this."

"Maybe she can see it." Willow smiled. "I like to think

that people in heaven get sneak peeks sometimes. After all, I believe God is big enough to facilitate such things."

"That's an interesting theory."

She continued to lead him through the house and, even though George had been impressed with the changes before, he felt even more impressed now. It was really extraordinary. Finally, after they'd been in every room and on every floor, they were in the conservatory, which was lit only by candles and lanterns. George felt uncomfortably close to tears.

"Willow, you've made this house more beautiful than I ever thought possible," he said quietly. "And I feel so terrible about how I fought you each step of the way. I really do hope you've forgiven me."

"Of course, I have." She sighed. "Have you called any of the people who were interested in purchasing it yet?"

"No, no, not yet." George was about to tell her that he wasn't sure he'd be able to sell it now, but he noticed a couple of cars parking out front. "Looks like party time." He tried to keep the disappointment out of his voice.

"Let's go greet them." Willow kept her arm linked in his. "Just smile and be friendly, George. It's not that hard. They're basically good people."

As usual, Willow understood his general discomfort with social situations, but she probably didn't know his real reason for reluctance right now. It was simply that he wished tonight's party had only two on the guest list.

Willow stayed close to George as guests began to arrive. But to her surprise, he acted much more at ease than she'd expected, especially as he discovered that he already knew a number of them. Besides Collin and Josie and Willow's employees, he was happy to see several other acquaintances. He also seemed glad that she'd invited Hal and Beth. Before long, Willow felt George was managing just fine on his own. As a result, she could relax and enjoy the festivities herself. All in all, it was turning into a lovely evening—albeit bittersweet, since she knew this was the last night to enjoy the house looking so happy and loved. But hopefully it would soon be adopted by new owners eager to continue what she'd begun.

Not only was George mixing and visiting with the guests, he even refilled their drinks, playing the role of a real host enjoying his real home. Of course, she remembered, he did own this house, but she'd never felt he was truly at home here. It was nice to see him fully engaged tonight. It was like seeing a new side to him.

She grew a bit concerned when she noticed him interacting with Cliff in the conservatory. She wished she could hear their conversation, but seeing George smile with confidence was reassuring. Apparently he was not intimidated by Cliff. And when Cliff left early, Willow felt nothing but relief. She'd suspected from the start that Cliff was not the sort of man she wanted to get overly involved with. She'd sensed insincerity and was old enough to realize that an attractive exterior didn't necessarily reflect an attractive heart. She wished him no ill but was happy to move on.

To Willow's surprise, George had plenty to chat about with Donna and Betty. The three of them spent a fair amount of time in the den, talking and laughing as if enjoying a private party. Willow felt slightly left out but tried not to feel jealous as she went to the kitchen to pay the caterers and thank them for their efforts. Still, she was proud of George. He was making real progress. And by the end of the evening, George appeared to have many new friends.

As they stood in the foyer, Willow smiled to see George sincerely thanking their guests for coming—and thanking them again for their help with his house. He was being so friendly that she wondered if he wanted the party to stretch later. But she was tired and eager to kick off her sandals as the last of the guests slowly trickled out. Finally it was just Josie and Collin.

"I've got to be to work early tomorrow or I'd offer to help clean up," Collin told Willow.

"That's okay," she assured him. "I think I'll leave most of it until tomorrow."

Now Collin turned to George. "Just one week before I head off to college," he told him. "I can't wait."

"You're going to enjoy it." George gripped his hand. "I look forward to hearing what you think."

"Maybe I can help you with the cleanup tomorrow," Josie said in what seemed a halfhearted offer.

"Thanks." Willow smiled. "I'd like that."

Josie shook a finger at George. "I really don't get how you can let this house go. Especially after we got it looking so awesome."

"Thank you again for your help," George solemnly told her. "I really appreciate it, Josie."

"Well, I kinda owed you one." She gave a sheepish smile. "You helped me with my apartment—and all that cool junk you gave me."

Willow and George waved goodbye as Josie and Collin walked down the porch steps together. "It's such a relief seeing them not tearing into each other for a change," Willow said quietly.

"They've come a long way." George closed the door.

"Haven't we all."

"Thank you for including me tonight," George said with what sounded like sincere gratitude. "I actually enjoyed myself. Much more than I expected."

"I'm so glad." She sat down on the foyer bench. "My feet have been begging for this—I hope you don't mind." She pulled off her sandals and sighed.

"Not at all."

She stood and stretched. "I just want to check on a few things and extinguish the candles before I go home." She paused to blow out the candles in the foyer.

"I'll help," he offered, following her into the living room.

She paused, looking around and trying not to feel sad about leaving. "By tomorrow afternoon, the only things left here will be your grandmother's furnishings," she reminded him. "And then you can—"

"Not necessarily . . ."

"What do you mean?" She turned to peer curiously at him.

"I'm making an arrangement with Donna and Betty," he explained. "To leave things in place."

"Oh, is that so it will look nice while you're selling it?" She nodded. "I suppose that makes sense."

"I'm not selling it."

"*What?*"

He shrugged. "For the first time in a very long time, I feel at home here, Willow. I don't want to sell it."

She smiled. "Oh, George. That's so wonderful. Does that mean you'll live here?"

He nodded. "I think so. Betty and Donna agreed to send me invoices for all their pieces. If their bills aren't too outrageous, I'd like to keep everything just as it is. Although I can't afford all the art you've brought in, I would like to keep a few pieces." He pointed to the painting above the console. "I actually like that painting, but it's far too expensive to even consider."

"No, it's not." Willow chuckled. "I priced it like that because it's mine. It used to hang in our home in Sausalito, and even though it's too massive for my apartment, I haven't been able to part with it. But it can hang here in your house for as long as you like, George."

"Really?" He turned to her. "And would you come around to enjoy it?"

"Of course."

"Because you've shown me that I need color in my life. You've shown me that it's healthy to take risks . . . and that there are people around me worth knowing." He spoke quietly but with what sounded like conviction. "I know I'm an old stick-in-the-mud and as stubborn as a mule. But I think I can change, Willow. I think I am changing."

"Oh, George." She went over to him, placing a hand on his cheek. "I would hate to see you change too much. I think you're pretty wonderful already."

"Thanks." He grinned. "I think you're pretty wonderful too."

Then he kissed her . . . and she knew this was just the beginning.

Melody Carlson is the beloved author of well over two hundred novels. She has been a finalist for or the recipient of many awards, including the *Romantic Times* Career Achievement Award. She lives in central Oregon.

"Carlson kicks off her new series with this heartwarming and uplifting novel about taking a chance on fulfilling your dreams."
—*Library Journal*

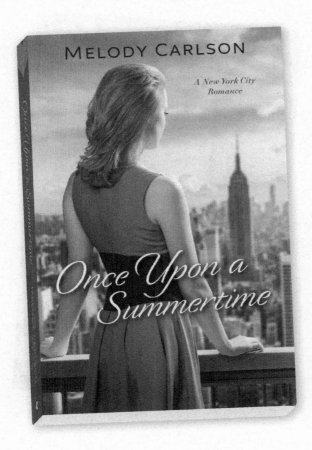

Anna moved to New York City looking for her big break and hoping for love—she just didn't imagine both would depend on a familiar face.

She's anticipating a quiet summer
surrounded by beauty. She never expected
a fresh chance at love.

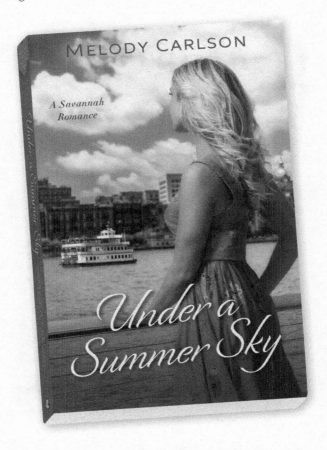

When a young art teacher moves to sultry Savannah to manage an art
gallery for the summer, she finds far more than she anticipated as two
handsome brothers vie for her attention.

Meet Melody

f Melody Carlson

MelodyCarlson.com

Printed in the United States
By Bookmasters